# KATE IN WAITING

# KATE IN WAITING

## BECKY ALBERTALLI

BALZER + BRAY

*An Imprint of* HarperCollins*Publishers*

Balzer + Bray is an imprint of HarperCollins Publishers.

Kate in Waiting
Copyright © 2021 by Becky Albertalli
Emojis by Carboxylase/Shutterstock
All rights reserved. Printed in the United States of America.
No part of this book may be used or reproduced in any manner whatsoever without
written permission except in the case of brief quotations embodied in critical articles
and reviews. For information address HarperCollins Children's Books, a division of
HarperCollins Publishers, 195 Broadway, New York, NY 10007.
www.epicreads.com

Library of Congress Control Number: 2020948140
ISBN 978-0-06-264383-4

Typography by Jenna Stempel-Lobell
21 22 23 24 25   PC/LSCH   10 9 8 7 6 5 4 3 2 1
❖
First Edition

For Adam Silvera, of course

# OVERTURE

It really feels like an ending, in every way possible. With the curtains pulled closed, the stage might as well be another planet. A well-lit planet full of giant foam set pieces, inhabited only by Andy and me—and Matt.

Coke-Ad Matt.

"It's now or never," whispers Andy. He doesn't move an inch.

Neither do I.

We just sort of stand there, in the shadow of a papier-mâché Audrey 2.

There's nothing sadder than the end of a crush. And it's not like this was one of those distant-stranger crushes. Andy and I have actually talked to this boy. Tons of words, on multiple glorious occasions. No small feat, since Matt's the kind of gorgeous that usually renders us speechless. He's got one of those old-timey faces, with blond hair and pink cheeks. Our friend Brandie collects Coca-Cola merch, and I swear the vintage ad in her bathroom looks exactly like Matt. Thus the nickname. The ad says, "Thirst stops here." But in our case, the thirst doesn't stop.

It's basic Avril Lavigne math. We were the junior theater counselors. He was our cute townie vocal consultant. You truly could not make it any more obvious. And for a full six weeks, he's been the sun in our solar system. But he lives up the road from camp, in Mentone, Alabama.

Which is just about a hundred miles away from Roswell, Georgia.

So Andy's right. Now or never.

Deep breath. "Hey. Uh, Matt."

I swear I can feel Anderson's surprised approval. Damn, Garfield. Just going for it. Get yours.

I clear my throat. "So. We wanted to say goodbye. And. Um. Thank you."

Matt slides a sheet of music into his tote bag and smiles. "Thank me?"

"For the vocal consultation," I say. "And everything."

Andy nods fervently, adjusting his glasses.

"Aww, Kate! You too. So cool meeting you guys." Matt hoists his tote bag over his shoulder, shifting his weight toward the door, just barely. Exit posture. Crap. I'm just going to—

"Can we take a selfie?" I blurt. I'm already cringing. You know what would be cool? If my voice would stop shaking. Also, Anderson. My dude. Anytime you want to step up, be my guest.

"Oh, sure," Matt says. "Let's do it."

Well then.

We squeeze into the frame, curtain tickling our backs, and I stretch my arm out at the up angle, just like Anderson trained me. And we smile. I mean, I'm trying to. But I'm so flustered, my lips are trembling.

It's worth it. Even if I come out looking like a dazed fangirl, it's worth it. Raina and Brandie have been begging for photographic evidence of Coke-Ad Matt's cuteness, and God knows Instagram's yielded nothing.

But this picture isn't for the squad. Not really. Honestly, they're both just going to make fun of us for having yet another communal crush. According to Raina, Anderson and I are enmeshed, which basically means we're codependent. Apparently some people believe falling in love is a thing you're supposed to do on your own.

And yeah, Raina aced AP Psych so hard, she's practically a licensed psychologist already. But here's the thing she doesn't get. It's not about Matt. Or Josh from last summer, who had very strong opinions about breakfast. Or Alexander from the summer before, who was really into being from Michigan. It has nothing to do with any of them.

It's about Anderson and me. It's about scheming in the prop closet and reading way too much into every flicker of eye contact. It's about brushing our teeth six times a day, always prepared for the unexpected makeout scenario. And in the end, when the makeout scenarios never materialized, it hardly mattered. It didn't matter. Because the makeouts weren't the point.

The giddiness was the point.

And I feel like this all sounds like a Bit Much, but that's just Andy and me. We bring it out in each other. And truthfully, summer crushes make for a surprisingly fun and robust team activity.

Less fun now that summer's over. Now it's just that sinking-boat feeling of a crush lost too soon. A crush cut down in its prime.

But that boat's so much less lonely when your best friend's on board.

# SCENE 1

Five minutes into junior year, and I'm done. No, seriously. Let's burn this whole year to the ground.

For one thing, I can barely keep my eyes open. Which doesn't bode well, seeing as I haven't even entered the building yet. Or left the school parking lot. Or even unbuckled my seat belt.

And it's Anderson's fault.

Because Anderson Walker knows I need seven hours of sleep to not be a zombie demon on Xanax, and yet. And yet! This mess of a boy let himself into my house, into my room, and turned on my lights at five thirty a.m. Because he needed my input on his first-day-back cardigan choice. Navy blue with brown buttons, or navy with navy buttons. "Just give me your gut reaction," he'd said.

My gut reaction was hurling a pillow at his face.

Now, almost three hours later—right on schedule—he's spiraling again in the parking lot.

"You're sure the navy's okay?"

"Andy. It's fine."

"Just fine?"

"More than fine. You look perfect."

And he does. He always does. Anderson's honestly too cute for this earth. Smooth brown skin, dimples, and a short, tapered Afro, not to mention big brown eyes behind plastic-framed glasses. And he's got that nautical schoolboy aesthetic down to a science: crisp button-downs and cardigans and rolled-up pants.

He rubs his cheeks. "I just don't want to look like trash. It's the first day of—"

But he's drowned out by trap music blasting out of a Jeep. Make way for the fuckboys.

Unfortunately, Roswell Hill High School is fuckboy ground zero. Mostly the suburban athletic subtype. *Fuckboius jockus*. No joke. Just stand in the hallway and put your arm out for two seconds, and you'll hit a fuckboy, right in his mesh athletic shorts. They're everywhere, armies of them, all in RHHS team gear. So prolific we had to give them a not-so-secret code name. F-boys. Which doesn't exactly obscure the meaning, but at least it keeps Brandie's innocent ears from exploding.

I glare at the Jeep through Anderson's passenger window. The driver keeps cupping his hands around his mouth, megaphone-style, to holler at groups of girls who walk by. The f-boy mating call. But his car door's flung wide open and is therefore blocking my door.

The sheer audacity of f-boys.

"Kate." Anderson pokes me with his keys, but I snatch them. I love his Funko Rapunzel keychain so much, it almost makes me want to learn to drive. Almost.

Our phones buzz simultaneously. Text from Raina or Brandie, no doubt.

Andy glances at his screen. "Come on, they're already down there."

Okay, that gets me moving. We've seen Raina a few times since camp ended, but Brandie left for Mexico the day before we got back. Which means it's been over six weeks since the full squad's been together.

Anderson grabs my hand to help me over the gear shift, and then we cut through the parking lot, bypassing the front entrance entirely. Instead, we head for the side door, which has direct access to the theater hall. Straight to Ms. Zhao's room, where all the usual suspects have gathered.

Honestly, we theater kids are as instantly recognizable as f-boys. Though it's not so much about the clothes in our case. It's more like an aura. My brother said once that theater kids walk around like we're each under our own tiny spotlight. Pretty sure it wasn't a compliment.

It's true, though. Like, there's none of that forced nonchalance people have about the first day of school. Instead, we have Margaret Daskin and Emma McLeod near the accessibility elevator, butchering *Newsies*, and Lindsay Ward gasping into her phone, and Colin Nakamura using Pierra Embry's head as a drum. And of course, Lana Bennett's delivering an urgent lecture to Kelly Matthews, who I can only assume made the mistake of referring to the school musical as a play. There is literally nothing Lana Bennett loves more than explaining the difference between musicals and plays to people who . . . clearly know the difference between musicals and plays.

Brandie and Raina are relatively chill, though, just leaning against the back wall, reading their phones. I think it's generally understood that, out of our squad, they're the ones who mostly have their lives together. I used to go back and forth in my head about which one of them was the mom friend, but the truth is, they're both the mom friend. They're just the mom friend in different ways. Raina's the bossy mom who makes everyone stay healthy and hydrated and on top of their schoolwork. Brandie's the soft mom who'll let you cry all over her cardigan when your crush starts dating an f-girl from the volleyball team.

Today they're so distracted, we're practically nose-to-nose before they notice us.

"Boo," I say.

They both look up with a start, and Raina's eyes go straight to Anderson's keys in my hand. "Kate, did you drive?"

I laugh, tossing the keys back to Andy. "Yeah, no."

"Didn't you say you were going to—"

"Yup. And I will."

Raina narrows her eyes.

"I will! Really soon."

Technically, I could take the driver's test tomorrow—I've had my permit for almost a year and a half. But I haven't taken the plunge. And I'm not exactly dying to, either.

At the end of the day, I'm really a passenger seat kind of person.

Brandie hugs me. "Your hair looks so cute!"

So maybe Anderson's five-thirty wake up call paid off. Normally, my hair's a notorious mess. It's that halfway point between blond and brown, and left to its own devices, it's almost recklessly wavy. But right now, it's what Anderson calls white-girl-on-YouTube wavy. I do think it's worth the effort every now and then, given that I'm a person whose overall attractiveness is highly hair-correlated. But now I feel like I'm broadcasting to the whole world how hard I'm trying.

"How was Mexico?" I brush the ruffled sleeve of Brandie's dress. "I love this."

She smiles. "It was great. Really hot, though. How was camp?"

"I mean, none of our campers died."

"Well done," Raina says.

"And." I press my hand to my heart. "Matt knows our names."

"Cokehead Matt?" Raina grins.

"Okay, that's blasphemy." I scrunch my nose at her. "I'm serious, he's like an old-timey dreamboat—"

"Which they'd already know if someone was capable of

taking group selfies without decapitating people."

"Um, it's not my fault Matt's six feet tall," I say. "Did I mention he's six feet tall?"

"Literally ten times," says Raina.

Anderson turns to Brandie and Raina. "Did I tell you he knew how to pronounce Aeschylus? On the first try?"

"Sounds like boyfriend material," says Brandie.

"God yes," says Anderson. "Don't you want to just, like . . . wear his letterman jacket and let him pin you—"

"—to a bed?" Raina asks.

Anderson bites back a smile, and then shakes his head quickly. "Anyway." His eyes flick back to Ms. Zhao's door. "No updates?"

"Nothing," Raina says. "Not even a clue. Harold thinks it's going to be *A Chorus Line*."

Anderson whirls to face her head-on. "Why?"

"Gut feeling?" Raina shrugs. "Ginger intuition?"

"Is ginger intuition a thing?"

"I mean, according to Harold."

Harold MacCallum: world-class jellybean. Sunshine in boy form. Raina's boyfriend. They met about a year ago in this online trans support group Raina moderates. Harold's cis, but his twin sibling is nonbinary, and he actually lives pretty close to us. He's super shy, and kind of wonderfully awkward. Raina gets this smile in her voice whenever she talks about him.

"Okay, well I have a theory," Anderson says. "It's a medieval year."

"What?"

"Hear me out. Last year was *West Side Story*. Freshman year was *Into the Woods*. And they did *Bye Bye Birdie* when we were in eighth grade."

"I don't get it," says Brandie.

"I'm just saying. The PTA is super cheap, right? So we're just cycling through two sets of costumes. We've got the fifties costumes and the medieval costumes, and they alternate them so no one catches on. Just watch. Any minute, Zhao's coming out with the sign-up sheet." Andy's enjoying this now—drawing out the info, dimples activating. "And you'll see. It's a medieval year. Mark my words. *Cinderella, Camelot—*"

"Or it's going to be *A Chorus Line*," I say, "and you're going to feel like such a dumbass."

"Yeah, but." He lifts a finger. "*A Chorus Line* in medieval clothes. Follow the money, Garfield. Follow the money."

Raina and I snort at the exact same moment. But before either of us can make the requisite wiseass remark, Ms. Zhao's door creaks open.

And the whole corridor goes silent.

Anderson grabs my hand, and my heart's in my throat. Which makes zero sense, since there's no suspense here. It's the same every year. Ms. Zhao announces the fall musical on the first day of school. Then I spend a week or two freaking out for no reason, playing the soundtrack on repeat, letting my daydreams run wild. It's that same nonsensical thought every time. Maybe this is the year. Maybe this is when the switch flips. But the truth is, I always know exactly where I'll find myself when the cast list gets posted.

Bottom of the page. Nameless part in the ensemble. I'm an absolute legend in the category of Nameless Parts in the Ensemble.

But somehow this moment gets me every time. The way everyone freezes when Ms. Zhao steps out of the theater room. The way she keeps her face impassive and doesn't make eye contact with anyone until the sign-up sheet's officially on the door.

At least that's how it's supposed to go.

But when the door flings open at last, it isn't Ms. Zhao there at all.

# SCENE 2

Anderson's hand drops to his side. "Holy fuck."

Which is how I know I'm not imagining it.

It doesn't compute, though. He's not from Roswell. He's not even from Georgia.

My heart's lodged high in my throat.

Because Matt. Dreamboat Matt. Coke-Ad Matt.

Is here.

"You guys okay?" Brandie looks concerned. "Do we know him?"

"Shh!"

"He sees us." Anderson's voice is choked. "Oh God. What's he doing here? What—hiiiii."

He's walking toward us. THE Coke-Ad Matt is walking toward us, blue eyes flicking between Andy and me. And holy shit. The thirst did not end there. It did not end. It did not, it did not. "Um. Hey."

His faint Alabama accent.

"Are you . . ." I trail off.

"I just moved here." He runs a hand through his hair.

"You . . ." I blink. "You go here?"

"I'm a senior."

"Look at them. Look at their faces," Raina murmurs to Brandie.

"Love at first sight," Brandie whispers.

"Or some fucked up communal crush at first sight."

Wow, guys. Love that subtlety. And that judgment! Raina doesn't get it. Neither of them do, and I doubt they ever will.

Here's the truth: crushes are pointless without Andy. More than pointless, they're painful. Crushing alone is like running lines without a scene partner. No one to play off of, and your voice sounds fake and loud.

But neither my voice nor my brain are even functioning now. The conversation only partially registers. I'm too focused on the fact that Matt just shook Brandie's hand and introduced himself with his full name. Like a grandfather. It's adorable.

Matt Olsson.

I can't believe he's here.

I was heartbroken to leave him. It's so dumb, because it's not like we were even really friends with him. It's not like we were staying up late with him, swapping secrets in bunk beds. We literally learned this boy's last name five seconds ago.

But it felt like we knew him. And not just the correctly pronounced Aeschylus name-drop that got Andy so bonered. I don't care about Aeschylus. I just feel so—I don't even know. Discombobulated. That's the word.

Because here's Matt Olsson, looking like he stepped out of an Archie comic. Sandy-haired and straightforwardly beautiful, standing right in front of us. He's a senior in high school. MY high school. In my Roswell. Roswell, Georgia, twenty miles north of Atlanta, home of an impressively well-stocked Super Target, infinite Waffle Houses and a staggering number of f-boys.

He meets my eyes. "Your hair looks different."

"This is so weird," I say, barely out loud.

Matt laughs. "Yeah, I know. I was just coming down here for first period." He gestures vaguely at the theater room. "I didn't think—"

"You have Ms. Zhao for first period?" Anderson's eyes widen. "Advanced Drama?"

Advanced Drama, better known as Senior D. No idea why, other than the fact that the class is for seniors, and people like saying, "Seen yer D." It's the class of legends, though. Zhao won't even consider you unless you're serious about drama. And apparently the first two months are strictly about trust building, because stuff gets pretty intense, and it only works if you're vulnerable. Everyone says you basically come out of Senior D with an acting MFA. I don't know if I buy that, but I do know that class bonds people for life. Andy and I have been aching to enroll since we were freshmen.

"Anyway," Matt says. "I'm supposed to bring a form up to Mr. Merced's office."

"Right now?" Brandie nods toward the door. "But Ms. Zhao's about to announce the musical. Like. Any minute."

"Is it a secret?"

Raina whirls around to face him, eyes narrowed. "She told you, didn't she?"

Matt smiles the cutest, tiniest guilty smile I've ever seen in my life.

"Tell us." Anderson clasps his hands. "Please tell us."

Matt tilts his head. "Should I?"

Okay, how is he already teasing us? How is he this cool? I'm still trying to get my brain to stop spinning, and here's Matt, gently trolling the squad like he's known us for years.

"So you're saying if the musical was *Once Upon a Mattress*, you'd want to know that?"

"Motherfucker." Raina looks as gobsmacked as I feel. Zhao told Matt the musical. Wow. So much for tradition. So much for pomp and circumstance and secrecy. She just . . . told him. She told Matt.

Coke-Ad Matt. Who goes here now.

Okay, help me out here, yoga warm-up exercises. Let's do a subtle inhale. Hold for ten. Subtle exhale. Kate Garfield, you are cool as a cucumber. Totally not freaking out. Nope. No overload in this brain.

Matt looks at me and smiles.

16

Okay, yeah, now I can't think straight, can't even breathe straight, can't even hold my head up, can't even—

"I have to pee," Andy whispers.

I nod slowly, finally catching my breath.

I have to pee.

It's our magic escape code.

# SCENE 3

Okay, it's not much of a code.

It means private meeting in the bathroom. Specifically, the men's bathroom at the end of the theater hallway, also known as the Bathroom Time Forgot. The BTF. We're the only ones who ever use it. All things considered, though, it's a decent bathroom. Minimal wall graffiti, and the stuff that's there is pleasantly vintage—mostly Sharpied penises and pointy stylized iterations of the letter S. We head straight for our favorite stalls, side by side, using the toilets as chairs. I don't even remember how we settled on this arrangement. I just know it's strangely intimate, sitting like this—side by side in a pair of bathroom stalls, talking through the partial wall that divides them. I'm Jewish, but maybe this is what confession feels like. When we're in here, I always say a little more than I think I'll say.

"What. The. Fuck. Is happening?" Anderson says. Even though I can't see him, I can picture him perfectly—awkwardly straddling the toilet seat, like he's riding a donkey.

"Wait, are we freaking out about the play or about—"

"Coke-Ad Matt. I didn't just dream that, right? He's here? At our fucking school?"

"Coke-Ad Matt is at our fucking school," I confirm.

"But why?"

"Because he moved here?"

Andy exhales. "Why would he move here?"

"Maybe he followed us?" I slide my feet forward on the tiles.

"Oh my God. He fell in love with us and followed us home from camp."

"WAIT—"

"I mean, he had to have known, right?" Andy says.

"Right, no. Definitely. That's just too big of a—"

"But," Andy points out. "But, but, but. He was clearly surprised to see us."

"He could have been acting."

"He is taking Advanced Drama."

"This is so weird," I say, for what feels like the millionth time this morning.

"SO weird."

"How are we even—"

But my voice evaporates, because out of nowhere, the bathroom door creaks open. And then, a moment later, there's the sound of someone peeing in a urinal.

Text from Anderson: UMMMMMMM

I text back: trespasser!!!!!!!!!

INFILTRATOR. HOW DARE, Andy writes, and I giggle before I can stop myself.

The pee stream stops abruptly.

For a moment, it's dead silent.

"You can keep peeing," Anderson says finally.

This time I clap my hands over my mouth to keep from laughing.

The infiltrator clears his throat. "Am I . . ."

"You're in the right place," Anderson says. "Carry on with your business and have a wonderful day."

HAVE A WONDERFUL DAY?? I text Andy. You sound like a cult leader.

Okay but why isn't he peeing?!!

Because you scared him and now he doesn't want to join your "wonderful day" cult

You're just jealous that it's a wonderful day in my cult, he writes. Anyway you're the one who giggled from the stall. Who does that??

Uh obviously me.

Katy he's not leaving, what do we do???

Who do you think it is? I write.

OMG

WAIT

For a moment, it's just ellipses. And then nothing. And then a lightbulb emoji, followed by a close-up selfie of just Anderson's wide-open eyes.

Then: Is it MATT???

"Did I interrupt something?"

**That's not Matt's voice,** I write back.

"Nope," Andy says brightly. "Not at all. We're just. You know."

"Peeing," I say quickly. "Just peeing."

"Kate?" asks the interloper.

And just like that, I recognize the voice, though I doubt Andy does. I dethrone and unlock the door, pausing before opening it. "Are your pants up?"

"That is quite a question, Little Garfield."

Mmm. Guess how much I love being called Little Garfield by someone who's six weeks younger than I am?

"Verbal confirmation, Noah."

"Yes, my pants are up."

I crack the door open, peering out. "Why are you here?"

"In the men's room? Why are you here?"

Noah Kaplan, the f-boy next door. Okay, technically, he's the f-boy across the street, and just at Dad's house. He and my brother are basically inseparable, even though Ryan's a senior. I guess it's one of those baseball team bro friendships that know no age limits.

"This isn't the locker room," Anderson calls out from the stall.

Andy has no patience for f-boys. Or f-girls. Or anyone even remotely allied with the f-force. But who could blame him? The school fuckboy population didn't exactly throw a Pride parade when Andy came out. Noah's not so bad—he's the slutty kind of f-boy, not the homophobic kind. He's one of those guys who's always ostentatiously flirting, or PDA-ing, or getting loudly dumped in the hallway. Last year he had two homecoming dates, and it wasn't even a secret. He had two boutonnieres.

Once, Andy looked at Noah, apropos of nothing, and asked, "Are straight boys okay? Do they need help?"

The age-old question.

Noah smiles wryly. "Not looking for the locker room." He pulls up the sleeve of his hoodie—which is when I notice he's wearing a bright-white fiberglass cast, almost to his elbow.

"Whoa. What happened?" I ask.

"Distal radius fracture."

"Sportsball injury?"

"Something like that."

Anderson cracks his door open, peering out at us. "Too bad we're not doing *Dear Evan Hansen*," he says.

"That's a theater reference," says Noah.

"Noah Kaplan," says Andy. "I'm impressed."

"I'm just getting warmed up for first-period drama," Noah says.

"Hold up." I step out of my stall, shutting it fast behind me. "Like Senior D?"

"Whose D?"

"Senior D. The class. Advanced Drama. Andy, get out here." I lean against my stall door, staring Noah down. "You're a junior."

Anderson steps primly out of his stall like he's stepping out of a limo. He looks Noah straight in the eye. "How?"

"I was . . . assigned into it?" He looks from Anderson to me, brown eyes crinkling. Classic Noah expression. You know how people freeze-frame into your brain, almost like your mental contact photo? That's Noah in my head. Perpetually twinkly-eyed. It's not like we're friends anymore. But he's always around—at Dad's neighborhood block parties, or with Ryan, sprawled out in our living room on rainy TV-watching days.

Anderson, who has apparently transformed into a TV lawyer, begins his cross-examination. "Did they say anything about you being a junior?"

"Nope."

"Or the fact that you've never done theater? Ever?"

Noah shrugs. "Had to move out of PE, and there were spots available—"

"What?" Andy inhales sharply. "Why are there spots available?"

"There are never spots available," I say.

"Unless—" Andy cuts himself off, frantically typing on his phone. Then he shoves the screen in front of my face. "Kate, look, look, look!"

It's the Roswell Hill High School website. *Music department. News and updates.*

I look up at Andy. "Glee club is a class now?"

"Brand-new. Saw a flyer, but didn't put it together." Anderson sounds breathless. "Katy, it's first period—"

"So it conflicts with—"

"Yes! Okay, yes. No wonder—"

"You guys okay?" Noah asks.

"Never been better." Anderson takes my hand and tugs it, and the next thing I know, we're halfway to the counseling office.

# SCENE 4

"I'm not sure I follow," says Mr. Merced, the counselor. He's new—which is promising—and he's young. So maybe he's pliable. "You're both asking to be transferred into Advanced Drama."

My heart pounds. "Yes."

He pushes his glasses up, peering at the monitor. "I'm not sure the system will let me."

"But you'll try?" Anderson asks.

Mr. Merced's already typing. "Andrew . . . Walker?"

"Anderson Walker."

"Ah. Okay. Yup, here you are." Mr. Merced purses his lips, scrolling. "First period, I see you've got—"

"Study hall," Andy says. "Just study hall. Throwaway class. I mean, first-period study hall. Who's actually going to show up for that?"

Mr. Merced raises his eyebrows.

"ME. I would show up for that. Because I would never skip class," Anderson says quickly. "I would never do that."

"Never. Me too." I nod.

Anderson scoots to the edge of his seat and plants his elbows on Mr. Merced's desk. "And actually, studies have shown that participation in the arts helps students—"

Mr. Merced cuts him off. "Okay, Mr. Walker. You're good to go."

"Wait—what?"

"First period, Advanced Drama, Zhao, room—"

"No, I know. But . . . I'm in?"

"I'll print you a revised schedule, and you can head down there right now. Do you need a hall pass?"

Anderson's eyes flick toward me, jaw hanging open.

"What about me?" I say. "Kate Garfield."

Mr. Merced starts typing. "And you'd like to make the same move as Mr. Walker, correct? You're withdrawing from study hall and—"

"Well, I've got study hall seventh period. First period is Algebra II with—"

"Oh." Mr. Merced frowns. "Ms. Garfield, if your first-period class is a core academic subject—"

"Right, I know." The words tumble out. "But if I could switch into the third-period section—"

"That's not really—"

"Or if we moved chemistry to fourth period, maybe—"

26

There's a knock, and Mr. Merced stands. "There's my nine o'clock."

"Wait—"

"Right!" Mr. Merced points with finger guns. "Hall passes." He pulls a bright-pink pad and a pen out of his drawer. "Okay . . . Ms. Garfield." He uncaps the pen, still standing. "Time: 8:57 . . . pass to Algebra II . . . with . . . Ms. Evans. Here you go." He hands it to me, and my heart sinks all the way down to my sneakers. "And Mr. Walker . . . let's say 8:58 . . . pass to Advanced Drama . . . with . . . Ms. Zhao."

"Wait—wait—wait," Anderson says, shooting out of his seat. "There has to be something—"

But Mr. Merced's already walking us to the door. "I'll notify your study hall supervisor of the change. Don't worry."

Then, in one smooth move, he opens the door and directs us into the counseling lobby, where this boy Frank Gruber is waiting with a half-crumpled schedule sheet. I don't actually know Frank all that well, though we used to get paired together a lot for alphabetical reasons. But I had one of those blink-and-you'll-miss-it crushes on him in ninth grade. We'd talk in homeroom sometimes, and he had this way of trailing off mid-word while staring at my mouth. Like a satellite dipping out of orbit. And the fact that I, Kate Eliza Garfield, had the ability to throw a cute boy off his orbit was electrifying.

Except . . . Anderson didn't think Frank was cute at all, which made him instantly a hundred times less appealing. I know that's awful. But that's just how it is for me. If a crush is really going to take hold, Andy has to like the guy too. Otherwise, this switch in me flips—and suddenly it's not electrifying and the boy isn't cute and the whole situation goes sour. And Andy's almost as bad when it comes to me. Raina says it's yet another example of us being codependent, and that's why neither of us has ever dated anyone but each other.

Of course, Frank Gruber just drifts past us toward Mr. Merced's office. Doesn't even spare us a glance.

The door closes, and Anderson looks like he might burst into tears. "Katy, I'm so—so sorry. This is bullshit. I can switch back—"

"It's fine."

"It's not fine. This is Senior D. We were going to take it together."

"Yeah, well." I shrug, and he winces. And okay. I'm not proud of this, but a tiny secret part of me is glad he feels shitty. I know it's not his fault. And I know it's just a class. Up until ten minutes ago, I never dreamed I'd be able to take Advanced Drama this year. But I can't help but feel like something got snatched away from me, right under my nose.

Because it's not just Senior D. It's Senior D with Matt.

Anderson's going to have a class with Matt.

"Katy. Seriously." Anderson takes both my hands. "I'll get Mr. Merced to switch me back. We'll take it together. Next year. You and me."

"Andy, just stop."

He furrows his brow.

"It's fine. Take the class." I force a smile. "Someone needs to get intel on Matt."

He nods slowly. "That's true."

"And obviously you'll tell me everything."

"Everything. The full play-by-play. Promise." Anderson hugs me. "You're so—"

"Late for first period." I hold up the Pink Hall Pass of Algebraic Doom. "Gotta go."

# SCENE 5

It's long past dismissal. But Andy and I, world-class suck-ups, end up taping Ms. Zhao's audition flyers around the school for almost an hour. You know how there's always that one teacher you'd do anything for? The one you swear would be your ride-or-die BFF in any other context?

Ms. Zhao. No joke. The whole squad seriously worships her. She's in her forties or so, with a wife and kids and everything, but she's always up-to-date on the news and pop culture and basically all our dumb memes. And not in a try-hard way. You can just tell she thinks her students are cool and interesting people. Which shouldn't be a revolutionary stance for a teacher, but it kind of is.

By the time we get home, Mom's car is in the garage, with Ryan taking up the whole driveway behind her. Doesn't matter. Andy always just pulls into his own driveway next door, and we cut straight through our adjacent front yards, back to my house. We're given a hero's welcome by the dogs as soon as we walk through the door. Charles and Camilla, pupper and doggo, respectively.

Mom's at the counter, working on a snack plate, and her face lights up when we walk in. "Oh, hey! Katy, you just missed your brother. He's out on a run."

Of course he is. I swear, Ryan's a couch potato by nature, but you'd never know it these days, especially during baseball season. Full-on jock mode.

"Are you doing Goldfish cracker art?" Anderson asks.

I take a closer look at Mom's plate, and sure enough: multicolored Goldfish splayed in spiraling rainbow order. Normally, Ryan and I are kind of latchkey kids. Same with Andy—his parents are doctors, so they're usually seeing patients until dinner. And Mom's a middle school music teacher, which means she's on the hook for after-school choir and the variety show. But when Mom's home early, she likes to be as extra as possible.

She carries her Goldfish masterpiece over but sneaks in a round of cheek kisses first. "My boychick. Mwah."

It's funny—when it comes to me and Ryan, Mom's obsessed with not playing favorites. Everything's painstakingly equal— equal allowance, equal-sized bowls of cereal in the morning. I'm half convinced she named us Ryan and Kate so she could spend the exact same amount of money on each set of custom wooden letters she ordered for the door signs outside our bedrooms. I mean, I technically own half of Ryan's car, and I don't even drive.

But all that goes out the window when it comes to Anderson,

her true favorite. She goes full Jewish mom when he's here. It's slightly terrifying.

"So? What's the musical?" she asks, setting the Goldfish spiral between us. Anderson sinks into a chair, swipes a layer of red ones off the outer edge, and stuffs them into his mouth like they're popcorn. Followed by lots of vigorous chewing. All of this just to keep my mom in suspense for a minute, because this boy lives for dramatic pauses.

Anderson finally swallows, smiling grandly up at her. "*Once Upon a Mattress.*"

"Oh, no way!" Mom presses both palms to her chest. "I was in that at camp. I played Winnifred!"

Anderson's eyes widen. "Shut up."

"For real." Mom beams. "One of my favorite roles ever."

So here's the thing: I can kind of sing. But Mom can really sing. When she was my age, she was the lead in every single play she tried out for. Not just the school plays—she did community theater at the rec center, too. And of course, she was basically famous at Camp Wolf Lake in the summers. I think she pretty much ran their whole theater program from fourth grade on.

"*Once Upon a Mattress.* How exciting! I'll have to tell Ellen. Katy, you remember my friend Ellen, right?" Mom says. And just like that, she's off and running. " . . . grew up together, and we were absolute best friends at camp, but we fell out of touch for—oy. Twenty-five years?" Mom shakes her head sadly. "We had one of those ridiculous fights, you know? She was seeing this terrible boy, and you know me. I'm not going to hold my tongue. What a schmuck. Thank God that finally ended. Ellen's an absolute doll, though. You remember."

"Yup. Ellen from camp who dated a schmuckboy."

"Even worse, she married that schmuckboy," Mom says. "Oy gevalt. Thankfully, the divorce is almost finalized, and she's back in Roswell . . ."

My mind starts to drift. I love my mom, but she's a Talker, capital T. She can keep herself going for hours. When we were younger, Ryan and I used to quietly time her. Of course, Andy's nodding along politely like the perfect boychick he is.

"Shabbat dinner," Mom concludes. "Anyway, look at me keeping you here, when I bet you guys are dying to sneak off and listen to that soundtrack."

"Oh no—" Andy starts to say, but I cut him off.

"Yup. YUP. Gotta go work on the play. Thanks, Mom. You're the best."

Listen. When my mom shows you an escape hatch, you take it.

# SCENE 6

Unfortunately, AP US History is already putting a serious damper on my daydream schedule. I just think it's disrespectful of teachers to expect us to focus on Puritans when we're eight days out from auditions.

There are so many things I need to think about by then. Things like audition songs and breath support and how much Zhao's going to cast based on seniority this year. Every few years, Ms. Zhao gets it in her head that all the good parts should go to seniors. Which would be an excellent mindset down the line—like, Zhao, feel free to lean right the fuck into that next year. But if Ms. Zhao goes the seniority route this time, I don't even have a shot.

The thing is, I kind of have my hopes up again. Classic me, dreaming of spotlights. My name at the top of the cast list. My voice, soaring on the wings of a wireless microphone. Standing ovations. Booming applause. Every year I get entranced all over again by the idea of it.

Every year I fall short.

It's such a stupid thing to want. A leading role. A singing part. I've barely even had a speaking part before. I don't even think I could pull it off. Who cares if I sound good when I'm alone in my room. Everyone knows I'm a mess under pressure.

Everyone knows.

But I can't seem to turn off the daydreams. Every time I close my eyes, I can picture it. Me as Princess Winnifred the Woebegone. Me, center stage, in an artfully bedraggled medieval dress, singing about swamps. Me perched on top of a stack of mattresses, the rest of the cast fanning out around me.

Me, standing in the shoes of giants. Carol Burnett. Sarah Jessica Parker. Tracey Ullman. My mom. It's the kind of daydream I love to live in.

Inconveniently, Mr. Edelman wants to spend AP US History learning AP US History, and today, that's worksheet packets. You can tell a lot about a teacher's desperation level from how quickly he resorts to worksheets.

It's the third day of school.

At least he's got us in groups. But the groups aren't great. I've got Brandie, but instead of Raina and Anderson, we've got this random f-boy, Jack Randall. Needless to say, the worksheets aren't going so well. Partially because Jack's a douchebag and Puritans are insanely boring, but also because Brandie and I are lost to our research.

"How do we know if it's the original version or the revival?" asks Brandie.

"I'll revive you," Jack says. Because vaguely sexual nonsense is the native language of all fuckboys. Brandie doesn't look up from her phone. He leans closer, dramatically inhaling. "Brandie Reyes. That hair perfume. Me likey."

Okay, anyone who says "me likey"? Should be punched in the balls. That is my hill to fucking die on.

"It's called shampoo," says Brandie.

Out of all of us in the squad, Brandie's the most patient with f-boys, as evidenced by the fact that she did not, in fact, punch Jack in the balls. Raina's the opposite, of course—at this point, she really just has to glance at an f-boy, and the ball-punch is implied. It's pretty funny to watch it happen in the wild. There's just something about the sight of Raina and Brandie together that appeals to fuckboys on some sort of chemical level—my theory is that it's because they're both really cute, but in completely different ways. Raina's got one of those poreless cheekbone faces, and she basically looks like the sensible younger sister of every white brunette actress on the CW. Whereas with Brandie, it's the unpretentious girl-next-door energy and the dreamy boho wardrobe. Plus Brandie's pretty much oblivious to all flirting, in a way that's completely irresistible to a certain kind of fuckboy. Which is how we've arrived at this blissful scene of Jack doggedly inquiring about Brandie's hair routine. And absolutely none of us have cracked open the worksheet packet.

Jack peers over my shoulder. "Are you looking at porn?"

"Excuse me?"

"Upon a mattress. Daaaaaamn."

"It's a musical." I start digging in my backpack for my head-phones. Something tells me I'll need a little help making Jack's voice disappear.

"A porn musical?" he asks, totally unfazed. I hear Anderson snicker.

"You don't think I'm funny, Garfield?" Jack tilts his head, grinning. "Your boyfriend thinks I'm funny."

He means Andy, of course—though he doesn't actually think Andy's my boyfriend. At this point, Anderson's out to everyone at school. Except, the funny thing is, Anderson and I did date once, in seventh grade. He realized he was gay after our second kiss.

It kind of bugs me, though, the way people get weird about our closeness. If we were a couple, no one would even blink. But people are always saying that if they didn't know Andy was gay, they'd never believe we were just friends.

It's such bullshit. First of all, we're best friends.

Second of all, there's no just. Friendship isn't a just. Yes, Andy's gay. No, we're not a couple. But Anderson Walker is the most important person in my life, hands down.

"*Once Upon a Mattress*." Jack grins. "That can't be a real musical."

I shove my earbuds in and scroll through my music library. Better be Lizzo. She's the only one who could drown out this level of fuckitude.

"Google it," I say.

Then I press play.

# SCENE 7

Raina smacks her palms down on the lunch table. "Final inventory."

"Spotify has the soundtrack." I settle in beside her, unloading my paper bag. "We've got two versions of the movie—"

"Karaoke tracks?"

"All over YouTube," says Andy. "Plus Kate's mom was in it, so—"

Laughter erupts behind me and I don't even have to turn around to know which cluster of tables it's coming from. I'm not saying Roswell Hill's like one of those teen dramas where the camera pans around the cafeteria, zooming in on every perfectly differentiated clique.

But the f-force.

I don't know how to explain it. One on one, they're not so bad. Jack Randall is a human dildo, and I'm pretty sure Mira Reynolds and Eric Graves are actual supervillains, but the vast majority of them are fine in isolation.

When they're together, though, it's a whole different story.

I don't mean to be a judgmental asshole. I know I'm holding on to stuff that happened years ago. Middle school. Elementary school, even. But f-force wounds are no joke.

"Um," Andy says, staring at some point over my shoulder. "I think Chris Wrigley just violated your brother's hoodie."

"He just—what?" I whip my head around, spotting Ryan in an instant. I'd know his slouch anywhere. He's facing away from us, sandwiched between Vivian Yang and Chris Wrigley. "I'm not seeing this violation—"

Andy tilts his chin up. "Just watch."

For almost a minute, there's nothing—but then it happens, lightning fast. Chris Wrigley, fuckboy on a mission, stretches his arm out toward Ryan like he's going in for a side hug. But he's holding something—a french fry? I stare in bewilderment as Chris's hand hovers over Ryan's hood, pausing the way a claw machine does before releasing its prize.

Ryan doesn't notice in the slightest.

"He's put, like, fifteen fries in there," says Andy.

"But why?"

Andy shrugs. "To be an asshole?"

I twist around in my chair, peering back toward Chris and Ryan. I don't get it. I seriously don't. I mean, for one thing, Ryan's cool with Chris. He's cool with everyone. He's cool in general.

"Should I go rescue him?"

"From french fries?" asks Raina.

I shake my head, glaring fiercely at Chris. "From being trolled by some fuckboy."

"You mean his teammate?" asks Raina. "The one he's choosing to sit with?"

"He didn't choose to wear Chris Wrigley's lunch." I scoot my chair back. "I'm sorry, but this is bullying."

"Yeah, I don't know," Raina says. "I think it's just f-boys messing with each other."

"Ryan's not an f-boy." I swipe her arm, and she grins.

I can't help but grin back. It's kind of a running squad joke at this point. No one—I mean no one—gets to call my brother a fuckboy. I don't care if Ryan looks like an f-boy or plays baseball with f-boys. I don't care if he carves a big red F on his chest. Doesn't matter.

And yeah, if I'm honest, it bugs me that Ryan hangs out with assholes like Chris Wrigley. Or Eric Graves and Mira Reynolds. Especially Eric Graves and Mira Reynolds. I don't like it. I don't get it. But it's not like those are his best friends. I'd say Ryan lives in the hazy borderlands of the f-zone. He's vaguely allied with the f-force. But he's not a jerk. He's just a jock who doesn't like to make waves.

Chris, apparently all out of fries, tosses a napkin wad into the hood like it's a basketball. Ryan doesn't even flinch. But the move catches Vivian Yang's attention—and a moment later, she's scooping the fries and trash from Ryan's hoodie, dumping it all back on Chris's tray. Ryan laughs and shoves Chris in the shoulder, but Vivian scoots her chair out and stands. Somehow, she catches my eye and smiles faintly, and I can't help but smile back. Honestly, Vivian's not so bad for an f-girl. I don't even know if she counts as an f-girl. Maybe she's like Ryan, living in the borderlands.

The funny thing is, up until ninth grade or so, she was pretty close friends with Anderson. Not that Andy ever talks about that friend breakup. All I know is they were in church choir together, and they shared voice lessons twice a week, and their parents carpooled to auditions and singing competitions. But then Vivian joined the track team and ditched singing altogether. I guess she ditched Anderson altogether, too.

I twist back around, mostly just to see if Andy noticed her, but he's grinning down at his phone.

"What's so funny?"

"Oh. I'm just." He holds his phone up to show me. "Lindsay sent me a meme."

"Lindsay Ward?" I look at him. "Didn't know you guys text."

The meme itself is one I've seen a million times before, with some anime guy and a butterfly. But the text doesn't quite compute.

Anderson looks at me sheepishly. "Inside joke."

"Oh."

"From Senior D. But it's not—yeah. Sorry." He sets his phone down. "Sorry, we're not really supposed to talk about it."

"Right." My chest squeezes in a way I can't quite explain. Raina and Brandie have moved on to speculating about auditions, but my eyes are locked on Andy's. It's like there's a tiny force field around us.

"Kate, it's not . . . no." Andy leans forward. "We just all kind of agreed not to talk about it, you know? Like what happens in Senior D stays in Senior D. It's a circle of trust thing."

"I'm not part of the circle?"

Andy doesn't say anything.

"Wow."

"Katy, it's not like that."

"Then what's it like?"

"It's not like anything. It would be shitty for me to talk about that class when we specifically agreed not to. That's all."

"Right." I exhale, more loudly than I mean to. "It's just that you said you'd—"

"I'm sorry, okay? I know I said I'd give you the play-by-play, but I'm literally not allowed to. It's not—"

"Andy! Okay, I get it. Sheesh."

He smiles at me tentatively. "You're not pissed?"

"No, I'm not pissed." I bite my lip. "It's just weird, you know? I'm not used to being on the outside of your inside jokes."

"I know—"

"And I'm not used to there being off-limit topics between us."

I mean, Anderson knows when I'm on my period. I know his glasses prescription and his top five Chrissy Teigen tweets. He knows my wavy hair type. By number. I don't even know my own hair number. And not to be morbid, but we know each other's Instagram passwords, just in case one of us dies. Seriously. We know everything about each other.

Anderson reaches across the table and squeezes my hand. "I'm not used to it either."

And maybe it's just a reflex, but I can't help but squeeze back.

# SCENE 8

Andy has a voice lesson after school, and my brother's ghosting my texts. Which makes it a bus day for me. The one downside to not driving.

I've got my laptop crammed in my bag on top of my school stuff. I used to carry around this neon duffel on Dad's house days, big enough to hold three nights' worth of stuff. At this point, though, I barely have anything to drag around with me. Ryan and I tend to have two of most things—two phone chargers, two toothbrushes, two closets of clothes. And my guitar pretty much stays in the trunk of Ryan's car. It's pretty seamless by now.

When the bell rings, I get caught behind a pack of f-boys kicking a textbook across the floor. So I end up running to catch the bus, which leaves me breathless. Of course, I'm the last one on board.

Of all people, Noah Kaplan's in the front seat, cheated out with his back to the window. He's got his arm in a navy sling today, tucked up tight to his chest. Normally, Noah drives. And even before he could, he wouldn't have been caught dead in the front. But I guess broken wrists put a damper on that f-boy life-style. I catch his eye, and he nods. "Bus life," he says.

"Bus life," I say. I settle in behind him and unwind my headphones. But the minute I tap into my music, Noah slides in beside me.

"So Anderson ditched you?"

"What? No—"

"Wow. He abandoned you." Noah shakes his head. "Sentenced you to bus hell."

"Anderson didn't ditch me! He's—"

"—moved on to bigger and better things. I get it. Sometimes we outgrow our friendships, Little Garfield."

"Oh my God, you doofus." I smack his shoulder. "He has a voice lesson."

Noah does this scrunchy-nose grin and scoots an inch closer. I make a big show of turning away from him and popping in my earbuds.

"Here's the thing, though," Noah says.

I swear, this boy can't go two consecutive seconds without talking.

He tips his palms up. "I don't really get the point of voice lessons."

"Great. You don't have to."

"Do they even work?" he asks. "Instruments, I get. You're teaching a skill—"

"How is singing not a skill?"

"But like, either you can sing or you can't, right? It's not like you can just keep practicing till you're Beyoncé."

"No, but you can train." I turn to face him. "You can improve your breath support, expand your range—"

"But why? What's the endgame? I mean, yeah, if you're going to Broadway or something, but 99.9 percent of people literally just end up singing in the shower, so—"

"Are you serious?" I yank out my earbuds. "That's like saying what's the point of playing high school baseball if you're not going to join the MLB."

Noah smiles hugely. "The MLB?"

"Major League Baseball?"

"Yeah, but you don't say 'the MLB.'"

"Why not?" I cross my arms. "You say the NFL, the NBA . . ."

Noah shakes his head, still beaming. "The MLB."

"Anyway." I side-eye him. "Unless you plan to play in the major leagues, you don't get to say voice lessons are pointless."

"Okay . . ." Noah nods, like he's considering this. "But hear me out. Maybe the point of playing high school baseball has nothing to do with baseball itself. Maybe the whole point is, say, impressing girls."

I shrug. "Maybe girls are more impressed by singing than they are by baseball."

I glance at his sling, feeling suddenly guilty. Maybe I'm

being too mean. Am I mean? Is it shitty to tease a baseball player about baseball when he can't actually play baseball?

The bus stops at our street corner, and Noah scoots out, pausing to wait for me in the aisle. "Hey." I look up at him. "Sorry you broke your arm."

"Ah, yeah." He smiles. "Life of an athlete. You know."

"I totally know." I make a grab for his backpack. "Hey, I can carry this."

He laughs. "Little Garfield, you are not carrying my backpack."

"You don't think I can handle two backpacks?" I follow him off the bus and fall into step beside him. "I can handle ten backpacks. You don't even know what I'm capable of."

# SCENE 9

Turns out, Ryan's home. Dad too—he leaves work early on Wednesdays when he can. He's a lawyer, but not the kind who sues people. He does family law, like divorces and custody and child support. Truly an area of expertise for Neil Garfield, PC, who himself is a divorcé, joint custodian, and child Supporter.

"Hiya, Peapod."

Why yes, I'm sixteen years old and my father calls me Peapod. Apparently, that's what I looked like when I was six weeks old in a swaddle. A pea pod.

The dogs burst into the kitchen, so Ryan must have picked them up from Mom's house right after school. Charles is so excited, he's vibrating. I'd say we're at threat level yellow for Charles peeing on the floor.

Dad scoops up Charles with one arm, letting him lick his chin long past the point where it's cute. And then Dad uses his other hand to give Camilla a deep tissue massage on her hips.

Now Camilla's leaning so hard into her butt rub, she's curved into a question mark, and Dad's entire neck is owned by dachshund spit. It's a classy situation.

"So how did it go?" Dad gently deposits Charles on the hardwoods.

"How did what go?"

"Auditions. The musical."

"Auditions haven't happened yet. Not till next Thursday."

Dad's not good with details. He's the opposite of Mom in that way. But he's the one I physically resemble. Ryan too. Everyone says that. Not in the hair, because he's pretty bald, though pictures prove he had a mop of hair just like Ryan and me when he was in college. But he's got the round cheeks and hazel eyes and heart-shaped mouth.

I ditch Dad and the dogs and head upstairs to my brother's room. Ryan gets one warning knock before I open it, but by now I know better than to wait for permission. He's a chronic knock-ignorer.

He's tucked into a gamer chair, thumbing an Xbox controller and wearing the headphones our grandma got him last Chanukah. Ryan's room is honestly a teen boy wonderland, even though the décor hasn't changed since elementary school: blank chalkboard walls punctuated by framed athletic jerseys, a Fathead decal of the Atlanta Falcons logo, and a giant Bulbasaur made from neon lights. But there's no mess anywhere, ever. I swear, Ryan's an even bigger neat freak than Anderson. His room at Mom's house has two twin beds, and even though he only sleeps in one of them, he always makes them both. If Ryan stays local for college next year, he'll probably come home every day, just to keep changing his unused sheets.

He cracks his eyes open when I walk in and slides his headphones off, looking at me expectantly, like *what do you want.* Like he can't even comprehend a world where a sister might pop into her brother's room with no ulterior motive. It's insulting. Also accurate.

"I need your keys."

He scoops them out of his pocket and tosses them to me, and I guess that's the upside of not driving. Pretty easy for Ryan to trust me with his keys when he knows perfectly well I'm not taking his car out.

"Thanks, Ry," I say, but he's already lost to his headphones. I watch him for a moment. Ryan never sings along to songs, or even mouths the words, but his lips always twitch like he wants to. He can actually sing—he just never does anymore, not even the heavily ironic falsetto some guys do on Snapchat or TikTok. That's the one thing I don't get about straight guys—okay, it's one of many, many things I don't get about straight guys. But seriously. Why are some guys so opposed to showing off their singing voices? If their goal is to hook up with girls, shouldn't they lean all the way into it? Even jock girls get melty over boys who can sing. It's a legit romantic superpower, and they don't even use it.

But Ryan's one of those guys who never really dates, even though he's got rumpled brown hair and long lashes and is objectively above average in cuteness. Andy calls Ryan a gorgeous waste of space. But he's kind of shy, and even though I'm pretty sure he likes girls, he's intensely weird about them. Not that it's the kind of thing we could ever talk about. Like. EVER.

My relationship with Ryan is kind of hard to explain.

Honestly, I don't even understand it. I swear there are times when no one gets me like Ryan does. Like when our parents are being weirdos, and we have a whole conversation with just our eyes. Or the way certain phrases, certain words, will hit us in just the same way.

But then he sneaks in late from some f-force party, or he fist-bumps Jack Randall in the hallway, and I get this pang in my chest. I guess I wonder sometimes—if Ryan and I weren't siblings, would we even talk to each other?

I mean, we used to be inseparable. We're only eighteen months apart. Mom calls us Irish twins, even though we're not Irish, and I'm pretty sure a year and a half is way outside the Irish twin window. Ryan turns eighteen next month, and I'll be seventeen in March. We used to play Hot Wheels and Playmobil dollhouse and Pokémon Rumble Blast and Pokémon cards, and we were Ash Ketchum and Pikachu for Halloween two years in a row, and okay, I don't want to name names or call anyone out for being obsessed with Pokémon, but only one of the Garfield kids still has a florescent Bulbasaur on his wall. I'm just saying.

Anyway. At least I've got his car keys.

I head straight downstairs, back through the kitchen, where the pups are snoozing on the floor. My guitar's waiting for me right in the trunk, next to a mitt and a few baseballs. I hoist the case up by its handle and hug the whole thing to my chest.

I love this stupid guitar. It used to be Mom's when she was younger, but Ryan rescued it from the basement a few years ago. He never actually learned to play—he just posed with it a lot for Instagram. Hashtag: "jammin." I'll never let him live that down. I don't think I could even call myself his sister if I did.

Though, to be fair, Ryan's the reason I play guitar at all. After what happened with Eric, I really thought I was done with music forever.

# SCENE 10

Eric Graves. The shittiest guy. My shittiest day. Even now, I want to throw up every single time I think about it. But it's always there. I guess it's kind of my origin story.

Here we go.

Once upon a time in eighth grade, Queen Kate the Clueless fell in love with Sir Dickbrain Fuckmonster Eric the Taintweasel, Level 69 F-boy.

It's hard to explain. Yeah, he was cute. But there were massive red flags from the start. For one thing, Anderson wasn't on board with it. It didn't matter how many times I mentioned the time Eric held the door for me once. Anderson couldn't be persuaded—his belief in Eric's dickbrained taintweasely fuckmonstrousness was unwavering.

It was the opposite of a communal crush.

But eighth-grade me didn't care what Anderson thought about Eric.

I let my crush brain soar. I wrote Eric's name in notebooks.

I orchestrated drive-by encounters in the hallways. I stared at the back of his head so long in social studies, I memorized his neck freckles. And in the evenings, I was even more of a love story fiend than usual. It was practically a chemical craving. I mainlined *To All the Boys I've Loved Before* almost weekly. I inhaled every YA rom-com in the library. And then the squad discovered *Ella Enchanted*, which I watched so often, for so many months that my dad could quote it. Obviously, I had Queen's "Somebody to Love" totally memorized, and I could sing it just like Anne Hathaway in the movie. I had it down to a science. Every inflection, every pause, every tiny dynamic shift. Even King Perfectionist Anderson was impressed.

I mean, here's how much I was feeling myself: I performed it for my mom.

And she loved it. She acted like I'd performed a solo at the Kennedy Center. She sprang up from the couch, full-on applauding, dropping brava after brava. There were seriously tears in her eyes. For weeks afterward, I'd hear her bragging to her music teacher friends about the crispness of my consonants, or my stage presence, or how much my voice had matured.

So I guess I should have seen the whole variety show thing coming.

It wasn't exactly a new conversation. Mom had been trying to talk the squad into singing in the variety show since sixth grade. "You four are so all-in on the musical. Why on earth are you so shy about the variety show?"

I could never quite explain it. Maybe it was a matter of

context? When you sing in a musical, you're a character. There's a script. You're telling a story. You're being directed.

In the variety show, you're you.

But Mom can be kind of a bulldozer when she wants you to do something. And I guess she got it in her head that I should do Ella.

Okay, that's not entirely it.

She wanted me to, yeah. And at first I said no. But then I kept picturing Eric Graves in the audience, staring up at me, entranced. He'd be in the front row. He'd think, how have I never noticed Kate Garfield before?

It was pure cliché nonsense.

I guess I let myself be bulldozed.

My hair was so long back then, it took me an hour to dry and straighten it. I dressed like Ella, too—at least the second-rate mall version of Ella: white peasant top, blue maxi skirt, thick belt. The variety show was just one night, always a Friday. But we did our dress rehearsal as an assembly during the day for the school. I was so wrecked with nerves, Mom had to play the opening notes twice. My voice trembled at first, but I shut my eyes and kept going.

And then the song did what songs do. It took over. It pushed me out of the driver's seat. I was Freddie Mercury and I was Ella and even Rachel from *Glee*, and I'd never felt so beautiful, ever. I opened my eyes after the first chorus, and there was Eric. Front row, center. The house lights were down, and I couldn't quite make out his expression. But he wasn't sleeping or whispering or even texting, like Mira Reynolds was doing beside him. He was paying attention. And when I finished, he clapped and whistled.

I just about bubbled over with joy.

For the rest of the day, I floated through the halls, feeling quietly triumphant. I didn't breathe a word to the squad. But I could just picture Eric on the walk back to homeroom, trying to explain it to his friends. *Her voice. I think I'm falling for her.*

I kept thinking he'd text me. Not that we were on texting terms. But maybe he knew someone who knew someone who knew someone who had my number. Maybe he'd look me up. Maybe he'd follow my Instagram. It's funny—I remember almost nothing about the variety show itself. I just remember being backstage, checking my phone over and over.

Nothing, nothing, nothing.

But as soon as we got home, my brother followed me straight to my room. That's how I knew something was up. He passed me his phone, already open to Mira's finsta page.

There I was.

Thirteen-year-old me, my peasant shirt coming untucked, and a crease I hadn't noticed on the side of my hair. It was the shittiest possible angle—tilted up from below, making me look like a front-facing camera meme in motion. And my painstakingly modulated Ella voice sounded as high as a six-year-old, with round choir-girl vowels and overly enunciated consonants.

There were already thirty-two comments.

*yikes lol*

*saw it live, that was some good shit wow* 💯

*I'M SCREAMING*

*Is that Ryan garfield's sister??*

*What is her face doing at the 32 sec mark? haha*

*this is so embarrassing, I literally can't watch*


"Don't read those," Ryan had said, snatching the phone away.

I could hardly form words. "Mira filmed me?"

Ryan showed me the caption.

Shoutout to e-dawg @sirEricGeneric for this cinematic masterpiece

Everything froze.

E-dawg. Eric Graves.

"Don't sweat it, okay?" Ryan shifted awkwardly beside me. "It only has a hundred and three views."

"A hundred and three people have seen this?"

I remember I could barely breathe. I remember wondering if you could puke your own heart out.

"It's not actually that bad," Ryan said.

I didn't reply.

"I mean, at least you sound—"

"Oh my God, just stop."

Ryan stopped.

I flopped backward on my bed, arms crossed over my chest like a corpse.

The next day, someone started a new account on Instagram

called Kate Garfield Singing. It consisted entirely of ugly screenshots of me from Eric's video. Square after square of my jaw hanging open, lips curled, eyes half closed. The bio said simply: I die a little. I cried, texting the link to the squad.

FUCK THIS, Raina wrote. I WILL DESTROY THEM. HOLY SHIT

This is garbage, sweetie, I'm so sorry, Brandie wrote.

Anderson never wrote back to the text, because he was already at my door.

"That fucking monster," he said. He didn't even pause to say hello.

I wiped my eyes with the heel of my hand. "Which one?"

"Eric. Mira. Both of them. Every single fucking fuckboy who followed the page."

By then, there were seventy-eight. I couldn't stop checking. Some were faces I recognized from the f-force, but some were strangers.

Ryan was on the living room couch, but I plopped down anyway, peering up at Anderson. "I'm never singing again. Ever."

Ryan didn't even look up from his phone.

But I woke up Sunday to find Mom's old guitar propped outside my door.

Ryan was in bed still, but awake, thumbing through a textbook. He didn't exactly look surprised to see me.

I gripped the door frame. "You know I don't play guitar, right?"

"I'll text you a tutorial." He stretched his arm sideways, expertly plucking his phone from its charger. A moment later, my phone buzzed.

I glanced down at it and then back up at him, glaring.

"'Somebody to Love?'" I asked. "Yeah, that's not—"

"It's a good song. Don't let a bunch of assholes ruin it for you."

I pressed play, and the video was pretty basic—just some guy running through the chords and finger positions on an acoustic guitar. But there was something about how the threads of sound came together.

My eyes were glued to the screen. "Who would I even play for?"

"What do you mean, who would you play for?" Ryan said, shrugging. "Just play for yourself."

# SCENE 11

I think Mom's self-destructing. Cause of death: Shabbat dinner. She's got no fewer than eight printed recipes fanned out on the table, and she's making everything from scratch. I don't know if she realizes we have one oven. And she's one person.

Needless to say, we Garfields aren't exactly Shabbat-dinner-level Jews.

"Katy, stick the mini soufflés in the toaster oven. Can we do that? They'll cook, right?"

I survey the kitchen: cabinet doors flung open, pans on every surface, Mom's cheeks streaked with flour. "Wait, so how many people are coming to this?"

"Well. You said Anderson's busy, right?"

"If by busy, you mean at home watching *Tangled*."

"Hasn't he seen it twenty times?"

"Twenty-two."

Not that I'm one to judge. I'm closing in on that figure myself. *Tangled* happens to be the best movie of all time. It gives me legit *Ella Enchanted* vibes, but without the weird f-boy baggage. Plus, there's Flynn Rider—the animated floppy-haired wiseass scoundrel boy of my dreams.

"Okay, so us," Mom says. "Ryan, Ellen, and Ellen's bringing her son."

"So . . . five."

"Mm-hmm. Oh, you'll like Ellen's son. We got dinner the other night when you were at your dad's house. He's a cutie. Looks just like his dad, and let me tell you, Paul is handsome. A total schmuckboy, but handsome." Mom purses her lips. "Very conservative. He grew up right in Mentone, right by camp. But he's turned into one of those Fox News Republicans. It's very sad."

"He went to camp with you guys?"

"Oh, no, he was a townie, and of course, that was this whole other thing. Ellen thought I was being a snob about him living in town, but it wasn't that. No ma'am. I didn't like the way he talked to her. Very condescending. I don't know, it all seems so silly now. Can you imagine losing your best friend over a guy like that? I'm just so stinking grateful for Facebook—otherwise Ellen and I would never have reconnected. I'd never have known she was back in Georgia."

I'm just so stinking grateful for Facebook. There's a phrase never uttered by anyone younger than forty.

". . . like no time had passed. It was remarkable. There's just something about old friends. And her son, Matthew, is absolutely lovely."

Every cell in my body freezes. "Matthew?"

Okay, that squeak you just heard? Was my voice jumping a full fucking octave.

Mom's as oblivious as always. "Such a sweetheart. Oh, he was telling me some story about—"

Deep breath. "Is his name Matt Olsson?"

"Oh, that's right! I forgot he's a senior. You and Ry might have run into him at school. He's—"

"Matt Olsson's coming here?" I grip the back of my chair so hard, I can see my knuckles. "Tonight?"

"Any minute." Mom exhales, glancing back toward the oven. "Oy. Okay. No good."

"I'll help. Sorry. Give me . . . one second." I've already tapped into my text chain with Anderson.

RED ALERT RED ALERT 🔔 My mom's friend Ellen? IS
    MATT'S MOM
    AND HE'S COMING OVER
    COKE-AD MATT
    IS COMING OVER
    TONIGHT 🗣

"Kate! Can you get water on the table? And where's your brother?"

I set my phone down. "Ice or no ice?"

The doorbell rings.

"Goddammit," Mom says. She heads straight to the door, still in her apron, still flour-faced, and by the time I catch up, she's hugging Ellen in the doorway.

Ellen, for what it's worth, is like a clone of my mom. They

even look alike—brown hair, big brown eyes, and they both have those hyperanimated, expressive faces. Ellen gasps when she sees me. "Is that Kate? Oh, honey. You look just like your Facebook pictures."

"Oh. Uh. Thank you?"

"Look at those gorgeous cheeks. My God, Maggie. Your girl. And this is my son, Matthew. Matthew, Kate's a junior—"

"We've met." He smiles. "Hey, Kate."

His voice. Saying my name.

The moms, the house, the soufflés, everything. All of it evaporates.

I am officially a puddle on the floor.

# SCENE 12

Mom keeps the mini soufflés and the hand-breaded chicken tenders and ditches all the other recipes—but she adds a veggie platter and a frozen pizza to the mix. It's an absurdly un-kosher Shabbat dinner. The kitchen's a disaster zone, with the exception of the gleaming, freshly mopped floor. And for once, the mop in question wasn't Camilla's tongue. Garfield family hospitality at its finest.

Mom pops open a wine bottle Ellen brought and digs out the candles, and we're just about to light them when the front door creaks open.

"Helloooo?"

"That must be the escort I hired," Mom says, she and Ellen just start cackling.

I catch Ryan's eyes for the barest split second. "Mom, stop," he says flatly.

Whereas I'm just sitting here loving the fact that Mom said

"escort." In front of Matt. You know what's really awesome? Your mom and your crush's mom talking about escorts.

Anyway, it's not an escort. It's Anderson.

"Heeeyyy." He peers into the dining room. "Am I too late?"

"Oh, of course you're not too late, sweetie. Ellen, this is Anderson Walker from next door. He's Kate's best friend. Look at you, boychick. I love that little bow tie."

Anderson, you absolute thirst machine. This boy literally changed into a fresh button-down and bow tie and straight up waltzed in here for dinner.

"Got your text," Andy says, eyeing me slyly.

"I can see that."

And okay. I'm glad he's here and everything, but can we just take a moment to recognize that he's ditching Rapunzel and Flynn for Matt? Because he definitely wasn't planning to ditch Rapunzel and Flynn for me. And, like, I get it. It's just insulting.

"So nice to meet you, Anderson," Ellen says. "I feel like I'm in the presence of Maggie and Ellen, the next generation."

I almost choke on my water.

Back up a minute. Andy and I aren't the next Mom and Ellen. Mom and Ellen are the opposite of friendship goals. They didn't even talk to each other for two decades. More than two decades. I'm sorry, but the thought of meeting Andy's kid for the first time as a teenager makes me want to curl into a ball and cry. And if I ever tell Anderson's kids they look just like their Facebook pictures, just go ahead and kill me.

We add an extra place setting for Andy at the head of the table, and Matt's directly to his right. So now they're giggling together over something that happened in Senior D this morning. Apparently Noah Kaplan had to pretend to be a mime. I don't really get what's funny about it, but Matt and Andy seem to think it's the height of comedy. Guess it's one of those things where you had to be there. Of course, Ryan doesn't even bother feigning interest—he's just scrolling through his phone.

Meanwhile, Ellen and Mom are basically just complaining about Matt's dad. "He wanted to get him a BB gun. Can you believe it? Matthew was six. I said, 'Absolutely not. Not in my house.'"

"Oh my God. Yes. No, of course. It just makes me so angry. And those hyperrealistic toy weapons. Hate them. Oh, and paintball!" Mom's in full rant mode now, about the eighth-grade paintball trip the athletic association sponsors every February. "It's so dangerous. I always tell Ryan and Kate no. Absolutely never. Not at home. Not at camp—"

"Oh, that's right!" Ellen turns toward me in her chair. "Matthew tells me you guys all worked together at camp this summer. What a neat coincidence!"

"I know." I smile, but my eyes flick back to the boys. Anderson's telling some story, tapping his fingertip to his palm. Ryan's staring into space. But Matt's hanging on every word.

"Well your mom and I loved doing the plays at camp. And you know, we grew up together around here, too. Different schools, but we were in a few shows together at the rec center."

Out of nowhere, Andy and Matt burst out laughing. So

fantastic. So glad they're having such a fantastic fucking time together.

But oof. I don't like this feeling. I don't know where that little voice in my head is coming from. It doesn't even make sense for me to be jealous—I'm the one who invited Anderson. This morning! Literally today! And in what universe would I ever prefer his absence to his presence? I mean, it's Anderson. So maybe I should stop beaming stink eye down the table with my mind and step up to the plate.

"Hey, do you guys want to—"

A burst of laughter from Andy and Matt. My words disappear.

"You don't even know." Anderson shakes his head. "And he had this whole thing with Lansing. You should have seen his face when Kate thought Detroit was the capital—"

"Wait." I lean in. "Are you talking about Alexander from camp—"

"Remember how you couldn't call him Alex? Had to be Alexander," Andy says.

"Oh, but I liked that," I say. "It was sweet."

"He was insanely hot, though," Andy says. "I'd wife that, for sure."

And there it is—that tiny indentation in Andy's cheeks. The Dimple of Self-Consciousness. I know this moment. It took me a few years to recognize it in the wild, but this is Andy coming out. He glances sideways, and I can almost feel him holding his breath, waiting for Matt to react.

"I mean, you'd have to move to Lansing if you wifed that," Matt says. "No question."

Andy grins. "I hear Lansing's pretty amazing."

"According to Alexander," I say.

"We both know you googled the shit out of that town," Andy says. He turns to Matt. "For the record, Kate had just as big of a crush on that dude as I did."

And of course—of course—Andy's words land smack-dab in the center of one of those random conversational pauses.

Mom turns to Andy, openly delighted. "Kate had a crush?"

I shoot Andy my most violent death glare.

He bites his lip. "Um, it wasn't really—"

"You know what?" I stand abruptly. "I need . . . something."

"I'll come with you." Andy practically leaps out of his chair. "Be right back," he calls over his shoulder, already well on his way to my bedroom.

I shut the door behind us. "What was that?"

"Katy, I'm sorry! She was having her own conversation over there. I didn't think—"

"You realize she's going to remember this forever, right? I'll be hearing about Alexander from Michigan for the rest of my life." I sink onto the edge of my bed.

"Do you think maybe you're overreacting? Just a little?" He settles in beside me, hooking his arm around my back.

"No!" I lean my head on his shoulder and sigh. "Shut up. I just don't like people knowing about my crushes. You know that. Come on, that's privileged information."

"Katy, it's a two-year-old crush."

"Yeah, well, the Code of Secrecy has no statute of limitations—"

"Technically, it's not a code violation unless I tell Alexander."

I glare at him.

"I still think that dude was gay," Andy says. "Remember when he touched my hair?"

"Didn't you say that was some racist microagressive bullshit—"

"Oh, it one hundred percent was." He pats the top of his Afro and sends a side-eye out into the universe. "But the way he did it so tenderly? I was like, sir, you're gay—"

"What? No. He was bi. He had that girlfriend!"

"In Lansing," says Andy. "His fake-ass girlfriend from fake-ass Lansing—"

"Excuse me—"

"EXCUSE ME, LANSING, MICHIGAN, IS REAL, AND IT'S THE CAPITAL."

I crack a smile.

He hugs me sideways. "I love your face, Katypie."

"I love your stupid face, too." I roll my eyes. "Come on, let's go see if dessert's ready."

# SCENE 13

Saturday's weather is pure liquid nonsense. I'm admittedly kind of a brat about rain. It's essential, and that's fine. I support its existence. I just don't get why rain has to be so rude. It doesn't care about your plans, your hair, anything. Rain just slides right in, like some ecological fuckboy in your DMs. No permission asked or granted, leaving you no choice but to roll with it.

Which is why today is a don't-leave-the-house day. A pajama day. An official squad homework accountability day. Andy's off doing audition prep with his voice teacher, but the girls are here, and Brandie's even doing real work. She's sprawled on my bed, thumbing through a massive paperback—*Les Misérables* in its original French. Brandie's in her own league when it comes to languages. She's always been fluent in English and Spanish, and even though she didn't start French until middle school, she's fluent in that now, too. She's too advanced even for AP, so now she's taking an independent study in French literature. But Madame Blanche lets her pick her own books, so Brandie can pick stuff she actually likes. You'd think other teachers could be that thoughtful, but weirdly, no one's letting me pick *Les Mis* as my algebra textbook.

Raina's got algebra due, too, so we've taken over my bean-bag chairs in the corner. We've got our books in hand, but that's about as far as we've gotten. I don't mean to be a slacker. But it's just hard to focus on math when there's an audition to obsessively speculate about.

"No, there's precedent," Raina's saying. "Harold's school did *Once Upon a Mattress* freshman year. Female Jester and Minstrel. They just transposed a few notes."

"And it's all tenor, right? Brandie, you could probably sing the Jester stuff as is—"

"Confirmed. I've heard her do it," says Raina. "But Minstrel goes a little low sometimes—"

"Okay, who do we think is gunning for the Minstrel? Probably Colin, right, but I don't think he'll be able to nail the dynamics—"

"Oh, it'll be Lana Bennett," says Raina.

"Ohhhhh. Yup. You're right."

"And Brandie, just think!" Raina says. "If you get Jester, you and Lana are going to get to spend so much time together! Yay!"

"Mm-hmm. That's a lot of ifs, but okay," Brandie says.

"Best friends." Raina smiles slyly. "Best, best friends. You and Lana."

Brandie ignores her, which is her general MO when we troll

her about Lana Bennett. But trolling Brandie about Lana is the most delicious pastime on earth.

The problem is, Brandie gives off such buttercup angel energy. She can't help it. It's who she is. But Lana seems to take Brandie's fundamental essence as a specific appeal for lifelong best friendship. So she's always inviting Brandie to hang out and sending her long, confessional texts about boys, to which Brandie mostly just replies with periodic polite emojis. It's pretty wild, because Lana seems to vaguely hate the rest of us.

Brandie sets down her book and covers her eyes. "We're seeing a movie the Friday after next—"

"Brandie, no!" Raina gasps. "How did this happen?"

Brandie peeks through her fingers. "Well, okay. So, Emma was telling me about that movie with Kristen Wiig, and I was like, 'Oh, I want to see that.' And then Lana overhears that, and jumps in—"

"The ambush," says Raina.

"Yeah. I didn't really know what to say, so I just tried to be vague, like, 'Yeah, maybe.'" Brandie bites her lip. "But then she starts suggesting specific dates—"

"Uh-oh." I wince.

"And then you set polite but firm boundaries." Raina raises her eyebrows at Brandie. "Because you don't owe anyone your friendship."

"Well I said I was busy, but then she kept suggesting alternative dates, so I felt kind of trapped . . ."

"Oh, that's hard, B. I'm sorry."

"And now she's already ordered tickets, and I'm just like, okay. So, that's happening." Brandie frowns. "I feel so mean."

"Brandie, oh my God. You're the opposite of mean." I shake my head.

"I'm just saying—"

There's a knock on my bedroom door. "Come in!" I call out, expecting Mom.

It's not Mom.

"Hey."

It's Matt. In my doorway.

"Hi!" I spring up from the beanbag chair and make a bee-line for my bed, kicking approximately six pairs of underwear underneath it. And of course, my phone jumps out of my hands in the process. I don't even just drop it like a normal person. Somehow it ends up skidding across the hardwoods like a hockey puck. I look up at Matt with my best I-meant-to-do-that smile. "Come on in!"

"Your mom said you were here. She told me to tell you something about . . . six inches?"

"The door," I blurt, blushing. Why does the phrase *six inches* sound so . . . penile? Wow, I sure hope Matt thinks I'm speculating about his penis size. With my mom.

Also, what on earth is Mom smoking? Raina and Brandie are here! Like, what the fuck kind of orgy is she even envisioning?

"Anyway." Matt's blushing too. "I was just returning a Tupperware. What are y'all up to?" he asks.

My phone starts buzzing—undoubtedly Anderson—but I stretch my leg out to kick it under the bed with my underwear. Andy texts are dangerous. For all I know, he's just discussing the play, but even then, it could change on a dime. At any moment, he could switch right on over to the topic of Matt's general gorgeousness and awesomeness and whether or not he's single. Which would be a recipe for total disaster if Matt happened to glance at my phone.

I plop onto the edge of my bed. Matt hovers beside me, hesitating. "Okay if I sit?"

"Oh, of course! Here." I scoot closer to Brandie to make room, but she slides off the bed, grabbing her phone. "Raina, we should probably head—"

"Yup!" Raina jumps up. "You two have fun. Be good."

Then she catches my eye for the barest split second and makes a big show of leaving the door six inches open.

# SCENE 14

Matt turns to me as soon as they leave. "Hey, you're auditioning for the musical, right?"

I choke back a laugh. "Yup."

I mean. I've only built my entire world around the school musical, last year, and the year before that, and every other year since sixth grade. I seriously wake up every single morning thinking about the best ways to deliver Winnifred's lines. I think I've listened to the soundtrack from start to finish—I don't know—thirty times.

"Okay, cool," Matt says, leaning back. He's sort of halfway lying down now, legs hanging off my bed. "So, do most people end up getting cast?"

"I think everyone gets cast. Even if you totally suck, Zhao will just stick you in the background. Not you, like you." I blush. "I don't mean you suck. You don't suck. Like, at all. Ha. Yeah, no. I've heard you sing."

Kate. For the love of God. Get your shit together.

"Anyway." I swallow. "Are you trying out?"

He shrugs, smiling. "It's a requirement for Advanced Drama."

"Wait—really?"

Okay, Anderson never mentioned that—which is weird, because Matt being in the play is a pretty big deal in Kate and Anderson world. I mean, yeah, I kind of thought maybe he would be. But now it's official, which means hours of rehearsal, cozying up backstage and at set design. And it's more than just the time together. It's hard to explain, but there's a certain kind of closeness that comes with working on a play. Maybe it's the we're-in-it-together team feeling, or the vulnerability that comes from creating something, or the slaphappy intimacy of tech week. Maybe it's hormones. I don't know the science behind it. I just know it's a different, leveled-up kind of friendship. Almost like you're siblings. Except for the part where you get caught making out in the lighting booth, cough, cough, Pierra and Colin.

Uh. I'll just state for the record, though, that I wouldn't mind making out with Matt in the lighting booth.

I sit up straighter, cheeks burning. "So."

"So."

"So you moved here."

He smiles. "I did."

Awkward silence, and it's a big one. One for the history books. But listen—talking and crushing simultaneously isn't easy. It's a whole lot for one brain. Because obviously, you can't just spew what you're really thinking, which in this case is

76

basically a bunch of heart emojis. And you don't want to cast yourself as Generic Stranger Number Six, who speaks only in basic-ass questions like—

"How do you like Roswell?" I ask.

Nailed it.

But Matt leans back a little, staring up at the ceiling. "It's good! I mean, it's really different. I think the weirdest part is my dad not being here."

"Oh." My stomach flutters. "I'm sorry. I shouldn't have—"

"No, it's fine. We're not close. At all. He's not very . . ." Matt trails off.

For a moment, we're both silent.

"Divorce is just weird," he says finally.

I nod. "So weird."

"I mean, you get it. How long have your parents been . . . ?"

"Seventh grade. So I'm pretty much used to it."

"Good to know you get used to it."

I scoot closer—close enough that our pinkies are touching—which feels insanely brave, but also right. "Do you miss your dad?"

"Mmm." He smiles slightly. "Not really."

And something clicks in my brain. Nothing earth-shattering or game-changing. Just this one tiny detail.

Matt Olsson smiles when he's sad.

I don't mean it like he's in denial. It's more like he's pushing it back, tucking the badness away. It's strangely moving. And it makes my whole body feel warm.

Maybe it's just the intimacy of knowing this tiny thing about him. It's not a thing you can know from Instagram. It's something real.

He turns toward me. "Where does your dad live?"

"Oh, just like ten minutes away."

"That's really nice. Are you and Ryan there a lot?"

"Wednesday and Thursday nights, plus every other weekend."

"Is that hard?"

"Sometimes? I don't know. Mostly it just . . . is."

He nods. "I know exactly what you mean."

# SCENE 15

And now I can't get that out of my head.

*I know exactly what you mean.*

It tugs at the edge of my mind the whole time Matt's here. And even after he leaves, it's there, stealing my brain away from algebra, and making my squad texts so short and distracted, even Brandie calls me out.

But I can't stop thinking about it. It's the most underrated sentence on earth. *I know exactly what you mean.*

Translation: no, you're not weird. Even your weird stuff isn't weird. You make sense.

The thing is, I don't usually talk about the divorce, apart from the logistics.

It's not a secret, of course. I just never want to be a brat about it, especially the whole joint custody thing. Because I know how lucky I am. My parents live three miles apart from each other. It isn't a tragedy. It's just my life. Split in half.

But it's hard to explain the way that wears on you. The

feeling of constant motion. The fact that you're never one hundred percent home. The way it falls into this unsettling new normal. It's just life. It just is.

And somehow Matt already gets that.


Mom and Ryan head out for a college info session, and it doesn't take me long to give up entirely on algebra. When I'm in this kind of mood, there's only one thing I'm good for. I tune my guitar, and then I strum until a song takes shape. "Hold Me, Thrill Me, Kiss Me," which I've loved my whole life. It always gives me this soft, enchanted feeling, like I'm in an English rose garden, or some rustic meadow dance floor strung with fairy lights.

Once upon a time, it was my parents' wedding song. You'd think that alone would suck out all the romance for me. But it hasn't, not even slightly. Maybe some songs are just unruinable.

I sing the first verse with my eyes closed, feeling my way through the chords. My mind keeps drifting back to Matt. Smiling, sad Matt, holding my hand as we stroll down a winter path, right at dusk. I'm dressed like Elizabeth Bennet, and my hair's collecting snowflakes. "But they never stood in the dark with you, love."

I know I'm singing too loudly. I know my voice is too earnest, too ardent. But I'm so moonstruck, I can't help it. I think my heart's wrapped in clouds.

Someone knocks—and everything freezes. My hand goes rigid against my guitar strings.

"Hello?"

My heart's hammering so loudly, I can barely hear my own voice. *Hello?* Maybe I didn't say it out loud at all. Just in my head. Maybe this is all in my head. I glance out the window—no cars in the driveway. So, the only person who could feasibly be here is Andy, and he's still with his voice teacher. Ergo, no one's here. No one's knocking on my bedroom door. My mile-a-minute brain made the whole thing up, just to troll me.

"Little Garfield?"

Oh my God.

"Um." Nope. Nope. Not real. "Noah?"

Of course, he takes that as an invitation.

So now Noah Kaplan's in my doorway, grinning like a T. rex. "Why'd you stop singing?"

You know those stoves where the knob makes a flame shoot straight up? Zero to burning. That's my face.

"How are you here?" It comes out like a croak.

He crosses the room in two strides, plops onto the edge of my bed. "What do you mean, how am I here?"

"This is my mom's house."

"I'm not allowed at your mom's house?"

"No, I mean, how did you get here? Where's your car?"

"At home. I can't drive until this comes off." He lifts his cast arm.

"So, what, you just walked here?"

Noah pops his sneakers off using only his feet. I always forget he can do stuff like that. Picking up stuff off the ground with his toes, and then sort of tossing it up into his hands. He says it helps keep him lazy. I don't even get how he's an athlete.

He scoots back beside me by the headboard. "Of course I walked here."

"You walked here from your house."

"Mm-hmm."

"That's like an hour-long walk."

"It was nice." He pats the head of my guitar, yawning.

"In the rain."

"I like rain."

"You're, like, completely dry. You're not even—okay, you're just making stuff up, aren't you?"

"Possibly."

I shove him hard in the shoulder.

"Okay, okay! Little Garfield. Sheesh." He glances at me sidelong, eyes crinkling. "If you must know, I'm here because your brother, Ryan Kevin Garfield, stole my phone—"

"He stole your phone."

"Well, I left it in his car yesterday."

"Ah."

"And unfortunately, my sources have informed me that it's still in his car, which is currently parked at Georgia Tech, and will be for another"—he checks my wall clock—"forty-six minutes."

"Which is why you're here . . . now."

"My ride had places to be, Little G."

"Your ride. You mean your mom?"

"No, it was definitely a limo. Like a big limo full of hot girls."

"Don't call your mom a hot girl. That's weird."

"It is weird." He wrinkles his nose. But then he smiles and taps the head of my guitar again. "Anyway. Sorry I interrupted your whole thing. What were you singing?"

"Nothing. I wasn't."

"What? Come on, you should keep going. I really like that song—"

"Nope." I set my guitar down, pushing it toward the foot of my bed.

"Come on, you're so good, though! It sounded amazing. It was the MLB of singing. I was like—whoa. She really means it—"

"I don't."

"You totally do. Who were you singing about? Wait, let me guess. Shawn Mendes. No. No, wait. Who's that guy from that movie?"

"That guy from that movie." I bite back a smile. "Very specific."

"You know who I mean. The cheekbones guy. With the French name—"

"I have no idea where you're going with this."

"I'm going to start leaving my phone in Ryan's car more," Noah says. "If it means I get to experience Kate Garfield singing to Timothée Whatshisname . . ."

All the air whooshes out of my lungs. Noah's smiling expectantly, but when he looks at me, it falters.

Kate Garfield Singing.

His eyes widen. "Kate—"

"It's not funny." I scoot off the bed, grabbing my guitar and shoving it into its case. "Okay? You're not funny."

I slam the case shut. And Noah's mouth falls shut, too.

# SCENE 16

Of course, the minute Andy and I walk into school on Monday, there's Noah, ready to pounce. "Kate!" He intercepts us in the lobby. "Hey, Anderson."

"Hiiii." Anderson glances at me sidelong, eyebrows raised.

"How's it hanging?" asks Noah.

"You mean my testicles?" Anderson asks. "They're fine, thank you."

For once, Noah's speechless.

Anderson smiles and elbows me gently. "Love you. See you in history." Then he adjusts his messenger bag—backpacks ruin Andy's aesthetic—and disappears down the hall.

Noah blinks. "Why are we talking about testicles?"

"You brought them up." I blush. "I mean, not up, physically—"

"This conversation needs to be, like, a hundred percent less literal," says Noah.

"Yeah." I nod quickly. "Yup. Anyway—"

"Anyway," he says, suddenly serious. "About yesterday. I just wanted to apologize again—"

"No, no, no. You're good. I overreacted. It's fine."

"No, it was a stupid thing to say. I just wasn't thinking about that whole mess. Not—I don't mean the singing was messy. Just the Instagram stuff."

"Noah?"

"Yup?"

"I don't want to talk about it."

"Okay." He nods. "Great. So we're good?"

"Good. Great."

"Great," he says. "Perfect. Because I need your help."

"My help?"

He smiles slightly and nods. Then he squares his shoulders, looking right into my eyes.

Aha. I recognize this maneuver. The eyegasm. An f-boy classic. It's this extra split second of eye contact, but with the intensity ramped up to eleven, typically ending in a makeout. Even Jack Randall pulls it off, and he's so stoned half the time he can barely keep his eyes open. But Noah's, like, unsettlingly good at it.

"My help with what?" I say flatly.

I refuse to succumb to the eyegasm.

But man. Noah's got these huge, gold-brown eyes, and his eyelashes are ridiculous. It's honestly unfair. F-boys should be required by law to have that muscly jock hotness that does nothing for me. Like, I truly, sincerely don't care about six-packs. Six-packs are meh.

But pretty eyes? Those are not meh.

"Well, I was thinking," says Noah. "Maybe you could teach me how to sing."

"How to sing?"

"Preferably by Thursday."

"You're trying out for the play?" I raise my eyebrows.

"For Senior D. They're making me."

"Right."

"I just kept thinking yesterday, like. Wow. Kate's such a good singer. Maybe she could tell me her secrets. But I was like, no, you can't really teach someone singing." He rubs his hands along the length of his cast. "But then I remembered what you said on the bus—"

"Oh. Noah. No, that's not—"

"And I thought, you know what? I'm not great, but maybe I could get better with some training. Right? Always room for improvement."

"Yeah. There's room."

I don't quite know what to say. I don't even know if he's serious.

Here's what I do know: Noah's not one of those guys like my brother, holding back wells of untapped talent. Noah Kaplan singing sounds like a goose slowly dying. We were in Temple choir together for over two years, and even the cantor gave up on him. She flat out stopped in the middle of "Oseh Shalom" and asked Noah to mouth the words. And instantly, the whole choir sounded fifty times better. If it were me, I'd have been mortified, but Noah seemed to find the whole thing hilarious.

"Are you actually required to try out for a singing part?"

"No idea. I didn't ask."

"I think you should ask."

"What if I want to try out for a singing part?"

I laugh. "Why?"

"Because."

"What, is there a hot girl in that class or something?"

"Is there a hot girl." Noah pats my shoulder. "Kate. It's theater. I'm basically swimming in hot girls."

"But do you mean hot girls like hot girls, or hot girls like your mom's limo—"

"Nope. Nope. That's gross." He shakes his head firmly. "I'm talking about hot girls. Just regular old—okay, not old hot girls. Age-appropriate hot girls. It's a class full of age-appropriate hot girls."

"And Anderson and Matt," I point out, feeling suddenly nauseated.

Matt. And hot girls. I was so busy being jealous of Andy, I didn't even consider the hot girls.

"So you'll do it?" Noah asks.

"Wait—what?"

"This afternoon sound good? I'll get Garfield to drive us— other Garfield, I mean. Big Garfield. Bro Garfield—"

"Noah." My lips tug at the corners. "I can't teach you to sing."

He looks stricken. "Why not?"

"Because you couldn't carry a tune if it jumped into your arms?"

"Little Garfield. Wow. Tell me how you really feel—"

"Okay, remember when you and Ryan tried to teach me sports?"

Sixth grade, right after Noah moved here from Texas. He and I used to hang out a lot, but it's not like we were ever really in sync. Noah always wanted to do stuff. But not my kind of stuff. Not stuff like reading with color-coded sticky tabs or singing the *Les Mis* soundtrack from start to finish. Noah just wanted to kick soccer balls and run drills with my brother, and I could never keep up, no matter what I did. So I tried to make them teach me.

He nods gravely. "That was so sad."

"Okay, no. You're sad. This isn't about sports. That was an analogy. That was me trying to explain to you why I can't teach you to sing."

"Really? Because it actually sounds like a reminder that you owe me one." Noah flips his palm up, the one with no cast. "So. This afternoon?"

"I'm at my mom's house."

"Tomorrow?"

"Mom's house."

"Wednesday?"

I pause—for like a split second, not even—and Noah lights up. "Wednesday it is! Sweet. We'll make Ryan drive us."

"He can't. Dad's taking his car in for an oil change. Also, doesn't Ryan have baseball on Wednesday?"

"Ohhh. Right, he does. Yup."

"So Wednesday's out."

"Oh no it's not. Little Garfield, come on. We'll live the bus life. Wednesday's perfect." He wrestles his bag onto his shoulder and glances back before he leaves. "Seriously, you're the best. Thanks for offering this."

"I didn't."

"See you Wednesdaaaaaaay," he warbles.

# SCENE 17

All week, I'm a yarn ball of nerves. I can't focus on anything. On the drive to school Wednesday, I'm so queasy, Anderson has to pull over.

"Breathe in and out." He rubs my shoulder. "You okay?"

"Why am I always like this?"

"Oh, Katy. It's just theatrical morning sickness. You know that."

I make it through algebra, which is a miracle under the circumstances. Not that Ms. Evans cares in the slightest. She is all about polynomials today. Teachers never get it. Like, come on. It's audition week. In a just world, they'd turn off the lights, skip the academic bullshit, and just let us all curl up in fetal positions with the *Once Upon a Mattress* soundtrack on repeat.

By lunchtime, the squad has officially descended into panic mode. All of us. Brandie's too nervous to eat. Raina's convinced she's losing her voice, so she's taken a vow of silence.

She's actually carrying around a spiral-bound notebook with common Raina phrases to flip to, like: *Nope. Hell the fuck yes. I'm judging you. Bye, f-boy.*

But for whatever reason, Anderson's the eye of the hurricane today. Calm amid the chaos. He slides gingerly into his seat, cupping his chin in one hand.

"Matt wants to get together and rehearse," he says, and my heart—

Just.

Plummets.

Wow. Matt and Andy. Rehearsing together. And making out, probably. Romantic multitasking. My best friend and my crush.

It's just weird. Our communal crushes have always been so safely contained. Like a row of dolls on a shelf. We take them down when we want them and put them back when we're done.

But Matt's Pinocchio. He's this real-life guy who walks and talks and makes plans, and apparently those plans are with Anderson. Just Anderson. Not me.

It's just great. Absolutely great.

"Have fun with that," I say, aiming for casual. But it comes out spiky and short.

Anderson rolls his eyes. "Okay, sourpuss, it's not a date. Y'all are all invited. Right after school, my house."

Raina holds up her notebook. *Hell the fuck yes.*

"Oh, fun. I'll bring snacks," says Brandie.

"Nothing dairy," Andy says firmly. "None of us are having

dairy until after auditions. Actually, Katy, can you bring tea? Your dad has all that herbal tea, right?"

My chest feels tight. "I can't come."

"Oh no! No, I'll drive you. Don't worry about the tea. We'll leave straight from school."

"No, it's not that. It's just—I promised . . . Noah."

Raina snorts. "Noah Kap—" she starts to say but quickly clamps her mouth shut, flipping frantically through her notebook. *Bye, f-boy. Bye, f-boy. Bye, f-boy.* She stabs the words repeatedly with her pointer finger.

I cover my face. "I knooooooow."

"I don't get it," says Anderson.

"I'm supposed to teach him how to sing."

"Okay, that's random." Andy reaches for my hand across the table. "Can you get out of it?"

"No. I don't know."

God. Of fucking course. The one day—literally the one day I make plans without the squad, Matt Olsson enters the picture. And yeah, I guess I could ditch Noah. One afternoon certainly won't make or break his singing voice. But this kind of situation throws me. I'm allergic to making choices. At least I'm allergic to choosing between people. I mean, on the one hand, I have my best friends, my whole squad, and the cutest boy in the universe, all of whom would like me to spend my afternoon with them rehearsing for the musical I can't stop daydreaming about. On the other hand, there's Noah, a literal f-boy, who basically tricked me into hanging out in the first place.

The thing is, I'm not a person who blows off commitments.

Holy shit, though. The thought of the squad and Matt rehearsing without me.

I guess a tiny part of me is relieved it's not just Andy and Matt. Raina and Brandie will keep things cockblocked. But even that thought is so strange. Cockblocking Anderson. It's never even crossed my mind before. Why would it? It would be like tripping my own dance partner. Pointless and absurd, practically a self-own. But maybe it's different with Matt. I don't know what the rules are here. We've never had a communal crush turn into a real crush before.

"I'm so mad at myself right now." I sigh into the sleeve of my flannel.

"You'll be fine. Just remember, no dairy." Anderson narrows his eyes slyly. "Noah can have dairy."

"You're evil," says Brandie.

"What? I don't care if he's Kate's protégé. He's my competition."

"Noah's not my protégé." I can't help but smile, just a little. "And he's definitely, definitely not your competition."

# SCENE 18

In fact, Noah's even worse than I thought.

"Middle C," I say. "Just—" I sing a quick quarter note, no frills or vibrato.

Noah's perched on the edge of my bed, arm tucked into his sling. And yeah, his back is straight, so he gets points for posture. But vocally?

"Ahhhhh . . ."

"You sound like you're getting a strep test."

Noah beams. "Is that good?"

"No."

"Ahhhhhhhhhhhhhh . . ."

"Maybe just hum it."

"Mmmmmmmmm." He glances up at me. "How's that?"

"Better."

It's not better. He's basically picking notes at random. If I hadn't been in choir with him, I'd swear he was messing with me.

"This room's so different from your mom's house." He leans back on his good elbow, peering up at my canopy. "It's like a little kid's room."

"Um, okay. No one asked—"

"I don't think this room has changed since middle school. Like, you haven't moved a single piece of paper on the desk, have you?"

"So what?"

It's true—my room at Dad's house is a museum of me. I've got my most loved teddy bear twins, Amber and Ember. The walls are pink, still covered with Rapunzel decals, and the bed's a canopy, because I was That Kid. There's a ceramic tea set on my dresser, a massive bookcase, plus a giant bin full of doll clothes, featuring a few too many hand-sewn togas from Brandie and Raina's short-lived American Girl Fashion Designer phase. I mean, it's nothing Noah hasn't seen before. If it were Matt, though, I'd die.

Of course, Matt's currently at Anderson's house without me.

"Let's try singing along with the soundtrack," I say quickly.

"Aye-aye, Captain."

"All right. Which one are you using for your audition?"

"No idea."

"Okay . . ." I hook my phone to my speaker and start flipping through my music library. "Which songs do you know the lyrics to?"

But when I glance back at Noah, he's lying all the way back, with his arm behind his head and his eyes closed.

"Noah?"

He sits up with a start. "Wait, what?"

"Did you just fall asleep?"

"Nooooo." He smiles crookedly. "Maybe."

"Noah!"

I just gape at him. This is unreal. I'm missing the ultimate squad rehearsal for this. For this f-boy, who's literally sleeping through the favor I'm doing for him. Seriously? I'm not asking you to be Josh Groban. Just be, like, physically awake. Not a high bar to pass.

"I'm up!" He nudges my arm. "Come on. Katy. What was the question?"

I blink slowly. "Which songs do you know the lyrics for?"

"Which songs in general?"

"From *Once Upon a Mattress.*"

"Oh, right." He nods. "None. Haven't listened to it yet."

I laugh flatly. "You're joking."

"No one told me I had to memorize it."

"Well you don't, but." I just look at him. I mean, it's baffling. Maybe this is just that aggressively casual f-boy mentality. But if you're going to be that unprepared, why bother auditioning? Okay, technically, he's required to audition, for Senior D. But Noah's the one who was so dead set on getting a singing part.

Which isn't happening, by the way. Like, super not happening.

I shake my head. "Noah, how—"

But I'm drowned out by squealing tires and a deep thudding bass, followed by a car door slamming shut.

"Sounds like someone's home from practice," I say.

A minute later, Ryan appears in my doorway, wearing a baseball hat that he promptly takes off. "How's the lesson going?" He smooths his hair down and sits gingerly at my desk, like he's trying to minimize the sweat-to-chair contamination.

"You mean how hard am I nailing this?" Noah says, and then he pauses like he's really considering it. "Pretty hard," he concludes.

I just shake my head. Nope.

"Did you get a ride from Sean?" asks Noah, and Ryan nods.

Wow. Sean Sanders, a true fuckboy icon. A boy who spends most of his time posting shirtless selfies that show his V-line, with captions that use "your" and "you're" completely interchangeably.

"Gross." I wrinkle my nose.

Noah looks intrigued. "You think Sean's gross?"

"I mean, he's not gross. He's just an asshole."

"Really! How so?"

"You want me to explain why Sean Sanders is an asshole?"

"Yeah, what did he do?"

What did Sean do? I don't even know how to respond to that. Is Sean an asshole? Of course. But it's not his actions, per se. He's just a fuckboy. It's just his basic fuckboy essence.

But even I have to admit, fuckboy essence is kind of nebulous. Probably wouldn't hold up in a court of law as a murder defense, for example.

I shake my head. "The real question is, why are you guys even friends with him?"

"With Sean?" Ryan says. He and Noah exchange glances. "I mean, I'm not, like, super tight with him."

"He drove you home."

"He was dropping someone else off nearby. He's not a bad dude." Ryan pauses, meeting my eyes. "Right?"

"Right. No, you're right." Something tugs in my chest. "He hasn't done anything to me."

"Okay, good." He hesitates. "Let me know if he does."

I stare up at my canopy, feeling thick-throated and strange. It's not that I mind when Ryan does the protective big brother thing. It's just, my heart never quite knows where to land with it. Because at the end of the day, Ryan still lifts weights with Eric Graves. He still sees Mira Reynolds at parties. And sometimes I just want to scream in his face. Did you forget? Do you not care?

"You know what the issue is?" says Noah.

I blink. "That you guys have shitty friends?"

"Good guess. But no." Noah grins. "Little G, the issue here is that you don't understand sports."

"Oh, yay. This again—"

"Hear me out. I'm talking about team stuff, okay? Take Sean, for example. You asked why we're friends with him, which I get. Super legit question, because, to the untrained eye,

99

sure. That's what it looks like."

I sit up straight, scowling. "I don't have untrained eyes."

"I'm just saying. You don't know what it's like to be on a team."

"Excuse me? I used to play soccer."

"You were six," Ryan reminds me. "You cried every game because you were scared the ball would hit you."

"Because it did! Right in the foot!"

"That's the game," says Ryan. "Like, that's the whole entire game."

"Okay, well, so what? I know what teams are—"

"But." Noah raises a finger. "You don't get team dynamics. You're trying to compare it to friendship, but it's not the same thing. It's like this." He grabs my teddy bears, Amber and Ember. "These two. They fucking hate each other, right?"

"Um, no. They love each other—"

"But let's say, just for the sake of argument, that they hate each other. Wait, no. Okay, it's more like a vague mutual dislike." He turns the bears to face each other. "But the thing is, they're kind of stuck together, right? They're hanging out here together in your bed all day, and—you sleep with them, right?" He looks at me. "Yeah, you totally do. So all day and all night, these two little dudes—"

"They're girls!"

"Pardon me! These two ladies. These pretty, pretty little lady bears—"

"Why are you doing this?"

"Just listen! So, what I'm saying is, you've got these two fine young women who are basically forced together twenty-four seven. And let's take it to the next level, okay? So Beary and Bundles here—"

"Amber and Ember! Show some respect—"

"All right, so Amber and Ember are not only constant companions, they also have to work together, right? Let's say they have some common task to complete. Like . . ." He looks at Ryan, who shrugs. "Okay. I don't know," says Noah, "I don't know bears. I don't know their lives. But the point is, even though they're not friends, and they may not even really get along, they pretty much have to find a way to be generally cool with each other. Otherwise it just sucks for everyone."

I snatch the bears back and hug them. "Got it. Cool story."

"So what I'm saying," Noah continues, unfazed, "is that when you're on a team—"

"You realize this is the exact same dynamic as a theater ensemble, right?"

"No, no, no. It's different. It's more like—Ry, help me out here. You know what I'm saying, right?"

"Something about teddy bears?" Ryan rests his chin on his fist.

"Shut up. No. You guys are both—ugh."

Ryan and I exchange the tiniest smiles.

"You know what?" Noah slides off the bed, turning to

face me. "Here's what has to happen. Kate, you need to go to a game. One game, okay? Promise me. Doesn't even have to be baseball."

"I'm not—"

"Football. All right? I'll make a deal with you. Little Garfield, you go to one football game with me, and I want you to really pay attention to how the players interact. Okay? On and off the field. The whole dynamic. I'll talk you through it. You'll get it."

"How is that a deal—"

"I'm not done! So, if you do that—one game, but you have to really focus, okay? And in return . . ." He pauses thoughtfully. "I'll sing a whole song onstage."

I laugh. "That's not an incentive."

"Just think about it." Noah gestures vaguely at Amber and Ember. "You three ladies talk among yourselves—"

I throw both bears at his head before he even closes his mouth.

# SCENE 19

Three and a half minutes after the final bell rings on Thursday, Andy and I are in the auditorium. Center section, six rows from the front, carefully calculated to be the ideal seat for audition spying. Andy sinks into his chair. "How are you holding up?"

"Fine. Good. Are you nervous? I'm nervous." I drum my hands along the armrest. "Why does this never get easy?"

Anderson nods without speaking.

"You got this, though. You're going to be so good, Andy. I swear to God, you'll get Dauntless. It's not even a question—"

He cuts me off. "I think Matt's going to get it."

"Why do you think that?"

"Seriously? You've heard him sing."

"I've heard you sing, too," I say.

But Anderson just sighs. "Like, what if Zhao does the seniority thing again this year? Or what if I just fucking bomb it?"

"You're not going to bomb it!"

"You don't know that. You're not psychic."

"Andy, you've never bombed an audition in your life."

And it's true. If Anderson wants to play Prince Dauntless, I'd be shocked if he didn't get it. After all, he's a triple threat. An obnoxiously talented triple threat.

They should make a word for the mix of pride and envy you get when someone you love is really good at a thing. It's like you want them to win so badly it feels personal. But also the thought of them winning makes you almost sick with longing.

Because when it comes down to it, I'm not as talented as Andy. I'm just not. I've never been. I don't have the magic singing voice or the comic timing or the charisma. I've never been the last to bow at curtain call. Maybe I'm just not a final bow person.

I'm more of a "this is so embarrassing, I literally can't watch" kind of person.

Raina slips in through the side hall, amped and ready. She pats her phone. "Harold says break a leg."

"Aww. Thanks, Harold. Cutie."

"I know." She leans over Anderson and me, craning her neck. "Where's Zhao?"

"I guess she's—"

But she cuts me off, eyes narrowed toward the entrance. "And why is Vivian Yang here?"

"What?" I twist around, stomach sinking. It's not that I dislike Vivian. I mean, I'm not exactly a fan of the way she ditched Andy out of nowhere to join the f-force, but I get that it was ninth grade. It's just that Vivian's not exactly a theater kid. I don't think she's ever tried out for a musical before in her life.

But she can sing. That I know, and not just from Anderson's voice studio performances. Vivian did the national anthem every few months at elementary school assemblies. And all those singing competitions Vivian and Andy carpooled to back in the day? Vivian won them. I mean, she pretty much won all of them. It's not exactly surprising, given that her parents are both legit professional musicians. Her mom's R&B group even opened for Blaque once in the nineties. Vivian sounds a lot like her mom, too. She's got one of those voices where she sounds like an alto tonally, but she's not. She's an uber-soprano. I'm pretty sure she can sing notes only my dogs could hear.

I sigh. "Fuck."

"Okay, where's Zhao?" Raina asks. "And where's Matt?"

There's a honk of piano notes, so loud we all jump. I glance up at the stage, and go figure—it's Noah. I don't know what it is about f-boys and musical instruments. It's like they have to touch everything and be as disruptive as humanly possible. Noah looks so startled, you'd think he was just now learning what happens when you press the keys of a piano.

The after-school late bell rings, and I spare one last glance at the auditorium doors. Brandie rushes in, and then Ms. Zhao and the music teacher both emerge from the wings, talking to Devon Blackwell, the student director—cute in a grungy, floppy-haired musician kind of way, with a double-blink tic I've always found really endearing. We used to talk a lot at rehearsals last spring, mostly about music, and for a while, I thought . . . maybe. But Andy wasn't feeling him. So. Yeah.

Anyway, most of us know the drill. The music teacher, Mr. Daniels, takes the bench, while Zhao and Devon sort of hover beside him. And then they call people up to sing, one by one. You have to hand it to them, though—they're not assholes about auditions. In movies, you always see people having to perform alone on a stage like they're on Broadway or *The Voice*. But Zhao, Devon, and Mr. D keep it chill. Just you and them on the stage, no microphone. And yeah, everyone's listening from the auditorium seats, but the piano accompaniment hides some of the messiness. Zhao's really big on not humiliating students, which is surprisingly rare for a teacher.

Lindsay Ward is up first, and I try not to look super obvious about leaning forward. She's singing "Happily Ever After," which means she's going for Winnifred. She's not bad. I sneak a glance at Mr. D's face behind the piano. He does this thing sometimes where his lips purse in and out while he's playing. Raina calls it the Suckle. He only does it when he's super in the zone.

I'd say Mr. D's giving Lindsay a basic polite head bob. Definitely no Suckle. But then again, Lindsay's a senior, which makes her a threat. You never know which way Zhao's going to go.

"Hey," Matt says breathlessly, sinking into the aisle seat beside me. "Am I late?"

"You're good. How are you feeling?"

Anderson leans over me to high-five him. "Made it."

Matt grins. "Phew."

"He had to finish an English quiz," Anderson says, because apparently Andy's the keeper of Matt's schedule now.

But then Matt leans closer, lips an inch from my ear. "So, Anderson tells me you've got Winnifred in the bag."

My heart flips. "He said that?"

Matt smiles and nods.

"Excuse me. You sweetheart." I shove Anderson lightly. Anderson winks.

"All right, Lindsay's done," Brandie whispers.

Onstage, Ms. Zhao's glancing between the sign-up sheet and the auditorium seats. "Raina Medlock, you're up."

"Fuuuuuuuuck."

"Love you, Rain. You've got this." I tuck my legs up so she can squeeze past me.

After Raina is Emma McLeod, and then Colin Nakamura, then Brandie, then Lana Bennett, then Anderson, who absolutely crushes it—total theatrical domination, followed by a goose massacre from Noah. Though even I have to admit he's kind of hilarious up there. Noah Kaplan has stage presence. Who knew?

Suddenly, I'm up.

I cross paths with Noah, who pauses to high-five me. "Good luck."

I freeze. "Noah! No! It's break a leg."

"How about an arm?"

"Okay, first of all, it's just an expression—" But I cut myself off, because Ms. Zhao's up there looking at me expectantly, and now my heart's skittering all over the place. "Hey," I remember to add, after a moment. "Good job up there, Noah."

"Why, thank you." Noah grins like he knows I'm lying, but he approves of the lie. "Okay, Little Garfield, you've got this." He taps his cast grandly.

"All righty," says Mr. Daniels. "What are you singing for us today?"

Deep breath. "'The Swamps of Home.'"

Ms. Zhao nods slightly, and even that acknowledgment makes me blush. It's this funny, unspoken thing. Zhao wants us to be flexible, so we're not technically allowed to try out for specific parts. But we send her coded messages with our song choices. If there's a part you want, that's who you sing—and we know it, and Zhao knows it, even if it doesn't always pan out.

So now everyone sees me wanting Winnifred. Now they all know.

"Whenever you're ready," Zhao says, leaning toward Devon. Then she whispers something, taps a spot in his binder, and he scrawls a note.

Mr. Daniels catches my eyes and plays the opening bars, pausing expectantly.

*Kate Garfield singing*, my brain makes sure to remind me. *I die a little.*

I take another deep breath.

And then my mind exits my body and floats up to the ceiling.

# SCENE 20

So now we wait.

"They're both impossible to read," Brandie says, for the twenty billionth time. She plucks a Coke bottle off Anderson's nightstand and sips. It's one of those personalized bottles: *Share a Coke with Braden!* True story: if Brandie sees anything remotely close to her name, she'll buy it and save the bottle. Raina calls it her garbage collection.

Anderson leans against his headboard. "Right?" He sighs. "Zhao's a Scorpio, so yeah, that tracks, but you'd think Mr. D would have some kind of tell."

"There's the Suckle," says Brandie.

"Yeah, but what does the Suckle really tell us?" Andy says. "B, I distinctly remember you freaking out last year when Mr. D didn't suckle—"

"Oh my God. Please stop talking about Mr. D suckling." Raina shudders.

"Rain, you're literally the one who—"

"I know." Raina pokes Andy's ankle. "But not as a verb."

Andy pokes her back. "Anyway. I'm just saying, I'm one hundred percent positive that Mr. D didn't do the Suckle for Brandie last year, and, hmm, oh yeah . . . what part did Brandie get?"

Brandie can't help smiling into the mouth of her Braden bottle.

"Maria, Maria, Maria, Maria," Anderson sings.

"Right," says Brandie. "But remember, he did suckle for Raina—"

"Ewwwwwwww."

Brandie ignores her. "And this year, he definitely did it when Vivian was singing."

"But not Kate," Andy says, "and Kate was—"

"Nope." I squeeze my eyes shut. "I don't want to talk about it."

A straight-up lie. I totally want to talk about it, and they know it.

It's the traditional audition postmortem. We spent the car ride here dissecting every moment, from every angle. And since Anderson's mom was home, we ran through the whole thing again for her benefit. She didn't even ask questions. She pretty much just sat there working on her cross-stitch, letting us monologue, like the hero she is. And now we've taken over Andy's crisply made queen bed, going for round three under the watchful two-dimensional eyes of Billy Porter, Lizzo, and Lena Waithe—Andy's Gallery of Icons.

"Kate." Raina stretches and yawns beside me. "You know you were amazing."

"What? No." I hug my knees. "Y'all were amazing."

Andy scoffs. "Excuse me, you three were amazing. My high note sounded like a shriek having sex with a grunt."

"Would that be a squawk?" Brandie sips her Coke.

"At least your first verse didn't sound like a sheep masturbating," I say.

"At least you didn't sound like a toad farting out of its mouth."

"This is the single most fucked up interaction I've ever witnessed," says Raina.

"We're not fucked up," Andy says. "We're just competitive. In a healthy way."

"You just said your voice sounded like a toad fart."

"Because it sounded like a toad fart," Andy says.

"What it sounds like," says Raina, "is a little boy named Anderson Walker fishing for compliments."

"Hey," Andy says. "I don't fish."

And it's true. Andy doesn't fish for compliments. He just gets like this when he's anxious. He goes into pendulum mode, swinging between cocky and self-deprecating. It's like he simultaneously does and doesn't know how talented he is.

"Anyway, I'm calling it," Anderson says, reaching past Brandie for a bag of Skittles on his nightstand. "Brandie as the jester, Raina as the queen—"

"Stop! Don't jinx me." Raina's cheeks flood with color.

I swear, some people's faces are legit neon signs. Raina has always been like that. She doesn't blush all that often, but when she does, it's so loud.

Raina wants to be the queen, and she wants it badly.

I probably could have guessed that. Raina's always had a thing about queens. It's why she picked the name Raina. I still have this crystal-clear memory of the first day of second grade, the year she socially transitioned at school. Her parents are so wholly and utterly extra, they'd bought her a whole wardrobe of skirts and dresses. But that day, Raina just wanted jeans and one of her sister's old T-shirts, with a picture of Elsa from *Frozen*. The shirt said Snow Queen. And every time Mira Reynolds and Genny Hedlund deadnamed her or misgendered her, or asked weird intrusive questions, Raina pretended to be Elsa. She explained it to me once. She said the secret was acting confident—unimpeachably confident. Queen-level confident.

And it worked. Mira and Genny moved on pretty quickly, and I think that was about the worst of it. Even in middle school, the f-force mostly left Raina alone. Honestly, I think a lot of people just forget she's trans. She's totally out, but she doesn't talk about trans stuff much, except with us and Harold. Because even though Raina's Elsa powers successfully repelled Mira and Genny, she'll still never trust them. She has a hard time trusting anyone in the f-force, to be honest. And she's probably right.

"Oh!" Anderson nudges me. "Matt wants to know if we're going to Sean Sanders's party tomorrow night."

Raina laughs—but stops abruptly when she catches Anderson's eye. "Oh, honey. You're serious."

Anderson swallows a Skittle. "Why wouldn't I be serious?"

"A party." Raina squints. "With Sean Sanders."

"And other people!"

"Right, right," says Raina. "I'm sure the whole gang will be there. All six of his abs—"

"Actually, eight," Brandie says.

Anderson smiles sheepishly. "I don't know. It could be fun."

"I would." Brandie smiles wryly. "But I have that movie."

"With your bestie," chimes Raina.

"Okay, that's—"

"And it's not a movie." Raina says solemnly. "It's a film."

Brandie swats her arm. The two of them are so funny, I swear. My dad calls them the Odd Couple. They're total opposites, but I actually think, in their own way, they're as enmeshed as Anderson and I are. For a while, Andy was convinced Raina and Brandie were secretly dating. He had all this evidence lined up, like the day Raina showed up to school smelling like Brandie's shampoo—or the way Raina lost her mind checking every grocery store for Cokes with Brandie's name on the label. In retrospect, it was maybe a bit of a stretch, but I swear it made sense at the time.

But no. It was just Anderson being full-throttle Anderson. Raina and Brandie laughed for hours when he told them. Raina's bi, but she made herself perfectly clear: dating Brandie would be practically Oedipal. And to this day, we have no idea how Brandie identifies. I mean, there was one time she blushed and called Harry Styles "adorable," but that's it. That's all we've got.

Andy turns to me. "Kate, you're coming, right?"

"Of course I'm coming," I say. "Like I'd miss out on all those fuckboy abs."

But Andy just snorts. "Like you'd miss out on Matt," he says plainly.

It's like he pulled the words straight from my brain.

# SCENE 21

When the last bell rings on Friday, I head straight to the Bathroom Time Forgot. Andy's meeting me there so we can walk down to Ms. Zhao's room together. I can't imagine looking at the cast list without him. Andy has a way of making bad news suck less. And he makes good news feel real.

He's already there, waiting in the bathroom doorway. No time to bother with stalls. The minute I arrive, he grabs me by the shoulder, rotates me around, and ushers me straight out the door.

I laugh. "I take it you're ready."

"I was born ready."

We're only a few yards from Ms. Zhao's room, just around the corner. But it's impossible to see Zhao's door, even as we approach it. There's a throng of theater kids blocking it. People keep pushing their way through—everyone wants to get close enough to photograph the full cast list to analyze later. But here and there, people peel away to high-five or text or cry. Margaret Daskin stalks straight past us with both hands covering her face.

"Okay, it just got real." Andy exhales. "Should we push our way in?"

I nod quickly. To be honest, we kind of have to. Otherwise, someone like Lana Bennett is bound to spill the news, and if I'm getting cast in a shitty background role yet again, God knows that's not how I want to find out.

"I see the back of Brandie's head," Anderson says. "Let's do this." He takes my hand and threads our fingers together, and moments later, we're weaving through the crowd toward Brandie. She turns around right as we reach her, almost like she sensed us. She's beaming.

My heart leaps into my throat.

"Good news?" Andy asks.

Brandie clamps her mouth shut and nods. It's hard to know what to make of that. Good news, for sure. But good news for who? Brandie obviously wants to be the jester, since there's that dance scene, but maybe her excitement is Anderson-related. Or Raina-related.

Or me-related.

I flush and look away quickly, homing in on the back of some freshman girl's head. We're dangerously close to the door now. Already, I can glimpse white paper against wood. Anderson pushes through, all the way to the front, and my breath hitches. For a moment, the typed list dances blurrily before my eyes.

Then it clicks into focus.

First character name on the list: Princess Winnifred.

The name beside it: Vivian Yang.

"Oh, Katy." Andy drops my hand, hooking his arm around my waist instead.

I nod numbly. "It's fine."

Princess Winnifred: Vivian Yang.

Wow. So Vivian gets the dream role. First time auditioning ever, and boom. She gets the final bow, the swamp dress, the showstoppers, the kiss with—

Prince Dauntless: Anderson Walker.

Wait.

Prince Dauntless.

Anderson Walker.

"Andy, you did it!" I hug him. "I told you. Holy shit. Mazel tov."

He laughs. "Mazel tov yourself."

"Me?"

My eyes flick back to the list.

Queen Aggravain: Raina Medlock.

King Sextimus: Noah Kaplan.

I grin. "Oh, Noah."

King Sextimus spends most of the play mute from a curse. Would that it could carry over to real life. Would that the curse could extend to all f-boys.

Anderson nudges me. "Keep reading."

Lady Larken: Kate Garfield.

"Wait . . . what?"

I turn slowly to Anderson, covering my mouth with both hands.

He hugs me sideways. "Not so bad, right?"

I mean, I'm pretty sure my throat's caving in. No big deal. Just a little touch of choking to death.

It honestly doesn't compute. Me. A leading role. Lines to learn. Center stage. Rows of eyes. Lights in my face.

Lady Larken. An actual named character who talks and sings and does stuff. My voice, but underlined. Me, but bolded.

"It doesn't seem real," I say finally.

I've always thought theater was the unrequited love of my life. All those roles I wanted that didn't want me back. All those auditions leading nowhere. It was starting to feel like shouting I love you into a black hole.

Turns out, getting a lead role feels a lot like I love you, too.

Anderson studies my face. "Are you happy?"

"Yeah." I nod. Then I peer up at him, smiling. "I mean, I'm bummed that I don't get to marry you."

"Uh, look at your Harry."

"Oh, right!" My eyes dart back to the list, scanning past my own name. And there it is, right beneath it.

Sir Harry: Matthew Olsson.

Holy shit.

Sir Harry: Matthew Olsson.

Sir Harry: my love interest. Matt Olsson is my love interest. And not even a casual love interest. It's not even subtle. Our characters literally have a love child together.

Forget learning my lines. I need to relearn how to breathe.

# SCENE 22

The closer we get to Sean Sanders's house, the faster my heart beats. "Remind me why we're about to walk into an f-boy party?"

"Because we were invited by the father of your unborn child."

All evening, Andy's been calling him that. My impregnator. My baby's dad. And yeah, Andy's just being a wiseass, but I swear, there's this edge to his voice. Like maybe if he jokes about it enough, no one will know it bothers him.

Anderson hooks his arm through mine. "Shall we do this?"

I nod firmly. "Let's do this."

So, wow. A real, bona fide house party. Music thumps through the front door, and my heart tracks to its bassline. Through the window, I catch a glimpse of people swaying into each other, tipping back red plastic cups. I glance sideways at Andy, who's paused on the stoop, staring ahead with giant brown eyes. He looks so utterly lost.

"Psst. You're a badass," I whisper.

"I know."

"A cute badass."

He looks me up and down, and grins. "You too."

And okay, yeah, that makes me blush. Because even though admitting it makes me cringe, cute badass was definitely the goal aesthetic. My hair's fairly well tamed and clipped back at the sides with bobby pins. Anderson talked me into a skirt—short and pleated—with ankle boots and an oversized cardigan. And I'm wearing blush, mascara, and ChapStick, which is about the only makeup I can handle without looking like I let a bunch of toddlers and/or f-boys scribble on my face.

He unhooks his arm, opens the door, and grabs my hand to tug me inside.

And—oof.

The party slams into every single one of my senses. Wall of sound. Smell of beer. Multicolored Christmas lights, proving Sean Sanders to be a festive hero among f-boys. My whole body drapes onto Anderson, almost without me realizing. "Do you think Matt's here yet?" I ask.

"I dunno. Let's do a lap."

Do a lap. Anderson, wow. Just whipping out that party language.

I try hard not to look too terrified at the prospect of weaving through this thicket of fuckboys. Funny how only hours ago, Anderson elbowed us through a crowd of theater kids. Same maneuver—but now, instead of dyed hair and *Hamilton* shirts, it's gray sweatpants and jerseys and tiny skirts and crop tops. I spot my brother in the corner with a group of baseball guys, laughing. I've never been to a party with Ryan, but I've seen pictures on Instagram where he's smiley and pink-cheeked. I guess a part of me figured Ryan probably drinks, but I wasn't entirely sure. After all, he's never holding a cup in any pictures.

But there we go. Mystery solved: my brother is definitely drinking. And something about it being confirmed makes me feel weird and small and a million miles away from him.

A bulky blond guy hulks his way in front of us, flexing his muscles, and yelling, "LES GOOO."

"Oh dear God." Anderson clutches his throat.

Something crashes down in the next room, followed by laughter and howling and lots of drawn-out cuss words. It's all a little louder than it needs to be. Even the couch squatters are startled out of their makeouts.

Maybe we've stepped into an alternate universe. Everything's slightly off its axis. Take the baseball caps, for example. It's like the minute an f-boy walks into a party, he forgets how hats work. Maybe f-boys don't want to commit to fully wearing them, so they just flip them around backward and perch them halfway on their heads. It's the only possible explanation.

"We should turn a fan on," Andy says, reading my mind, as always. "Just like, whoosh, oh no! Did your hat just fly off? Maybe you should have, I don't know, actually pulled it down onto your fucking head."

I blink. "Is Matt . . . anywhere? I don't see him."

"Maybe he's in one of the other rooms. Should we divide and—"

"Are you insane?" I gape at Anderson. "Don't you dare leave me. I could get killed."

As if on cue, a girl in a tie-dyed crop top staggers into me, barely catching her drink before it tumbles. "Oh my God." She puts her hand on my shoulder. "Oh my God, I'm so sorry. I'm so, so sorry."

"It's . . . fine," I start to say, but she's already mowing back into the crowd.

"Okay, let's be systematic," says Anderson. "Why don't we start moving toward the drinks table?"

"You're drinking?"

"No!" Anderson presses his lips together gingerly. "But we should get red cups of water or something, to blend in. I don't know. I don't like this any more than you do."

"Ugh." I wrinkle my nose. "Fine."

I swear, there's a bubble around us. We move through the party, and no one talks to us. Occasionally, someone steps out of our way to let us pass—otherwise, I'd be convinced we were actually invisible.

As it turns out, Vivian Yang is hovering in the doorway near the kitchen, clutching a red cup to her chest. She's wearing a tank top, maxi skirt, and makeup, which kind of throws me. At school, she basically lives in track gear. Vivian's so pretty, though, with her golden-brown skin and dark eyes and halo of hair. She just may be the only person in the world who makes florescent kitchen lighting look like sunshine. She looks up with a start when we join her. "Oh, hey."

"Hey," replies Andy, too brightly.

"Hey," Vivian says again. "So this is really—"

"Hey, congratulations!" Anderson says, at the exact same time.

"Hey, you too!"

Five heys in the span of ten seconds has to be some excruciating new record. Honestly, I don't get their weird chemistry. It's not romantic chemistry, but it's something.

Andy hesitates. "Really cool hearing you sing again," he says finally.

It's hard to know where they stand. I don't know much about what happened between them, other than the basics. Ninth grade. Vivian liked this guy Jeff Jacobs, from the track team, and I remember it being this whole big thing. Maybe it was supposed to be a secret crush that people found out about anyway. Or maybe Jeff had a girlfriend. I legit can't remember. But the point is, Vivian joined track and basically stopped talking to Andy. And that's it. There wasn't even a fight. It was more like turning the volume down on their friendship.

Vivian tucks a lock of hair behind her ear. "That audition was intense. God. I was so nervous."

"It didn't show," Andy says.

"Well." Vivian looks from Anderson to me. "You guys were both incredible."

My cheeks go warm. "No, you were! Oh my God. You were seriously wonderful."

"Oh!" She smiles sheepishly. "Thank you."

She's so sincere, I'm almost startled. I mean, how badass is Vivian? Just a plain old thank you, with no deflection or denial. Maybe I'm just wired wrong, but I don't even know if I'm capable of that. When someone compliments me, I always, always feel the need to counter it. I take your compliment . . . and raise you a BIGGER compliment.

But Vivian just let the compliment land—and it makes me feel so weirdly buoyant. Like maybe my compliment actually meant something to her. Maybe she cared about my opinion enough to let it touch her.

"Anyway," says Andy. "Have you seen Matt?"

Vivian tilts her head. "The new guy? I don't think so."

I peer past her into the kitchen. No blond Matt heads, not even half hidden beneath an improperly anchored baseball cap. Not that Matt would ever wear an improperly anchored baseball cap. He would never. And he's apparently nowhere. Though—wow. Or as my mom would say: oy.

I raise my eyebrows. "Is that . . . Noah?"

I mean, it's definitely Noah, back pressed against the refrigerator, enthusiastically making out with some girl with long dark hair and patches on the butt of her shorts. His non-cast hand is sliding up and down her back, almost methodically, and he keeps switching between glomping her neck and glomping her mouth. I can't look away. Wow. I mean, I knew he was skanky, but wow, Noah.

"Oh please," says Anderson. "In front of the fridge?"

"They were going to get drinks," explains Vivian, "but they didn't make it."

I blink. "We're in hell."

Suddenly, Anderson's face lights up. "Hey, Matt's here."

"Where?"

Andy taps his phone. "He just texted. He had to rescue a drunk guy on the back patio, but he wants to know where we are. I'll just tell him we're coming to the patio, okay?"

"Wait." I look up at Andy. "You and Matt text?"

"I mean, it's not a thing. It was really just to coordinate the audition rehearsal."

"Right." My voice comes out soft.

"Um," Vivian says slowly. "I'm going to run to the restroom."

I glance up at her, startled—and thoroughly, electrically self-conscious. Cool. No big deal. Just me and Andy being so transparently thirsty that people have to run for the bathroom to escape the radius of our awkward.

"Come on," Andy says, grabbing my hand. I lace our fingers together, out of sheer habit, even though a part of me wants to beam myself away from him, beam myself out of this party, beam myself home. Instead, I trail half a step behind Andy, feeling mostly numb. It always takes me a minute to acclimate to unsettling news. I always have to find the way back to myself again.

Not that this is even newsworthy. I mean. Two humans exchanged phone numbers to coordinate an activity outside of school. An activity to which I was even invited. And the fact that Matt hasn't asked for my number doesn't mean anything. No big deal. It's nothing.

Sean Sanders's back patio is mostly just a few squares of concrete, jutting out into the grass of his expansive backyard. There's a covered-up Big Green Egg grill off to one side and a whole bunch of plastic chairs arranged in clusters. A few f-boys are sitting there, drinking and smoking and laughing and watching other f-boys play flip cup at a table in the yard. But Matt's removed from the action—we find him sitting cross-legged with his back against the side of Sean's house. Sitting beside him is a flushed, baby-faced f-boy wearing a sleeveless jersey and the requisite unanchored baseball cap.

The boy grins up at us. "Hiiiiiiiiiiii, Fiona."

"He's been calling me Fiona, too," Matt says. "I'm just rolling with it."

"Who is this?" Andy asks.

"No idea."

"I'm driiiiink," the guy explains.

Anderson just stares at him for a minute, unblinking—and then he snaps back into himself. "Okay, buddy bro, I'm just gonna . . ." Andy squats in front of the drunk boy, reaching toward his head, and for a moment, I'm bizarrely convinced Andy's going to slap this f-boy's face. But instead, he grabs the drunk guy's hat, rotates the brim forward, and tugs the hat firmly onto his head. "Yup. Wow, okay. That was satisfying."

"So you just found this guy wandering around out here?" I ask Matt. "Is he okay?"

"Yeah. I mean, he seems fine. But I found him lying down on the concrete, which was kind of—I don't know. He said he was stargazing. I just don't want to leave him alone until we find his friends, I guess?"

Okay, so Matt's a literal angel. Just look at him. First party at an entirely new school, and he's already taking drunk strangers under his wing. I'm not particularly religious, but even I can recognize a biblical situation when I see one. Sacrificing his own night to help a stranger in need. Talk about a worthy crush. Eric Graves would never.

"Maybe we should go back in and look for someone named Fiona?"

"Nope." Anderson settles in across from Matt, so close their knees are almost touching. "I'd rather babysit this drunk f-boy disaster all night long than go back in there."

Matt laughs. "Totally one hundred percent agree. Kate?"

I sink onto the concrete. "Literally always up for not partying."

"Yassssss," affirms the drunk boy.

A cheer erupts from the flip cup table, and I look up in time to catch Chris Wrigley pouring a cup of beer over his own face. Ryan and Noah have drifted out to the patio too, hovering around the edges of the group. I don't see the butt-patch girl, not that I care, but Noah's certainly showing off that chaotically disheveled makeout hair. Of course, he catches me staring and shoots me a beaming, drunk smile.

I look away quickly, but that's a mistake too.

Jack Randall appears to be humping the Big Green Egg grill.

# SCENE 23

Nine in the morning on Saturday, and Noah Kaplan's in my kitchen. No Dad, no Ryan, no dogs. Just Noah at our kitchen table with a bag of braided challah, rolling a wad of it into a bread ball. The classic Noah technique.

"Sup, Little Garfield?"

I pause. "What are you doing here?"

I mean, it's not like it's the first time I've come down in my pajamas to find Noah helping himself to the contents of Dad's pantry. But today feels different, for some reason. I guess my mind keeps sliding back to that vision by Sean Sanders's fridge— the girl with the patches on the butt of her shorts, Noah's hand on her back. The way their faces kept squishing and unsquishing. Like, wow. That was sloppy. A cringingly, sloppily, vomity-gross kiss. The true kiss of an f-boy with absolutely no shame.

I guess it's just weird having that kind of f-boy in my kitchen.

"I live here now," Noah says calmly.

I roll my eyes. "Sure."

"Nah, I came back with Ryan."

"Ryan drove?" I sink into the chair across from Noah, remembering my brother's flushed, smiley face. The red cup. "He was drunk!"

"You can put your jaw back up, Little G. Madison drove. Good party, right?" He smiles. "You looked so cute. I like your hair like that." He pantomimes clipping his hair back on the sides. I never know how to respond when Noah says stuff like that. I can't tell if he's making fun of me.

So I change the subject. "Who's Madison? And please tell me she's not, like, in my brother's bed right now." I reach across the table to grab a chunk of challah.

"Nah, she went home."

"And why aren't you home?"

"Because Livy's having a slumber party, and you know I can't go scandalizing the youngsters."

As if Livy Kaplan could even be scandalized at this point. Not only is she a very worldly seven to begin with, she's the youngest of four. Noah and Livy have not one, but two older sisters in college.

"So." Noah props his chin in his hand. "I heard you asked about me last night."

My cheeks flush. "Excuse me?"

"Vivian said—"

"Vivian said I asked about you?"

He tilts his head back and forth, eyes twinkling.

"Okay, first of all, I didn't ask about you. I saw you suctioned to your girlfriend's face, and I asked if it was you—"

"Madison's not my girlfriend," he says. "We're friends."

"Friends?" I splutter.

"And also—" Noah cuts himself off, popping another bite of challah into his mouth. "Also, if you actually saw me suctioned to Madison's face—"

"I did."

"Then why did you ask if it was me?"

"What are you talking about?"

"You said you weren't asking about me, you were asking if it was me. But you also said you saw me, with your own two eyes, so I'm just asking—"

"Oh my God. Stop."

He shrugs—and for a minute, I just sit there, glowering at him across the table.

"Okay," he says, after a moment. "So what's second of all?"

"What?"

"You said, first of all, you didn't ask about me, which is absolutely debatable, in my opinion, but you never closed the loop. You never said what—"

"Second of all, maybe you should go practice your lines. Right now."

Noah shuts one eye thoughtfully. "But my character's mute."

"Exactly," I say, reaching across the table. Then I snatch away the challah, cradling it like a baby as I stalk out of the room.

# SCENE 24

My hype level for the first day of rehearsal is off the charts. I spend all of Monday trying to activate my clock telekinesis skills, but it's no use. I'm pretty sure at least ten years have passed by the time the three-forty dismissal bell chimes.

But as soon as I reach the auditorium, I know it's worth it.

First rehearsals are glorious. They just are. It's all of us here, even the techies, and the stage lights are off, so everything's cool and still.

"I'd like to get to our read-through today," says Ms. Zhao. "But first, I want to focus for a while on ensemble building. I want you to feel comfortable enough to take risks—which is a lot to ask, I know. But I need you to get to a place where you really trust each other."

Everyone nods solemnly, like this is some earth-shattering wisdom. And maybe it is. Or maybe wisdom doesn't need to shatter the earth. It just needs to feel true. And sitting here in a metal folding chair, tucked between Raina and Brandie, what could be truer?

"As we move forward, we'll be splitting into smaller groups sometimes, and we'll schedule intensive pair or trio rehearsals for some of the principals—Winnifred and Dauntless, Larken and Harry, etcetera."

Matt catches my eye and winks, and I swear, it makes my organs rearrange. I mean. I don't think my brain has fully grasped the fact that I've been cast in a musical opposite Matt Olsson.

I get intensive rehearsals with Matt Olsson.

And.

I get to kiss Matt Olsson.

"But." Zhao's hand goes still, and then she lifts a single finger. "Every week, every Monday, I'd like to come back to this. Full cast, full ensemble. And that may happen even more frequently than once a week. Take a minute to look around."

I do—everyone does. We all just sit there for a minute, peering around the circle of bodies onstage. There's Anderson, straight-backed and cross-legged in his chair; Vivian, in navy gym shorts; Matt looking like his usual dreamboat self. Next to him is Emma McLeod, fiddling with the wheels on the manual wheelchair she uses for theater stuff. Devon Blackwell, meanwhile, is idly threading his hair with the tips of his fingers, like his head is the prize in a claw machine.

And there's Zhao herself, tattoos poking out of her plaid button-down. "For the next two months, we're family," she says. "It's not always going to be easy, but we're going to build that foundation of trust as an ensemble. And that starts today."

Turns out, that means theater games. We play a couple rounds of The West Wind Blows, before moving on to the human knot, and then it's trust falls, which I suck at. Even when I'm paired with Anderson, I suck at them. I can't stop my body from trying to catch itself. But it's okay, and no one really judges me, and before I know it, we're moving on to that game where you have to silently arrange yourselves in order by birthday.

And then it's time for the read-through.

Pierra, Lindsay, and Margaret don't really have speaking parts, so they spend the whole time interpreting the script into a dance. A vaguely inappropriate dance, involving a fair amount of crotch grabbing, all of it happening right behind Ms. Zhao's back. At one point, Pierra lines the spine of her script to her breastbone, opening the pages in a sudden, sexy thrust, like she's yanking open her shirt. But when Zhao turns around, they all freeze. It's like one of those old Super Mario games with the little ghosts that look like cream puffs.

So now Anderson and Vivian keep smirking at each other, and the freshmen look completely delighted. Even Brandie's grinning in her self-contained way. But no one's enjoying this more than Matt, and it's the cutest thing ever. Like. I cannot get enough of the little skip in his voice, the way he keeps rushing through his lines to keep from giggling. It's not working.

Also, when he giggles, I giggle.

Which makes for some very giggly Larken/Harry arguments.

I swear, this is why I do theater. It's not about the tiny spot-lights or the attention or the final bow or any of that.

I mean, maybe it is sometimes. A little bit.

But mostly it's this. This filled-to-the-brim feeling, this absolute rightness. I don't know what it is about play rehearsals, but it's really like that sometimes. You get these moments that feel rare and gifted and almost too good to be real. That exact perfect half point between giddiness and contentment. Half roller coaster, half rocking chair.

And just when I think this moment couldn't possibly get any sweeter, there's Matt, scooting in beside me at the edge of the stage, our legs dangling down over the orchestra pit. Matt's jeans next to my jeans. "Hey, let me know if you need a ride home," he says. "You're right on my way."

I look up, turning to face him. "Oh!"

I mean. This can't be real, right? Did that actually just happen? Did Matt Olsson just offer me a ride home from rehearsal?

A ride home. Me. Kate Eliza Garfield.

But then again—

Anderson. Who's staring past us, stiff-backed and stoic, clutching his messenger bag a little too tightly.


"I'm just saying, I wouldn't have minded."

Anderson's eyes are glued to the road. He's squeezing the wheel so hard, I swear his knuckles might burst through his skin.

"You wouldn't have minded? Andy, you look like you're trying to choke the steering wheel."

"Excuse me for being a safe driver."

"Andy, come on." I poke him. "Come on! Stop being mad. I'm right here. With you. Do you really think I would have ditched you?"

"To ride with Matt Olsson?" he asks. Then he shrugs, like *I dunno, you tell me.*

And wow. Wow.

"Okay, when have I ever ditched you for Matt. Ever?"

Like, for real? Is Andy even serious right now? I could have had Matt completely to myself that night at Mom's house, but no. The second I found out he would be there, I texted Anderson. But Andy? Practiced for auditions with Matt when I couldn't be there. Joined Senior D with Matt. Exchanged numbers with Matt.

But somehow Andy's pissed at me because Matt offered me a ride home from rehearsal? A ride that I turned down?

You can kind of see Anderson putting all of that together—the way he exhales, the way his jaw clenches. And sure enough, when the light ahead of us turns red, he turns briefly to face me. "Katypie, I'm sorry."

"It's fine. I get it. It's weird."

"It's insane. I feel like this jealous monster. Every time he looks at you, I'm just like, fuck my whole life." He does this choked little laugh, and his lip trembles just barely, and oh. He looks so much like seventh-grade Andy right now, it makes my chest hurt.

It's a full minute before either of us speak.

"Kate, I like him," Andy says finally. "I think I really, really like him."

# SCENE 25

When we were younger, Anderson used to cry over every-thing—spiders and splinters and overly loud fireworks. Once he sobbed for an hour when he bit into a chunk of Oreo fudge that turned out to be blue cheese.

But by the beginning of seventh grade, the tears mostly stopped.

I'm not saying Anderson stopped being dramatic. He's like the sovereign king of rants. No one—literally no one—knows how to give a rant like Anderson. I've seen him obliterate GOP senators, racist beauty gurus, *Gone With the Wind*, you name it. And his takedown of Rachel Dolezal could legit be a TED Talk. My favorite is always the halfway point, where Andy says, "Okay, whatever, I'm done. I'm over it." But then, a split second later: "Okay, but ALSO, can I just say—"

I don't know. It's like somewhere along the line, Andy fig-ured out you could be funny and upset all at once. And that people are way less weird about hilarious rants than they are about crying boys. But the wobbly lip thing is another beast entirely. That I've only seen him do once before.

It was the Saturday after Eva Cohen's bat mitzvah. Anderson and I had been kind of bashful around each other all week. No one knew about the kiss. Definitely not Raina or Brandie, and I know Andy didn't tell Vivian. The whole thing seemed so surreal. The morning after the kiss, we kept sneaking our phones out in Sunday school and church. Andy asked me to be his girlfriend in a paragraph-long text, riddled with adverbs and nervous disclaimers. I said yes with an "I'll be your Batman" gif from *Teen Wolf,* Andy's obsession at the time. And I really meant it. I was on cloud nine the whole day.

But school the next day was like stepping into a funhouse. Everything was off-kilter. We tried holding hands on the bus on Monday, but it felt ridiculous, so we stopped. And then we mostly just hung out the same way we normally did, other than being a little bit shyer and more smiley with each other. It wasn't exactly what I'd expected. But I remember thinking, maybe that's how getting a boyfriend always feels. Maybe romantic relationships are just friendships gone weird.

Of course, it wasn't until Saturday that we were actually alone together. Normally I'd wander over to Andy's house after breakfast in sweatpants, but this time I'd blow-dried my hair and even whipped out my new cherry ChapStick.

But Andy was in the strangest mood that day—quiet and

preoccupied, almost broody. We ended up watching *The Maze Runner* on his laptop, and when it ended, he jumped up to brush his teeth. Then he asked if he could kiss me again.

And the kiss was nice. Calm and sweet. But when I opened my eyes, his lower lip was trembling. He looked like he was trying not to cry. "I'm so sorry," he whispered. "I don't think I can do this."

"Oh." My stomach twisted. "That's—"

"I'm so sorry."

"No, no. It's fine. I get it. You're my best friend, and it's weird. It makes total sense."

But Anderson was shaking his head. "I think I'm gay," he said softly.

When I hugged him, he burst into tears.

# SCENE 26

Anderson's words hang in the air the whole way home.

*Kate, I like him. I think I really, really like him.*

I swear, every friend bone in my body is screaming for me to suck the tension out of this situation. It would be incredibly easy. I could do it in one sentence.

"Andy," I say softly.

*Andy, this Matt thing—you should go for it.*

I could tell him I'm not interested in Matt. I could offer to be Andy's wingwoman. I mean, I can't make Matt Olsson like boys if he doesn't, but at least it could stop feeling like a competition. Everything could just be normal. Like a normal crush and a normal lovesick Andy and a normal best friend Kate.

The only problem is, I don't feel normal. Not about Matt.

"I think I like him, too," I say. I barely recognize my own voice. It's soft but certain. Like maybe my voice knew how I felt before my brain did. "I really like him."

"I know." He sighs.

"But we'll be fine, okay?" I drum on the armrest, eyes fixed to Anderson's profile. "Seriously. It's not like we haven't done this before."

"Done what?"

"Communal crushes. I mean, that's like our thing, right?" Andy shakes his head. "Not like this. Not for real."

We're both quiet, for what feels like centuries, until finally Andy turns on the car's Bluetooth player. Like maybe hip-hop will drown out the awkwardness.

But out of every song in the universe, the one that plays is—I'm not even kidding—"The Boy Is Mine." Like. Holy shit. This song is literally two decades old—more than two decades old. And I don't even think it counts as hip-hop. The only reason it's even in Anderson's music collection is because his mom gets really into Brandy when she's feeling midlife crisis-y. I cannot fucking believe this song just started playing.

"Is God speaking to us through your Bluetooth?" I ask.

Suddenly, Anderson pulls over, even though we're less than five minutes from Dad's house. He jabs the button to turn on his hazards, and for a minute he just sits there, hands over his face. Shoulders shaking. He's leaning so far forward, I'm legitimately concerned he might honk the horn with his rib cage.

It takes me a full sixty seconds to realize he's not crying— he's laughing. "Wow. Are we the biggest clichés ever?"

"I think so." I grin. "It's kind of our specialty."

"Well, we're not going to do this. Fighting over a boy? That is some grade-A f-force bullshit, and I'm not here for it."

My heart swells. "Neither am I."

"Katypie, I'm so sorry. I'm done being an asshole." He leans over the gearshift and wraps his arms around me tight. "I love you so much. None of this matters. The Matt stuff? Doesn't matter. I love you."

I lean into his hug, my eyes prickling with tears. "I love you, too."

"You smell like laundry detergent," Andy murmurs, into my shirt. "Just FYI."

I hug him even tighter.

And that's how we sit, for five minutes straight. Kind of like one of those drive-through movie makeout couples, but without the movie or the makeouts.

I am so platonically in love with Anderson Walker, it makes my brain hurt.

# SCENE 27

So we're fine. At least, I think we are.

But every time I talk to Matt, the Anderson stuff bubbles right back up to the surface. Anderson likes this boy. Anderson really likes this boy. But I really like this boy, too. And it's all turning out to be a little more complicated than I thought it would be.

Especially at rehearsal.

"So we've got Harry kneeling," says Ms. Zhao. "And, Larken, go ahead and stand right up next to him." I take a step down-stage, toward Matt. "Closer . . . closer. Right next to him, Kate."

Matt looks up at me, smiling the gentlest smile imaginable.

"And let's have you lean back a little bit and put your hand on your hip—other hand. Great. Okay, and Matt?"

"Yup!" He straightens his shoulders and does this dorky obedient nod. It's so cute, it almost hurts. Andy says Matt's like that in Senior D, too. Super respectful of Ms. Zhao. Like, soldier-level respectful.

"And, Matt, let's have you rest your head right there on her stomach."

My stomach. Wow. So now my heart's like a humming-bird. I know exactly what Zhao's going for. She's obviously recreating that iconic pose from the Broadway revival with Jane Krakowski and Lewis Cleale. It's an undeniably cute pose for a secretly pregnant lady and lord. Larken looks like a total boss mom-to-be, and I love the idea of Harry trying to listen to the baby through her princess skirt. So, artistically? I'm into it. It's just that I didn't exactly wake up today thinking Matt's cheek would be on my stomach.

Matt peers up at me, tilting his head. He's got this look on his face like he's asking permission.

Deep breath. I catch his eye and nod.

And . . . okay, so far, so good. I mean, it doesn't feel sexual or anything. I'm actually not as self-conscious as I thought I'd be. I guess Matt doesn't really seem like an abs guy. Which is good, seeing as I'm a generally squishy person with no abs what-soever. Anyway, I'm all layered up today, in jeans and a flannel, which makes for a nice, solid barrier. Honestly, the only weird part of the equation is Anderson.

Who happens to be down in the music room with Vivian and Mr. D, working on vocals. Thank God.

"Great. So, Matt, cheat out just a little bit—good. And put your hand on her stomach."

Again, he hesitates, catching my eye first—and if this isn't the most endearing thing in the whole entire world, I don't know what is. Matt Olsson is obviously the kind of boy who asks if he can kiss you before kissing you, which is a move that makes Anderson and me melt. God. The first time we saw *Call Me By Your Name*, Anderson had to bite his own fist when Oliver asked that, just to keep from screaming. Andy's got this whole soapbox about consent being sexy, and it's so fucking true.

But if I'm totally honest, it's the moment itself that appeals to me. Specifically, the moment right after the question gets asked. Just that breath of a second before the world changes its orbit. Every time I think about it, I literally sigh.

Okay, I'm literally sighing.

Which makes Matt yank his hand back, like my stomach's a hot stove.

I whisper, "No, you're fine."

And then apparently I'm possessed by some other Kate entirely, some badass total queen version of myself I barely even recognize. I find Matt's hand, hovering about an inch in front of my body. And then I press it back onto my stomach.

"This looks fantastic," Ms. Zhao says, nodding. "So, Larken and Harry, you'll hold this pose for a couple of beats after the song ends—good—applause, applause, applause. And then we'll have you exit stage right." She pauses to scribble a note in her script. "And . . . great. All right! Let's keep it moving. Why don't we skip ahead to . . . Act One, Scene Four, with Queen Aggravain and the Wizard. Raina and Emma, you're up!"

I drift behind Matt into the wings, and he turns toward

me—hands fisted, tucked sweetly beneath his chin. Then he shakes his head slowly, his voice barely a whisper. "I'm so sorry."

"Why are you sorry?"

"For all the groping. Are you good?"

"I'm good. Are you good?"

He laughs. "Yeah, absolutely." Then he reaches his hand out.

Wait.

Am I supposed to take his hand? Is he asking me to—oh.

Oh.

I get it. We're doing the shoulder thing, not the hand thing. He's sliding his arm around my shoulders in a nice solid side hug, easily the dreamiest side hug in history.

"Sorry if I made it weirder back there. I just didn't want to—you know—"

"You didn't." I shake my head quickly, trying not to get derailed by the fact that his arm's still hooked around my shoulders.

Neither of us speaks for a moment, and my heart squeeze-flips, like a roly-poly.

God. If Anderson were here.

And suddenly, Matt slides his arm off my shoulder, like my guilty brain sent him a telepathic message. Oy. Thank God Andy and I aren't going full Brandy and Monica over this guy, because I wouldn't stand a chance. Anderson has my own brain running interference for him. Unless—

Okay, maybe the side hug release isn't a big statement.

Maybe it's just phone related. After all, now Matt's reaching into his back pocket, and—

"We should exchange numbers," he says.

I'm rooted to the spot. I just stand there, blinking up at him.

"If you want to," he adds quickly. "Just so we can rehearse. But seriously, only if you want to—"

"Yeah, okay. Totally." I slide my phone out of my own pocket, trying to ignore my thundering heart. "Give me yours, and I'll text you."

There's this guilty twinge in my throat, but I swallow it back. I mean, Anderson already has Matt's number. He already gets to do the flirting over text thing. Not that I have flirting on the brain. Just—you know. Acting. And rehearsing. And being bros. Just one bro shoving his face against another bro's stomach.

Anyway. I'm just saying.

If Anderson gets to text with Matt Olsson all night, maybe I do, too.

# SCENE 28

But we don't text all night. In fact, Matt doesn't even respond to the text I sent him with my number. And yes, technically he was standing right in front of me when I sent it. But still. I can't text him again, since I'm the one who sent that first text. The ball is clearly in Matt's court.

All I can do is not check my phone fifty million times during breakfast. Or at least be discreet about it.

"Peapod, you expecting a call or something?" my dad asks.

Welp. I mean, Dad didn't even notice when I decided—a week after the eighth-grade variety show—that I was now a guitar goddess, and therefore needed blue-streaked hair. And that was the same week Ryan kept wearing turtlenecks to hide this red spot on his neck. Mom was pretty much obsessed with it—she must have asked Ryan a zillion times if it was a hickey. Personally? I think Ryan was experimenting with Mom's curling wand and didn't want to admit it. But Dad never even asked about it.

So there you have it: even blue hair and neck burns are more subtle than my thirst for Matt Olsson.

I don't see him at school in the morning at all, which sucks grandly. And there's no rehearsal on Fridays, so unless a miracle happens, I'll be Matt-less until Monday. It's so weird having a crush on someone you mostly see at rehearsal. It flips your whole world around. You start living for Mondays through Thursdays, and everything else is just filler.

Of course, I'm looking for him everywhere. I can't stop staring at doorways, like Matt's about to randomly stumble into my history class. I take the long way to the cafeteria, past the senior lockers. And I'm so zoned out at the lunch table, I hardly notice Lindsay Ward and Emma McLeod sidling up. "Hey, mind if we join y'all?"

"Of course!" Brandie scoots her chair sideways to make room for Lindsay.

Emma parks her wheelchair next to Anderson, but she grins right at me. "Kate, your face yesterday during the preggo pose. Oh my *God*."

Lindsay leans forward. "Right? You and Matt are so cute. I was like, whoa, I'm watching a rom-com."

"I mean, *Once Upon a Mattress* is pretty much a rom-com, right?" I say.

"Actually, it's a musical," says Raina.

"Actually, are you Lana Bennett?" I ask.

Lindsay's and Emma's jaws drop, but then they both burst

out laughing, and now I can't decide if I'm a comedy genius or an asshole.

Lindsay turns back to me, still smiling. "All I'm saying is, the chemistry was palpable. We were feeling it. Back me up here, Em."

"Definitely feeling it," says Emma.

Anderson scowls. "Pretty sure that's called acting."

"Pretty sure that's called Kate and Matt are going to be married by tech week," says Emma. "Mark my words."

"That's ridiculous."

Brandie and Raina exchange glances.

"You never know." Lindsay beams. "Lots of intensive rehearsals coming up on that schedule."

"Wow," Anderson says, opening a bag of chips with unnecessary force. "And here I thought it was possible for actors to—I don't know—act? And be professional? You guys are like those blogs that analyze paparazzi pictures for evidence of actors hooking up."

Raina snorts. "That's not a thing."

"Uh, yeah it is." He whips out his phone.

"Hey," I say, and my voice sounds hollow and bright. Because apparently I can't even land the delivery of one syllable. I plow ahead regardless, desperate for a subject change. "Do y'all know when set design is?"

"I don't know. Not till September, I think," says Raina. "Why?"

Andy's still tapping on his phone, peering intently at the screen. And there's this empty-ache feeling inside me, all of a sudden. Everything just feels so strange. Maybe the air pressure dropped.

Maybe Anderson's mad at me.

Even though he can't be mad at me. We already talked about this. About how the Matt stuff doesn't matter. And how we love each other too much to cave to f-force bullshit. We're not clichés. We're better than that.

But maybe there's some unspoken contingency here I'm not understanding. I should crowdsource for answers. Easy peasy. I'll just google: Is it cool to let your best friend's crush put his face on your stomach?

Yeah. Probably not.

# SCENE 29

Anderson leaves lunch ten minutes early, looking mopey and cross. Which means I spend the next few minutes staring at the door, trying to decide if I should go find him.

I almost do.

But just as I start to stand up, a crash from across the cafeteria stops me in my tracks. A tray clambering to the ground, plastic bottle thudding, fork spinning to a stop in the awful silence that follows. And then there's the inevitable *oooooooh*. Completely synchronized, almost choral.

It's the kind of moment that makes my stomach twist. I can't stand watching people get embarrassed, even strangers. Even fictional strangers. I honestly can't watch certain TV shows. I get this visceral secondhand shame reaction. It's like my brain can't tell where someone else's humiliation ends and mine begins.

And that feeling. You know that moment when your phone's front camera catches you looking like a swamp monster? Or when the bathroom smells bad, and then you catch a glimpse of yourself in the mirror. That little spike of wait-holy-shit-I'm-actually-horrible-and-gross.

It's like that. But applied to your whole entire being.

"Noah Kaplan. What a surprise," Raina says.

I twist around to follow her gaze, and there he is. Smack-dab in the middle of the cafeteria. His arms are still out in tray-holding position, and if he wasn't grinning his face off, I'd think he was in shock. A few f-boys have absconded with his water bottle—they're kicking it around the cafeteria like a soccer ball. But otherwise, Noah's tray's just sitting there, over-turned at his feet.

"Do you think he's just going to leave it there?" asks Raina.

I open my mouth and then close it. I guess I don't quite know what to say. I mean, on the one hand, Noah seems absolutely delighted with himself, really basking in the attention. And yeah, as far as I can tell, he's made no move to pick up his tray.

But then again, I don't know if Noah's arm situation is entirely ideal for picking corn kernels off the floor. Don't get me wrong, he could at least try. But I guess it bugs me that he's blatantly injured and nobody's helping him.

I stand abruptly and grab a fistful of napkins. "I'm going in."

Walking up the aisle toward Noah, it feels like the whole cafeteria's staring at me. It's awful. I feel prickly and self-conscious, and I'll never understand it. When I'm in a play, being watched makes me feel invincible, flooded with light.

But every other time, it's feels like—

*yikes lol*

*this is so embarrassing, I literally can't watch*

*I die a little*

*I die a little*

*I die a little*


"Little Garfield." Noah peers at me, twinkly-eyed. "I finally got your attention."

I'm sorry, but he's unbearable. This is totally a thing he does—this fakey lovesick banter he whips out of nowhere, just to unsettle me. Of course the punchline is that we all know an f-boy like Noah would never actually be lovesick. Or if he were, he'd be lovesick over some mega-hot queen bee f-girl. The kind who's destined for modeling or Hollywood or at least the *Bachelor* franchise. But f-boys don't exactly pine for flannel-wearing theater girls. Thus the joke. The absolutely side-splittingly hilarious joke of Noah pretending he wants to impress me. And that's not even touching the question of who would be impressed by a tray dropping.

"Kate. I'm just messing with you."

I don't respond. I just kneel down on the floor, collecting corn kernels into a napkin. And for once—for once in Noah's life—his little wiseass mouth is shut. I glance up at him finally. "Just so you know." I ball the napkin up forcefully. "I'm doing this for the custodians. Not you."

And before he can reply, I grab his hand, open it, and shove the corn napkin into his palm. His fingers close around it, but other than that, he doesn't move.

I look up at him. "Are you saving that for later or something?"

"Uhhhh, nope." He blinks. "Throwing it away. Right now."

"There you go."

I move on to Noah's chaotically scattered french fries—but suddenly, someone squats down beside me. "Hey."

I look up from the floor. "Oh. Hey."

It's a girl I've never spoken to, but I know I've seen her around the hallways. I think she might be a cheerleader. She definitely has that faintly floral smell that cheerleaders are prone to. And she has super-straight hair, like Raina's, but darker. More black than brown.

Pretty sure I've seen that hair before, actually. Pretty sure it hits just above the spot on jean shorts where a fashion-forward girl might sew a few patches.

Madison. Noah's "friend."

She cups her hand, running it along the floor like a snowplow. "You're so sweet to do this," she says. When she gets a bunch of fries piled up, I scoop them into another napkin. "Kappy's so weird about asking for help. He gets so embarrassed."

"Kappy?" I almost say—but then it hits me.

Kappy. Wow. I'll tell you one thing: I'm saving that one for the next time I get called Little Garfield.

"You're Ryan's sister, right? Katelyn?"

"Just Kate."

"Can I just say, I love your brother. He's hilarious."

"He is?"

"And he's such a sweetheart." She shoots me a megawatt smile. "He was just telling me about his dogs, and how they're named after the royal family." Madison laughs. "How cute is that?"

"It's cute . . . ish." As in, cute enough to get a surprised chuckle every so often at the dog park. But not cute enough to warrant Ryan being called hilarious by floral-smelling girls. And that's putting aside the fact that Mom's the one who named the dogs in the first place.

"Hey," Noah says, reappearing. He squats down between us, eyes darting back and forth almost nervously—which makes me wonder what kinds of secrets he thinks I'm telling Madison. I mean, if she wants secrets, I've got them. I could go full sabotage. Like I could easily tell Madison about the velocity experiment we did in eighth-grade science. Somehow Jack Randall managed to bounce a tiny ball into Noah's pants without him noticing, and it rolled right out through the cuff as soon as Noah stood up. "Hey, Madison," I can picture myself saying. "Want to hear about the time your boyfriend's balls dropped?"

Nailed it.

Though of course Madison and Kappy aren't even a couple. They're friends. Friends who suck on each other's faces at parties, like friends apparently do.

# SCENE 30

Today's the kind of weather that's too perfect to waste, so we end up in Raina's backyard, sprawled out in the sunshine. Harold shows up with a big Tupperware of grapes, which is just so Harold. He's like a quiet, scruffy Prince Harry, just with blue jeans and thicker eyebrows.

Before long, Brandie and Anderson have Harold cornered, and they're bombarding him with rehearsal photos. "Lana's the Minstrel," says Brandie, tapping her phone screen. "She's the one whose voice is so—"

"Annoying," interjects Anderson. "She has the most annoying fucking voice I've ever—"

"Mmm, I wasn't going to say annoying," Brandie says, tugging her phone back. "Just, like, kind of operatic."

Harold furrows his brow. "Is that not a good thing?"

"Can we please not talk about Lana Bennett?" Raina repositions herself cross-legged beside me, facing Harold. "Hi."

"Hi," Harold says back.

I swear, the way they look at each other makes me feel like I stumbled into their wedding vows.

I pop a grape and lean back on my elbows, watching Harold laugh along with Brandie and Anderson's banter. I'm pretty sure he likes us, even though he always seems a little nervous when we hang out in person. It makes me wonder: Are we intimidating? I've always assumed people see us as, like, a lovable band of nerds. But who knows? Maybe to Harold we're as insular as a pack of fuckboys.

Harold catches my eye and does this tiny, sharp inhale, like he's steeling himself for a new conversation. It seriously makes me want to hug him. I just love shy people so much.

"So, Kate." He clasps his hands and tucks them under his chin. "I hear you're pregnant."

Brandie gives a startled, short laugh.

"Um. Yes?" I grin. "Theatrically speaking."

"She got knocked up by some knight," says Raina.

I shrug. "It happens."

"At least you know it'll be a cute baby," says Brandie. She tilts her phone up toward Harold. "That's him. In the green, next to Kate. Matt."

"Sir Matt." Harold smiles. "You guys look nice together."

"Really?" I beam. God, I love Harold. I fucking love him.

"In case it wasn't completely obvious," Raina says, "Our Katy has a giant, raging crush on Sir Matt."

"As does our Andy," I say quickly.

"Matt's one of their communal crushes," explains Brandie.

"I don't think I've ever heard of that," says Harold. "Communal crushes."

Raina pats my back affectionately. "That's because these two ding-dongs made them up."

"Oh, okay." Harold tilts his head. "So it's like a competition? How does that work?"

"It doesn't," Anderson says flatly. "It's not working."

My heart plummets. Wow. I'm an asshole. I really am. Here I am, basking in the glow of being teased about Matt, without a single thought for Anderson. Matt and Kate look so nice together! Won't their babies be cute! Or Emma and Lindsay yesterday. Palpable chemistry. Married by tech week. Andy probably feels like we're all taking turns punching him in the face. I mean, God knows that's how I feel every time I catch Matt and Andy whispering in rehearsal. Even thinking about it makes my eyes prickle.

It's just not supposed to be like this. Not with Andy and me. God knows there are enough people out there just dying to hurt us. The Erics of the world, the Miras, the Gennys. Even the Vivians. The last thing we need is to inflict this shit on each other.

I should change the subject. To be honest, we should probably stop talking about Matt altogether.

Of course, talking's only half the problem. I don't want to get ahead of myself or anything, but what if Matt and I started dating? I could never in a million years keep that from Anderson. Which leaves me with two equally shitty choices. Option one: I declare Matt Olsson off-limits, kind of like a *Naomi and Ely's No Kiss List* situation. But then again, the No Kiss List wasn't exactly smooth sailing for Naomi and Ely.

Which leaves me with option two: I break Anderson's heart.

It's just unbearable.

Suddenly, as if he feels me pronouncing his name in my head, Andy glances up from his phone—he's been texting—and looks me right in my eyes. Then he nudges his glasses up his nose like a dork. And he smiles. I smile back.

My phone buzzes in my lap, and when I check it, it's confirmed. Anderson Walker can officially read my mind. Want to grab fancy waffles after this? Just us. I think we should figure out the Matt stuff, for real.

# SCENE 31

We leave just as the sun's setting and set out for the Belgian waffle place on Canton Street. Andy sets us up with some music—thankfully, no messages from God this time. It's just his Broadway and off-Broadway playlist, which I've heard fifty million times—*Be More Chill*, *Next to Normal*, *The Last Five Years*, the song order so firmly associated in my head, it's starting to feel more right than the actual soundtracks.

The song switches to "A Heart Full of Love" just as we pull into the parking lot, which leaves us no choice but to invoke the Formal Kate and Anderson *Les Mis* Protocol. Andy parks the car and turns the volume up, and we don't even bother taking off our seat belts, because there's no leaving the car until we've sung it all the way through. It's not even the best song on the soundtrack, but we're both suckers for anything with Éponine. Because Miss Éponine Thénardier is literally us. The true patron saint of trench coats and unrequited love. By the time we get to her verse, we're practically howling.

*He was never mine to lose.*

If anyone walked by Anderson's car right now, they'd probably run away screaming. God knows Kate Garfield Singing™ isn't exactly a vision of adorableness. But somehow when I'm with Andy, all the bullshit fades into the background. It hardly even exists.

"All right, Katypie," Anderson says, once we're inside and in line. "We have got to set some ground rules."

"Ground rules? Like a No Kiss—"

"No, come on. We're us. We have no game. We don't need a No Kiss List."

"That is an excellent point."

"I just think we need some guidelines. Because—I feel like we're on the same page with Matt, right? Like okay. We both like him. We both think he's awesome. But we're not letting this get in the way of us." He presses one fist to his heart. "We come first."

"Definitely." My heart flips. "Andy, I'm so sorry. I don't even know—"

The barista asks if we're ready to order, and my brain jumps straight to waffles. We order a whole bunch to share: strawberries and cream, pink drizzle, and chocolate dunked. They need a name to call out when it's ready—Anderson doesn't hesitate for a second. "Kandy with a K." Our portmanteau.

"So here's the thing," Anderson says, as we drift toward the water dispenser. "I know you're not trying to hurt me, obviously. And I'm not trying to hurt you."

"Of course. Yeah. I know."

"And we don't even know if Matt's into guys or girls or both or who or anyone, so obviously that's a thing, and then even if he is into whatever genders he's into, that doesn't mean he likes us."

"Uh, then he has no taste," I say.

"Obviously. But here's what I'm thinking." Anderson pauses to fill a cup with water, which he hands to me. Then he fills a second cup for himself. "We both know there's no point in trying to talk ourselves out of liking him. The heart wants what it wants."

"The heart wants Matt."

"Exactly," he says.

"So . . . what do you propose?"

"Why, Kate Eliza, I'm glad you asked." He settles into a chair, sets his cup down, and clasps his hands like a CEO. "After careful consideration, my proposal is this." He pauses. "I think we should be happy for each other. Like, let's promise each other—no matter what happens, we're going to be really, truly happy for each other. Even if we're disappointed."

"Even if we're disappointed." I bite my lip. "So you're saying . . . we both pursue him?"

He laughs. "Katy. When has either of us ever pursued?"

"Seventh grade. Eva Cohen's bat mitzvah. The choir robe room."

"Mmm. That was all you."

"Oh, that's funny, Andy." I cup my chin in my hands,

grinning up at him. "Very, very funny. Especially funny coming from a guy who went right for the boobs. Wham. Second base."

"Ahem. I was figuring stuff out."

"At synagogue. We were in a synagogue."

"You're the one who said it was a reform synagogue," Andy says. "Listen. All I'm saying is that, given that neither of us are particularly . . . aggressive when it comes to pursuit—"

"Kandy with a K?" There's the barista, beaming down at us. "Okay, plates are warm. Oops. You got them? Okay! Bon appétit!"

"Thank you so much," we both say. Like, in unison. With the exact same intonation. The barista raises her eyebrows and backs away slowly.

"Are we creepy?" I ask Anderson, setting our plates on the nearest table.

"Little bit."

We high-five.

"Anyway." Anderson plops into a chair. "Basically, what I'm thinking is we just roll with it and see what happens? Since we're both kind of shy"—I snort—"about this sort of thing. Shut up. I'm just saying we're shy about boys."

"Yes."

"So maybe we just let the situation play out, you know? We'll just be honest with each other."

"Even if we know the other person might not want to hear it?"

"Even then," says Andy. "Especially then."

"Okay, so we're happy for each other, we're honest with each other." I count it out on my fingers. "And what about this: our friendship is the most important thing."

"Well, duh."

"I mean it! Like, we could put it in writing. I'll text you right now, and you take a screenshot."

"A screenshot. Wow. Kate. Are we ready for that level of legitness?"

"Texting you now."

"And you want me to screenshot this?"

"Yup. And text it back to me. The whole thing. We're happy for each other, we're honest with each other, and our friendship comes first. No matter what."

"I like it." Andy grins. "Let's make it screenshot official."

# SCENE 32

But the minute I walk into Monday's rehearsal, there they are: Andy and Matt, in the very front row of the auditorium, heads a little too close together. Not close enough for kissing—anyway, Andy thinks making out on school grounds is both slutty and basic—but definitely close enough for secrets. Flirty secrets. Inside jokes. Love confessions.

Wow.

I'm just.

So happy for Andy. Super happy. Obviously. Didn't think I'd have to be happy for him so soon, but that's—

Okay, now Anderson is literally tousling Matt's hair, making it stick up in peaks. Man. Rehearsal's so fun. I'm so glad I get to witness this romance unfolding. It's going to be a great ninety minutes, a great month, a great forever.

It's like I can suddenly see our entire lives unspooling before me. Anderson texting me pictures from Matt's college campus next year. Or, like, an ironic-but-not-really-ironic photo of a sock on the doorknob of Matt's dorm room. Yeah.

But maybe I'll get numb to it. Maybe eventually this sort of thing stops hurting. I'll play guitar and sing at their wedding—something romantically offbeat, like "With You" from *Pippin*. And obviously I'll be ready to fight Anderson when he starts getting too attached to weird celebrity baby names. I'm going to be an excellent third wheel. Best third wheel in history. Maybe it's what I was built for.

"Okay!" Ms. Zhao calls, checking the time on her phone. "Let's get started. I need Dauntless, Winnifred, Aggravain, Sextimus, Wizard. Center stage. Let's hustle." She claps her hand around her fist like a coach, and Mr. D takes it to the next level by pounding out a frantic hurry-up song on the piano.

I reach the front of the auditorium just as Anderson's stepping onstage, but I can't exactly slide into the now-empty seat beside Matt. That's just too thirsty, even for me. But then again, if I sit in one of the rows behind Matt, he might not even see me. And I don't think we're scheduled to run any of the Larken/ Harry scenes today. So theoretically, Matt and I could go the whole rehearsal without interacting, and then I'll go home feeling growly and strange, and then Anderson will text me to tell me all the swoony details of their new romantic lives together.

And I'll just be so happy for him! Because those are the ground rules!

Whatever. I'm sitting in the front. It doesn't have to be thirsty. I'll just slide in here at the end of the row, a few seats down from Matt. Of course, if Matt wants to, he's perfectly welcome to scoot closer. I settle my backpack on the floor in front of me, making it my footrest, and then I glance sideways to see if Matt's noticed me.

He waves.

I wave back. And of course, my phone slides out of my hand, hitting the floor with a nice loud thud.

Oof. I mean the floor's linoleum, and I've got a decent phone case, and at least it was just phone-loud, not lunch-tray-loud. Though somehow I manage to catch Noah's eye onstage—he immediately grins, raises his eyebrow, and mouths, oooooooooooh. Just what I need.

But then Matt slides down the row, resettling right beside me. "Hey," he whispers. "Phone okay?"

"I think so. Nothing fatal," I say.

"Just a flesh wound."

Anderson's watching from the stage, but who cares? It's not like I'm breaking any ground rules. Matt is absolutely free to move closer to me and be cute and make cute Monty Python references, and I'm absolutely free to giggle and grin right back at him.

And hey. Anderson's free to feel happy for me.

# SCENE 33

Mr. Edelman, king of hands-on teaching, gives us another worksheet packet in history class. But with a twist. One, we have to work independently and in silence. Two, anyone who finishes the packet by the end of the period gets to opt out of Friday's pop quiz.

"How is it a pop quiz if we know it's on Friday?" Anderson murmurs.

"Who cares?" I've got my textbook open and my mechanical pencil poised and ready. I am very much a fan of opting out of quizzes.

"Hey." There's a tap on my back. "Psst. Little Garfield."

I glance over my shoulder. "What do you want, Kappy?"

That throws him.

He opens his mouth to reply, pauses, shuts it again, points a finger at me, and says, "No."

"No what?"

"Kappy. I don't like that."

I widen my eyes. "You seem to like it just fine when Madison says it."

"I do not like it just fine when Madison says it." Noah plants his elbows on his desk and leans forward, cupping his chin in his non-cast hand. "Okay, Little Kate—"

"Yes, Kappy?"

"Ha," he says. "Ha."

I shrug with my palms up and turn back to my worksheet.

He taps me again. "Okay, Kate."

"Shh. We're supposed to whisper," I say.

"No we're not," says Anderson. "We're not supposed to be talking."

"Whispering isn't talking," whispers Raina.

"Anyway," Noah says, leaning toward me.

"No talking, please," says Mr. Edelman.

"Anyway," Noah whispers. "Kate. Question." He doesn't wait for me to respond. "Are you going to the block party Saturday?"

"Why are you asking me that?"

"You should come!"

"Go with Ryan." I start to turn around, but Noah taps me again. I narrow my eyes. "What?"

"Okay, but hear me out."

"What?"

"Ryan has baseball," says Noah.

"No he doesn't."

Noah makes a face at me. "What happened to you not following sports?"

"Kappy, I live with Ryan."

"Touché! Also, hey, let's not make Kappy a thing."

"Please be quiet," Mr. Edelman says, rubbing his temples. "Please."

"Mr. Edelman has a migraine," whispers Brandie.

"So are you coming?"

"To the block party?"

Noah nods and locks eyes with me, clearly going for an eyegasm. Ha ha ha. No.

"Noah. What's your endgame here?"

He looks almost wounded. "What do you mean?"

"What's your endgame? Why do you need me to go to the block party? What do you want—more singing lessons?"

"No—what? I'm already great."

Anderson and Raina both snort.

"Kate." Noah sighs. "I don't have an endgame. I just wanted to thank you, okay? For the tray? I feel bad that you had to deal with my mess."

"You feel bad?"

He shrugs.

"Maybe you should thank Madison."

"Already did."

"Oh, I bet."

Anderson laughs out loud.

"So you want me to hang out with you at the block party," I say, "as a thank-you to me."

"Yes." He grins.

Wow, that is some f-boy self-esteem.

"So you'll be there?" he asks.

I roll my eyes. "Obviously, I'll be there."

Raina looks from me to Noah, eyebrows raised halfway to the stratosphere.

"It's a neighborhood block party," I remind her. "Right outside Dad's house. I'll be at Dad's house. Therefore, I'll be at the block party."

Raina flips her palms up. "Didn't say anything."

"You guys should come," I say, shrugging.

Brandie says she'll try to stop by, but Raina says she has a date.

Noah high-fives her. "Yeah you do!"

Raina rolls her eyes, but she's smiling.

"I can't come," Anderson says, pausing for the barest split second. "I've got plans."

Something about that pause.

He's staring at his worksheet, but his dimple caves briefly, like it does when he's feeling awkward. A tiny knot forms in my chest. Something like dread, maybe panic.

"Plans?"

Somehow, before Anderson even opens his mouth, I know just what he's about to say.

"Plans with Matt," he says gently.

And then I mostly just feel numb.

# SCENE 34

So, Dad's neighborhood has a bit of a fuckboy problem.

I mean, it could be worse. I could be Brandie, who lives walking distance from no fewer than eight members of the lacrosse team. But it's not great. We've got Mira Reynolds and her tween sisters over near the neighborhood pool, and there's a whole crop of baby-jock eighth graders one cul-de-sac over.

But I actually love the Remington Commons neighborhood block party, mostly because it's barely a party. It's just this dorky street event the neighborhood association started throwing a couple of years ago, every September and May. Half the time, the f-boys are too hungover to even show up.

Anyway, I can't just sit in my room thinking about Andy and Matt and their plans. So I throw on one of my mom's old Stacey Abrams campaign T-shirts, which wins a tiny smile from my brother. He's currently sitting at the kitchen table, eating cold pizza with one hand, and petting Camilla with the other.

Ryan sets down his pizza. "Making a statement?"

"It's a good statement."

"You're not wrong."

I grab some raisin bread and eat it standing over the counter. Then I round up the dogs, pop their leashes on, and step out into the ten a.m. early September heat.

It's pretty quiet this early—mostly just a bunch of dads in polo shirts hanging out in plastic chairs at the edge of their lawns, drinking bloody Marys. I spot my dad in a little chair cluster at the Kaplans' house, looking flushed and happy alongside both of Noah's parents, plus the dad who just moved in next door. New Dad, who's currently holding an extremely new baby, is the youngest in the circle by at least a decade.

Dad waves me over. "Peapod!"

The whole peapod thing. I should probably be mortified, but it's hard to muster it up when it's just a mom, three dads, and a newborn. Also, it's pretty obvious that this is the neighborhood dork crowd. Which is probably a weird thing to say about a bunch of parents, but it's true. All I know about the new dad so far is that he and his wife dress the baby exclusively in science pun onesies. Anna and Joe Kaplan are the type who post massive photo sets to Facebook without even removing the blurry ones. And Dad's just there with his pants tucked nice and high, and his shirt buttons off-track. Like, basically imagine the geek table from any high school cafeteria, then age them up twenty-five years.

But the funny thing is, in some strange, subversive way, I really think that makes them cooler. Like, if you're going to be forty-five, just be forty-five. Don't be those parents grasping for their glory days, trying to recreate them with tennis team hierarchies and their kids' sports schedules.

I let the dogs lead me over to Dad's dork squad and spend the next ten minutes fielding questions about school. And running interference against Camilla, who's apparently determined to snuffle deep into everyone's crotches.

"Noah's really loving the play rehearsals," says Anna. "He was so anxious at first, but he's really come around to them." Anxious. Noah Kaplan. It really is funny sometimes how parents get certain ideas of their kids.

"Peapod, you know what? We should grab the karaoke machine. I was just telling Bill here that you're a fantastic singer."

"She gave Noah voice lessons," says Anna.

"We could set up a whole karaoke station here. Line up some chairs or something. What do you think?"

"Absolutely not."

Wow. Speaking of parents getting certain ideas of their kids. Dad seems to have mistaken me for someone who spontaneously performs in public. Non-theater people never get the whole emotional preparation factor. And even then, you could be courting disaster. It could be Ella-gate 2.0. I mean, maybe someone like Anderson could pull it off without the cringe, because he's more consistently talented than I am and his voice doesn't shake when he's nervous. And he's just overall slightly more badass. Maybe that's why he suddenly has so much game now. Enough game to get the ball rolling on mysterious plans with Matt.

Saturday plans. I wonder whose idea they were.

Camilla makes a sudden move for Bill and the baby, so I quickly yank her leash back before her tongue gets involved. Then I move an open bag of chips from Charles. And then I end up just using the dogs as an excuse to leave, which is pretty much why I brought them in the first place. I'll just take them on a quick walk around the neighborhood and go home. After all, I'm well overdue for some moping time in my room.

I mean. I'm not moping. I'm not. Maybe it resembles moping from the outside, but it's really just rapturous excitement. It's me being wildly, extraordinarily happy. For Anderson. So happy that I'm just going to kneel here really fast and snap a quick selfie with the dogs. Who, by the way, make terrible models—Camilla's got one lip hooked up like Elvis, and Charles is just a blur of movement. But I text it to Anderson anyway. **We miss your face!!**

No response.

By the time I make it to the pool and back with the dogs, Brandie's car is in my driveway, and she's standing on our lawn beside Noah and my brother.

Noah hugs me. "Hey, Kate."

Okay. Didn't know we were hug friends. Noah's not a bad hugger, though—at least it's not one of those fakey loose hugs like Lana Bennett's known for. Also he smells good. Gotta love when boys shower. I'll give him extra props, too, because I've heard showering in a cast is complicated.

Brandie squats down to pet Charles, who goes straight into belly-up surrender position. "Charles, have some self-respect," Noah says. Then, glancing back at me, he adds, "So I was thinking we could all walk down to the playground?"

I stare at his arm. "Did you draw boobs on your cast?"

"No," he says. "Jack Randall did."

Of course he did. "So you're just going to walk around like that," I say, and then it hits me. "Wait, the play! How are you—"

"Okay, first of all, long-sleeved costumes exist," Noah says, looking extra amused. "Second of all, let's not forget my man is named King Sextimus, which is clearly the name of a king who appreciates boobs."

"Wow. You're gross."

"And third of all, I'm getting a replacement cast on Tuesday. Boob-free." He smiles. So I'm not going to ruin your play, Little Garfield."

"It's not my play, Kappy. It's my musical."

"Hey," Brandie reminds him. "It's your musical, too."

# SCENE 35

By the time we set out for the playground, I'd say it's a fairly-legit party, in the sense that the dads all seem to have acquired coolers of beer. Livy Kaplan somehow catches up with our group, which is pretty impressive for a seven-year-old in Disney heels. But Livy in heels is fast enough to keep up with Ryan and Brandie, who are at the front of our pack. They're too far ahead for me to make out what she's saying, but she's been talking nonstop since she joined us.

"Has she even taken, like, one breath?" I ask Noah. We're the stragglers, a couple of yards behind Brandie and our siblings.

"Absolutely not. That would be a criminal waste of valuable talking time—OH." Noah's voice drops. "This perv. Look." He juts his chin out, just barely, toward a yard at the center of Remington and Pine. There are probably twenty tiny kids there, plus their parents, all clustered around a duo of tiger mascots in hoodies.

"Isn't that—" I start to say, but then the words somehow vanish.

Because Noah's hand is on my hand. His right hand, the one without the cast. And just the back of it, not the palm. But still. Noah Kaplan's hand. Pressed all the way up against mine.

Which is weird. Next-level weird. Wow.

Except, as fast as it happened, it's gone. Total retreat.

"He wears. No pants," says Noah.

"Who, Daniel Tiger? Isn't he a child? And a cartoon?"

"His dad's not a child."

"So Daniel Tiger's dad is the perv."

"Kate, he's a grown man. A father. Wearing no pants."

"He is a cartoon tiger," I say, sounding calmer than I feel. There's still this fluttery knot in my stomach. "I hate to break it to you, but sometimes cartoons don't wear clothes."

"Then riddle me this. Why is he wearing the hoodie?"

"Did you just say 'riddle me this'?"

"Don't change the subject." Noah looks at me sidelong, grinning. And then he does the hand thing again! Wow. That split-second, back-of-the-hand contact—what is that? Some kind of new f-boy move? An alternative to the eyegasm?

"I'm just saying," Noah continues, "here we've established a world where the animals wear clothes, they talk, they walk around. They're anthropomorphized."

"How much thought have you put into this?"

"Years," Noah says. "Years of thought."

We reach the playground, and Livy flings herself onto a swing, stomach first. "Guys, this is gonna be epic. Noah! Come on. I want to film a YouTube."

"Hold on," says Noah.

"Don't forget to smash that like button!"

I turn to Noah incredulously. "Livy's on YouTube?"

"Livy thinks she's on YouTube." He pulls out his phone. "Future blackmail material."

"A-plus big brothering," I say, watching him drift toward the swings.

My own brother is standing a few yards away, arms crossed—not in an angry way. Just self-conscious, I think. He's talking to Brandie, who's already climbed into the play structure and is sitting at the edge of its platform, legs dangling down. Brandie's counting something off on her fingers, and Ryan's nodding along. It's funny. I'm not sure I've ever seen them interact before, other than Ryan mumbling hi from the couch when the squad comes over.

Speaking of the squad, it's been a good few minutes since I texted the dog selfie to Anderson. So I sneak a peek at my phone to see if he's responded.

He hasn't.

Which is a total gut punch. I know it's stupid to get this antsy over a text I sent twenty minutes ago, but in Kate-and-Anderson time, that's centuries. And it's a text with a selfie, too, which makes the lack of acknowledgment even worse. It's like when your scene partner's supposed to cut you off and overlap your line, but they don't. That same quiet beat of panic and awkwardness.

But I'm being ridiculous. Andy's probably just not checking his phone. And there are lots of reasons why he might not be checking his phone, reasons that have nothing to do with Matt. His phone could be charging, for example. He could be peeing. Or driving.

And today's so strange in general, that I keep feeling like I'm drifting along two steps behind my body. I blink, and somehow I'm sitting at a picnic table across from Noah, who's got both arms stretched across the table, illustrated boobs winking in the sunshine. And that alone is mind-boggling. Just being here with Noah Kaplan. It almost feels like a time warp.

The Kate-Noah friendship didn't last all that long, between Noah moving here and my parents' divorce and Noah becoming an f-boy. But we were briefly a duo, mostly due to Sunday school choir rehearsals, which we occasionally skipped in favor of prowling around the synagogue. Noah was really good at charming the parent kitchen volunteers into giving us extra pieces of that mushy, pre-sliced Hebrew school challah. Even now, when I think of Sunday school, that's what I think of. Me and Noah in the supply closet near the women's bathrooms, rolling challah slices into bread balls and eating them like popcorn.

I stopped going to Sunday school after my bat mitzvah. I guess I could have gone on to get confirmed, but I never felt like my parents wanted to drive me. And then Noah started dating Genny Hedlund, which added this whole extra layer of weirdness. Even more so when they broke up six weeks later. Apparently it wasn't like Anderson's and my breakup, which ended in us crying, hugging, and vowing forever friendship beneath Andy's eight *Teen Wolf* posters. All of which, I later noticed, prominently featured Dylan O'Brien's face.

But by April, Noah was dating Savannah Griffin, and after that, Gayatri Dawar. And then Mackenzie Yates, and Eva Cohen, and Ashlyn O'Shea, and Amy Austin. He just always seemed to have a girlfriend. Or an almost-girlfriend. Or, evidently, two simultaneous girlfriends. I don't even want to know what his deal was at ninth-grade homecoming.

Anyway, the whole thing just made Noah hard to be friends with. It wasn't that I cared who he hooked up with. And he's never been the type to drop off the planet when he's in a relationship. But it almost started to feel like we were from two different species. You had Noah, flirting and kissing, bouncing from sports games to parties. And then you had me, a slick teenager with slick teenage moves, blowing my hair out to look like *Ella Enchanted*. Or memorizing the Wikipedia page for Lansing, Michigan. Or playing love songs alone in my room and crying. I just felt so childish compared to Noah. It's like he moved on to French pastries, and I was still munching on bread balls.

# SCENE 36

It's getting warmer, maybe a little too warm, but I'm not quite ready to head back inside. Noah's winding up about the musical now, which is funny to watch—just hearing the phrase "intensive rehearsal" in the mouth of an f-boy. "Intensive is right. I was like, damn. Mr. D made Brandie and Laura sing the 'hey nonny nonny' part thirty-eight times in a row, I counted—"

"You mean Lana?"

Noah looks unruffled. "Well, yes and no. On the one hand, I know her name's Lana. On the other hand, I have to call her Laura because she keeps calling me Nolan."

"Fair," I say, yawning. Sunshine always makes me sleepy. And for a minute, neither of us speaks, but it's the peaceful kind of silence. Livy's still on her swing, though she's talked Noah into letting her play a game on his phone, and Ryan and Brandie are pretty much where we left them. And it's starting to feel like a moment I could settle into. Like, so what if Anderson and Matt have plans that don't include me. I don't have to stress about that. I can just choose not to think about it.

After a couple of minutes, Ryan and Brandie drift back toward the picnic table, and Brandie scoots in right beside me. And I'm flooded with some kind of feeling, some preemptive nostalgia. It's the kind of moment where I swear I feel a memory forming before I'm even done living it. Brandie must feel it too because she hooks her arm around my waist. So I do the same thing to her, and now it's like we're posing for a picture. It's such a soft, sun-soaked feeling, so quintessentially Brandie. She's like a walking, talking Xanax. I mean, it's actually weirdly easy to picture Brandie as a grandma.

Noah yawns, turning to Ryan. "You have your thing tomorrow, right? Georgia State?"

"Kennesaw," says Ryan. "Nine a.m."

"Yikes," says Noah.

Sucks to be Ryan. My parents don't agree on much, but they're both fanatical about college. Which means Ryan's been doing campus tours and info sessions practically every single weekend. I think he's pretty burned out on them. It's weird—I never see Ryan all that hyped about college, the way most seniors are. Honestly, I'm not so hyped for him to leave either. Even if he ends up staying local, it's going to make everything different. It's like when my parents split. You wouldn't think Mom moving three miles up the road would be the biggest change on earth. And it wasn't.

It was more like a million tiny changes.

But then again, Raina says she and her sister actually got closer after Corey left for college, because they started texting more. Though Ryan's a shitty texter, so maybe that doesn't apply. Andy thinks I should take over his room when he leaves and turn it into a dressing room.

Except I'm not thinking about Andy. Or Matt. Or their plans.

Of course, the minute I decide that, my phone finally buzzes in my back pocket. Four times.

But when I pull it out to check, not a single one of them is from Anderson.

They're all from Matt.

**Want to come over and run lines tomorrow?**

**Okay anyway I'm free all day tomorrow if you want to, so just text me!**

"Okay, you kind of look like you just won the lottery," says Noah, "but also like you're about to throw up."

"That's exactly how I feel."

Noah raises his eyebrows. "Must be some text."

# SCENE 37

It's almost noon, and Dad and Ryan still aren't back from Kennesaw—which sucks hard, because they were my top two choices to drive me to Matt's house today. I feel weird asking Matt to pick me up at Dad's house. It just tips the invitation too far out of the realm of casual, I think. And it's not like I can bum a ride from Anderson, unless I want Anderson present for the line running. And I don't. Maybe that's awful, but I don't.

In the end, I ask Mom. She picks the dogs and me up right after breakfast, which works great—until I casually ask her to drop me off at Matt's house.

"What?" She gasps. "Katypie, like a date?"

"No, like running lines—"

"And here I thought you liked that boy Alexander!"

"Who?"

"The one you and Andy were talking about at Shabbat dinner. Alexander from Lansing, Michigan?"

"Oh my God. How do you even remember that?"

"But you and Matthew! Now, how cute would that be? He's just such a sweetheart. And he's Jewish! Sweetie, grab Charles— he can't climb on the gearstick like that."

I scoop Charles back onto my lap. "Not that it matters, but I don't think Matt's Jewish."

"He is! Ellen's Jewish, so Matthew's Jewish."

"Does he go to temple?"

"Do we?" Mom drums the steering wheel, clearly delighted. "Does Ellen know about today?"

"How would I possibly know that?"

"Now, you know I'm going to call her." Mom's voice gets suddenly stern. "Six inches. You know the rule."

Ah yes. The most pointless rule ever. If I'm alone in here with any boy who's not Anderson, the door stays open six inches. And the same applies to Ryan's room with girls, or at least it would if Ryan ever had girls over. I have no idea where Mom got the impression I'm capable of sealing any kind of deal. There's honestly no need to cockblock me. I myself am the cockblock.

"Mom. It's not a date. We're running lines."

"Yeah, kiddo, that's how it starts. One minute you're running lines, next minute the script's on the floor—"

"Whoa. Can we not?"

Mom glances sideways, looking genuinely confused. "Can we not what?"

"Can we not, like, graphically imagine this hookup that isn't happening?"

"No kidding, it's not happening. Because that door's going to be six inches open."

# SCENE 38

Mom drops me off at Matt's house, which is in one of the newer neighborhoods near school. His whole street is a series of identical townhomes, all gleaming and well-maintained, with tiny patches of yard in the front. It's a different vibe from the swim-and-tennis McMansions in Dad's neighborhood, and it's very different from the quirky, woodsy older houses on Mom's street. But it's kind of charming and safe-feeling, and just the fact that it's Matt's street makes me gooey inside.

By the time Mom parks, my heart's bouncing around like a pinball. Ellen's car is parked across from their townhouse, right beside Matt's, and I can just picture this turning into a Mom Thing. Mom will be like oh, just one quick hello, and that hello will turn into three hours and several wineglasses, and Mom plus wine plus my crush is a nerve-racking equation.

But Mom doesn't walk me in, because she doesn't want to leave the dogs in the car. So I'd like to nominate Charles and Camilla Garfield as Dogs of the Year, canine heroes, saviors, and general MVPs. Mom does, however, wait in the car, like she does whenever she drops anyone off anywhere. "Don't ever leave until they're inside." She must have said this to Ryan and me a hundred times. "You know, your father dropped me off after a date once and sped off before I realized I'd forgotten my key. I was stranded out there for hours."

Mom barely ever talks about Dad, but when she does, it's always like this. She gets this lemon-mouth expression, and then she calls him "your father," and then she tells about something he did that was stupid or careless. But she never seems like she's actually mad about it. It's funny, I think a lot of divorces happen because someone cheats or there's fighting or something. But my parents just drifted apart. The way Mom describes it, they just weren't that close anymore. They stopped telling each other things.

It's kind of scary if you think about it. Just how easy it is for a relationship to dissolve. And how especially easy it is to stop confiding in each other. Like Andy, for instance. He never did respond to the dog selfie, but when I asked him how his plans with Matt went, he said they watched a bunch of superhero movies and went to Waffle House, and it was fun. And that's it. I mean, if this were a normal communal crush, Andy would be flipping out in my texts, unpacking every single interaction and shouting about the good parts in all caps. So his restraint, when it comes to Matt, is really unsettling.

But maybe I'm overthinking this whole Andy and Matt thing, especially seeing as I'm literally standing on Matt's doorstep. For a hangout he initiated. Of course, the word "hangout" is probably overly broad, seeing as we're just running lines. So in that way, it's more like a business meeting. It's just that I'm having trouble thinking businesslike thoughts. Also, this just in: freaking out on a boy's doorstep is extremely uncool, especially when your mom's still parked here, watching you. I have to breathe. I have to ring the doorbell.

Right away, footsteps. So now my heart's just putting a down payment on its new forever home, in my throat. Matt opens the door, smiling sweetly. "You made it!"

Mom honks and waves and finally, finally drives off.

Ellen's not home, as it turns out, despite her car being here. Matt says she flew to New Jersey for the weekend to help Matt's great-aunt Sylvia move into a retirement community. As soon as he says that, my brain splits off from my mouth completely. It's like, here I am saying soothing, heartfelt things about Aunt Sylvia, but underneath all of that, my mind's spiraling in two totally opposite directions. Because—holy shit—I am—oh my God—alone in a house with Matt Olsson. But on the other hand—

So was Anderson.

Whatever that means.

He gives me a quick tour, and my brain's sputtering holy shit, holy shit over and over, like the world's least articulate broken record. The foyer, the dining room, the staircase, the hallway, his bedroom. Matt's bedroom. Even the idea of it makes it hard to stand upright. I have this sudden urge to send a giddy freakout text to Anderson, and the fact that I can't makes me wistful. A month ago, a moment like this wouldn't have felt real unless I shared it with Anderson. But of course, a month ago, a moment like this wouldn't have been real. Because Matt wasn't real. Not to us. He was like a concept we invented.

Everything was a lot simpler a month ago.

Matt's room itself is fairly small and sparse, with just a few fantasy books and some Funko Pops on the dresser. There's also a big rectangular mirror, lined with unframed photos, like a group of hot, preppy boys sitting on a dock in bathing suits. And an old picture of a blond guy who's unquestionably Matt's dad—looks exactly like him, wow—alongside Ellen and Matt as a tiny blond toddler. So cute I could melt. I try not to stare too closely at a more recent one of Matt and a pretty blond girl, clearly dressed for a formal dance. She's wearing a corsage, and his boutonniere matches, and she's as straightforwardly gorgeous as any Roswell Hill f-girl. And it occurs to me suddenly how little I know about Matt. I don't even know if he's single.

"My room's so boring," he says, almost apologetically, coming up beside me at the window. Matt's room looks out onto a modest backyard—mostly just a deck and a small, fenced-in grassy area, with a few bushes and one tall tree.

"It's not boring. I think it's peaceful."

"We're renting month to month while Mom house-hunts, so we're supposed to keep everything neat in case the landlords need to show it."

I try to wrap my mind around that. I guess in the grand

scheme of things, it's a small inconvenience. But I can't imagine living like that. Even in their own home, Matt and Ellen hardly get to stretch their legs out. Which kind of defeats the purpose of home in the first place.

We head back down to the main floor, and Matt asks, "Are you thirsty?" I say no, because I'm not, at least not in the way he's thinking. So, we end up on the living room couch, with our scripts facedown between us. My eyes keep darting all around the living room, basically everywhere but Matt's face. The living room is as clean and uncluttered as the rest of the house, with extra-high ceilings like a magazine room. But right away, I recognize a series of those old-time film-camera camp photos, just like the ones my mom has. I open my mouth to mention them, but then Matt looks right into my eyes with a heartbreakingly sweet smile. So of course I forget how to speak.

"Want to see how far we can get without the scripts?"

Uh. Yeah, I'd like to see how far we can get. Maybe we can just slide these scripts onto your mom's coffee table there, and lean back and—

WOW. Okay. Maybe I'm getting a little ahead of myself.

But it's crazy, the way I can't stop turning every single moment here into the start of a love story. The way Matt goes soft-eyed whenever Harry declares his love for Larken. Sir Harry in the show is kind of a medieval f-boy, but Matt makes him into a guy you could really fall in love with. Which is useful. Strictly from a professional standpoint. Just, you know. Speaking as Lady Larken.

We run through the end of Act One, Scene One, where Larken tells Harry she's pregnant, and Matt doesn't miss a single cue. He does little movements and gestures, too, even though we won't officially be blocking the scene until Thursday. But he does them like he's caught up in the moment. He'll thrust his chest out like a knight, or he'll grab my hands and pull me closer.

And I can't seem to rein my heart in. I've got that giddy, bursting-at-the-seams feeling. Like the joy's too big for the moment. It keeps leaking out around the edges. We keep giggling in the middle of lines and having to start over. There's this one line where I'm trying to talk discreetly about the secret baby, and I'm supposed to say to Harry, *you know*, all knowingly. And for some reason, that line in particular is unbearably funny. I keep saying it in less and less subtle ways, just to make Matt laugh. Rubbing my stomach in circles and winking. You know. Pantomiming rocking a baby. Pointing back and forth between the invisible baby and Matt, like I'm delivering the news of a paternity test. You know.

Matt's so cute when he laughs. He scrunches his nose and flings his head back and shuts his eyes all the way. Like he's having a little private laugh-moment, completely with himself. And there's just this feeling in the air, this palpable energy. I swear, it feels like we could start kissing at any moment. He could scoot closer, or I could. Just a tiny shift in our blocking. But then again, the kissing part feels strangely tangential. Like the conversation itself is the kiss. Maybe some conversations are like that.

The only thing I can't quite settle my mind about is Anderson. What would he think if he could see Matt and me right now? I didn't even tell him I was coming here. I'm not entirely sure why. I guess I thought maybe he'd try to join us. Or he'd go weird and silent about the fact that it was even happening. Which, by the way, would be insanely unfair, coming from someone who's supposed to be happy for me. Especially someone who had his own plans with Matt yesterday.

But I have to admit, Andy and Matt's plans feel very far away right now. Superheroes and waffles. I mean, yeah, that sounds fun, but it couldn't have felt this charged. It just couldn't have. Though I guess there's a chance Anderson's given me some neutered, watered-down version of the day. Just like I'll probably do when I try to explain today to Anderson.

If I even explain it to him at all.

# SCENE 39

Of course, I end up blurting the whole thing out to Andy the minute he picks me up for school on Tuesday. For a minute, he stays parked in my driveway, eyes fixed on the windshield, looking vaguely confused. "You ran lines?" he asks finally.

"Yeah. Pretty much." I buckle my seat belt.

I mean, it's true. We ran lines. And it's not like anything physical happened, beyond hand-holding, and that was just character work. Except for one particular moment. Not that it was a moment. But Matt and I had finally made it through the whole scene without laughing, so we were feeling very smug and self-congratulatory. And somehow our eyes locked, just for ten seconds, maybe twenty, until he opened his mouth to speak. But the words never came.

Instead, he looked away, so I looked away too, and there was this whole electric minute where we were just sitting there in silence. Inches apart, not facing each other. But I kept sneaking glances at Matt out of the corner of my eye. He had this look on his face that reminded me of something.

I'm not telling Anderson that part.

"Are you upset?"

"What? Of course not." He glances up at the rearview. Then, carefully, he backs out of my driveway and onto the road. "Why would I be upset?"

"I don't know. You kind of seem upset."

"Well, I'm not."

For a minute, we're both silent.

"Did Matt mention he was inviting me over?" I ask finally.

Andy pauses. Pushes the turn signal. "Nope," he says.

"Maybe he just decided last minute."

"Maybe."

Kind of strange, in a way. Matt must have invited me right after Andy left on Saturday. Also strange the way, the whole time we were together, he didn't mention Anderson once. Not the superheroes, not the waffles, not anything. Almost like Matt wants to know us separately. Or at least there's something separate about us in his mind.

I don't know how I feel about that. I'm so used to Andy and me being this indestructible unit. Not that this Matt thing is destroying us. Destroying is definitely not the word. Because we'd never let that happen. We have ground rules. Anyway, Andy's not even upset.

I mean, he says he's not upset.

But I swear he's not quite the usual bright-eyed Anderson. He's not even the only-slightly-less-vibrant foggy morning Anderson.

In fact, he doesn't speak at all, the whole way to school.

# SCENE 40

But by history class, Anderson's completely back to normal. Even better than normal. He's the goofiest, bossiest version of himself, the kind that usually only surfaces for play rehearsal.

I guess Mr. Edelman's feeling sassy, too, because we're doing a study notes review game about Puritans today. He let us pick our own teams, so the squad squadded up. We even moved our desks into a pod as a display of team unity and gave ourselves the most atrocious name on earth: Team Massachusetts Bae. Of course, all the other teams immediately followed suit. Team Plymouth Raunch. Team Thomas Hooker. Team Devil's Playground. Team Cotton Mather's Cotton Trousers, consisting of Noah and three f-girls. And Colin Nakamura's group, the Colinists. Something about AP US History does this to people. Like, here we have a bunch of sixteen-year-olds from Roswell who all apparently think we're Lin-Manuel Miranda.

Each team gets a whiteboard, and Mr. Edelman stands at his podium with a few sheets of questions. Just your basic trivia competition game. Open-book, but no phones allowed. Twenty seconds after the question is read, each team holds up their answer. It's completely pointless, seeing as there are no prizes, not even extra credit, but it really starts to feel like your pride is at stake. Like somehow Thomas Hooker's legacy is contingent on whether four f-boys can answer questions about Calvinism. But you'd never know that, watching the room erupt into shouting, finger-pointing, and desk-banging, so loud I'm pretty sure Mr. Edelman will never recover. It is the rowdiest, most aggressive celebration of Puritanism I've seen in my entire life.

Team Massachusetts Bae is no exception. We're not above it. Brandie and I flip frantically through our textbooks, and Raina and Anderson keep yanking the whiteboard back and forth between them. "Okay, 1636," Brandie keeps muttering. "It's got to be Harvard, right?"

"Or Yale! Brandie, use the index."

"Here it is. The Puritans founded Harvard University in 1636." I slide the whole book toward Anderson. "Boom."

Something crashes to the ground right beside me, and I'm so startled, I almost leap from my seat. It turns out to be Noah, in a heap on the ground, blinking out from underneath his overturned desk.

"Oh my God, your arm." I kneel quickly beside him. "Are you okay? Let me see."

"I'm fine." He disentangles himself, looking slightly dazed, while two of the girls on his team tip it back upright. He thrusts his cast arm into my hand and lets me examine it.

"Um," I say, rotating it just a little, and bending his fingers up and down, like I imagine a doctor would. "Cast looks okay."

It's the same cast with the illustrated boobs, so Noah's doctor appointment must be in the afternoon. Maybe even during rehearsal. Not that I care. He shouldn't be missing full ensemble rehearsals though. I bet Ms. Zhao's going to be pissed.

It occurs to me, suddenly, that I'm still holding Noah's cast. And his fingertips too. I jerk my hand back and clutch it to my chest. "You can get up now," I tell him.

"But it's nice down here."

"You're on a real fucking roll, Noah," says Raina. "First the tray, now this. Holy attention-seeking behavior. Wow."

"You just fell out of your desk," Anderson says. "You really did that."

"I actually fell with my desk."

Anderson narrows his eyes. "Were you trying to eavesdrop?"

"Whaaaaaat?" Noah's voice jumps an octave. "Of course not." Wow. I have literally never seen anyone look more over-the-top, comically guilty than Noah Kaplan in this moment.

"Noah, it's open-book," Brandie says gently. "You don't have to cheat."

"I wasn't cheating. Just collaborating."

I shake my head. "Noah."

Anderson climbs onto his chair, clearing his throat. "Excuse me," he says.

Everyone falls expectantly silent.

"Ahem. Team Cotton Mather's Cotton Trousers are a bunch

of filthy cheaters, and they should be disqualified. That is all." Andy steps down, with a final haughty glance for Noah—who beams up at him from the floor.

Something bubbles up inside of me, some inexplicable warm relief. Because Andy and I are us again. We're back on the same team. And it feels like flipping on a light switch or finishing a puzzle or pressing the cap back onto a tube of Chap-Stick. Like everything clicking into place at last.

# SCENE 41

Thursday's one of those insane weather days where you don't think it's the apocalypse, but you're not one hundred percent sure it's not the apocalypse. It's just nonstop booming thunder and flickering lights. I'd be legitimately freaked out if I were home alone. But at school, it just gives me this vaguely excited, anticipatory feeling, like the universe could deliver pretty much anything.

To be fair, that feeling might have something to do with the fact that this afternoon marks the first official Larken/Harry intensive rehearsal. Ninety minutes. With Matt. Just me and Matt. And, okay, Ms. Zhao and Devon and Mr. D and probably some of the tech crew. But still. And that's not even getting into the fact that we're blocking "Yesterday I Loved You," which happens to involve a kiss.

It's weird. I keep half-forgetting it's happening, but then I'll remember it out of nowhere—in the hall, or in class—and I get this jolt. It's a butterflies in the stomach feeling, but super intense. Butterflies on steroids. To be honest, I can barely keep myself from floating between classes. Everything about today feels infused with magic.

Case in point: Andy and I slip out of class for a carefully coordinated rendezvous in the Bathroom Time Forgot, and who do we run into? Matt Olsson himself. At his locker. In the middle of a class period. I mean, I never see Matt in the halls, even walking between classes. But here he is, and here we are—just the three of us, in an otherwise empty hallway. He hugs both of us, looking genuinely delighted. He's wearing this soft navy V-neck, more fitted than usual, and something about that color makes his eyes look like denim. After we part ways, Anderson and I spend twenty minutes in our bathroom stalls, pretty much hyperventilating.

It's happiness overload. So much joy, it barely sinks in. It's everything—the thrill of being at school in a thunderstorm, the diminishing hours until rehearsal, seeing Matt in the hallway, how extra cute he looked. And it's the secret thought in my head that maybe—maybe—the extra cuteness on today, of all days, is somehow deliberate. Deliberate in the same way my own outfit is deliberate—swingy short dress, black with flowers, and a jean jacket. Because if you don't put in that extra ten minutes of effort for an intensive romantic play rehearsal with your crush, what's the point? I mean, I'm probably overthinking it, and who even knows if boys have that degree of self-awareness. But maybe. Maybe?

Even the thought makes me unravel.

Out of everything, though, the best part's the bathroom freakout with Anderson. We could barely catch our breath, there was so much to discuss. Those denim eyes, Matt's lightly tousled hair, and that shirt. That. Shirt.

I don't know. It was just really nice how, for those twenty minutes in the bathroom, Matt was ours again. Both of ours.

# SCENE 42

By the end of the school day, the storm's even worse. Matt walks in sopping wet to rehearsal—cheeks flushed, hair slicked straight against his forehead, like he just stepped out of the shower. I stare at him, almost speechless.

"Left my script in my car," he explains.

Andy, Raina, and Brandie have all had their first intensive rehearsals already, so I kind of know what to expect. Thirty minutes of vocal rehearsal with Mr. D, thirty minutes of blocking and fine-tuning with Ms. Zhao, and then thirty minutes running through the whole scene, vocals and blocking together. According to Anderson, it can get a little repetitive. But I'm not so sure that's a bad thing.

I mean, I wouldn't mind getting a little repetitive with that Harry/Larken kiss. Not that I've been obsessing about the kiss, the kiss, the kiss, the kiss, the kiss, the kiss, the kiss, the kiss.

The.

Kiss.

Wow. I'm so totally chill right now. Just so normal and fine and not losing my shit.

"Harry and Larken, come on down," Mr. D calls, and then he starts playing the theme song to *The Price is Right*. Mr. D is so extra, and I love it. "Okay, let's warm up. Starting on ah."

We settle in at the edge of the piano, side by side, singing along to all fifty million scales Mr. D gets in his head. Everything. Major key, minor key, up to the top edges of our ranges, and back down again.

"Now ooh."

There's something wonderful, almost conspiratorial, about running through silly warm-ups with Matt. Not to mention the fact that silly warm-ups make Matt even cuter. He stands perfectly stick-straight, like a choirboy, clutching his hands to his diaphragm. And his wet hair's curling so sweetly around his ears, winging out slightly in the back. My heart can't take it.

"Great. Let's do . . . bah!" But as soon as Mr. D suggests it, there's a massive clap of thunder. "Hmm. No bah?" He peers up at the ceiling like he's consulting with God.

The lights flicker.

"No bah," says Matt.

Mr. D nods. "I can take a hint. Better hop straight into the songs while we still have power, am I right?"

We start with "In a Little While," and Matt leans over to tell me it's his absolute favorite of our songs.

It's my favorite, too. I actually think it's my favorite song in the show. It's hard to explain why it's so relatable, but it is.

It really is. Like, on the one hand, yeah, it's about a medieval knight secretly knocking up a lady-in-waiting. But I think it's really about anticipation and certainty and that feeling you get when you imagine your best future. The precious secret future, the one you carry around in daydreams.

It's a Rapunzel kind of feeling. A when-will-my-life-begin kind of feeling.

Matt's so close to me now, by the piano, and I keep expecting my voice to go haywire or disappear altogether. But I push through, and I sound much more okay than expected. Not like I'm perfect or anything, but I get the lyrics mostly right. And Matt's as dreamy of a Sir Harry as ever, even though he can't quite nail the octave leap at the end of the second verse. But somehow this little vocal glitch makes him even cuter.

Mr. D is terrible at time management, so we only have time to run through "Yesterday I Loved You" once before he hands us over to Ms. Zhao. By now, we've already blocked bits and pieces of the scene with "In a Little While"—Ms. Zhao's really good at squeezing little moments into the margins of full-cast rehearsals. But it's the first time we've ever run through it from the beginning of the scene, and Zhao keeps stopping the action to adjust us. "Matt, step forward. Good. Kate, lean back into him and put your hands over his hands. Yup."

Cheesy prom pose for the win. Matt keeps quietly apologizing for the dampness of his shirt, which is so sweet, it makes me giggle—at least it would make me giggle if my lungs were even kind of working. But no, apparently my entire brain and body are closed for business, except that little spot on my rib cage where Matt's hands are pressed.

I mean. These intensive rehearsals are something. They really are.

"Okay, great," Ms. Zhao says. "Devon's taking all of this down, so you can sit down with him later to add the notes to your script. But I say let's keep it moving and knock out 'Yesterday I Loved You.' Who's ready for that kiss?"

Um, apparently Mr. D is. Because now he's playing that "Kiss Me" song, the one with the line about milky twilight that Anderson swears is about semen. And wow. I sure do love associating that thought with Mr. D. I'm probably super bright red now, and even Matt looks flustered. He shoots me this tentative look, like, are you ready?

Um, I was born ready. I was conceived ready. For the kiss, though, not for Mr. D's milky twilight. The kiss.

The Kiss.

Deep breath. I nod.

And . . . thunderclap. It catches me so off guard, I jump. "That's a loud one," says Mr. D.

But Zhao acts like she didn't even hear it. "Let's get started. Okay, Act Two, top of scene six. It's the middle of the night. Harry, you're there pacing. And Larken, we'll start you"—she pauses to write something—"downstage left. Good. So Kate, you're actually leaving the castle, running away to Normandy, but Harry hears you, and he turns around and says—Matt, go ahead and say your line here."

Matt puffs his chest up. "Friend or foe?"

"Friend," I say.

"Okay, great. And let's have you both stop in your tracks. Right there, yup. Center stage. And you'll stand there for a beat, looking at each other, and then Larken, you take a step toward him. You're drawn to him. And you'll say your line there, and then we have Harry's line, and we move into the song."

I glance up at Matt, and then back at Devon, who's got his head down, writing, and I don't even want to know what I look like right now. I feel like someone hollowed out my insides and replaced my bones with marshmallows. How am I supposed to survive blocking this song? Especially when this song is the only thing standing between me and the Kiss. The third kiss of my life. And since the first two were with Anderson, this is definitely my first kiss with potential. I'm standing right at the edge of my happy ending. I just know it.

Maybe this is the kiss Matt and I will tell our kids about in thirty years. We'll line them up on the couch, *How I Met Your Mother*–style, and describe every single moment in detail.

Blocking the song out feels like a dream. Like I'm sleep-walking. Face each other. Now clasp your hands together. Now take a step closer and draw your hands up between your chests. Then cheat out, so you're holding hands but facing the audience. And Matt, you step behind her again. Kate, you turn . . .

"Good," Ms. Zhao says firmly, and everything blinks back

into focus. "Okay, let's block this kiss. Everyone feeling good?"

"Great," Matt says, smiling. He looks straight into my eyes when he says it.

"Okay! So let's start from where you are. Kate, you're turned all the way into his embrace, and let's put your arms around his shoulders. Perfect. And Matt, let's have you put your hands on her face. Really swoony and romantic."

"Okay." Matt cups my cheeks. "You good?" he whispers.

I nod. "Good."

"Hmm. Actually, Matt, why don't you slide your hands a little farther back, just so we're not losing her face. Good. Yes! Perfect. Kate, tilt your head up just a little bit—"

I honestly can't believe this is happening. Like. Holy shit. HOLY SHIT. And I know it's onstage, and I know it's being choreographed by a teacher, but the feeling in my stomach, in that spot below my belly button? That's real.

Matt's lips are so close now. Inches away. I can feel his breath.

Ms. Zhao looks up from her notebook finally. "And . . . they kiss."

"And we kiss," Matt says softly. Suddenly his lips are on mine.

And okay. It's not a makeout—more like a slightly extended peck. But it's so achingly sweet, I could melt. I could seriously melt on the spot.

Matt Olsson just kissed me. He really did that. And now I'm standing here tingling from my head to my feet, and he takes a single step closer—

BOOM.

Thunderclap. I'm close enough to feel Matt's startled exhale. Then, a split second later, the lights cut out completely.

"Oh, that's not good," says Mr. D.

For a minute, we all freeze in place, like we can somehow coax the lights back if we stand still enough. But nope. Total pitch-darkness. There are no windows in the auditorium. And I've been backstage before in varying levels of darkness, but never like this. I reach out for Matt's hand, and when I find it, I squeeze it. He squeezes it back, and he doesn't let go.

"Okay," Zhao concedes. "This doesn't look good. Why don't we stop here for the day? Take it nice and slow coming off the stage, please. Do you guys have flashlight apps on your phones?" I nod, even though I know she can't see me.

Wow, though.

It's so easy to imagine how we'll retell this moment. Our first kiss. The lights went out. We held hands. Used our phones. Even as it's happening, it's like it already happened. That same preemptive nostalgia feeling. Like it's a story we'll tell in some not-so-distant future.

# SCENE 43

Matt drives me home in the rain, and he doesn't seem to mind the extra few minutes it takes to get to Dad's house. In a moment of unprecedented courage, I ask if he wants to come inside. But he tells me his mom's been calling him all afternoon, and he holds up his phone with the missed calls to prove it.

"Oh wow. Everything okay?"

"Yeah, I think she forgot I had rehearsal."

"Parents," I say, even though that is not a parental mistake I can relate to. I mean, my dad would definitely forget my rehearsal schedule—he wouldn't have known it to begin with—but he wouldn't be frantically calling all afternoon. Whereas my mom's all about the frantic phone calls, but she'd never misremember my rehearsal schedule. She actually photographs the call lists Ms. Zhao sends home and stores them in her phone to refer back to. She does the same thing for Ryan during baseball season. Total supermom move.

The storm's mostly ended by the time I settle in at Dad's,

though settle maybe isn't the word, seeing as I'm now a human jumble of wires. I change into sweatpants and flop back on my bed, staring at my canopy for a full ten minutes. I feel simultaneously normal and radically strange, like my brain's switching between two tracks. There's Normal Brain, which remembers I have algebra homework and wants to eat yogurt and watch *Tangled*. But then every few seconds, I-Kissed-Matt Brain takes over, and wow, I-Kissed-Matt Brain is not a chill brain. I-Kissed-Matt Brain wants to swoon and explode and replay every second of today's rehearsal, ad nauseum, ideally over the phone with Anderson, because apparently I-Kissed-Matt Brain is a total asshole.

I can't do that. I can't tell Anderson about today. Ground rules or no ground rules, that's just cruel. I don't even want to tell Raina and Brandie. God. It's going to be so messy if Matt and I start dating. Like, as a squad, how do you even navigate that? What do you prioritize? Celebrating with me over my first real boyfriend? Or consoling Anderson over his first real heartbreak? I mean, I'm sure Andy will joke around and yammer on about the ground rules and act like he's totally fine.

But he won't be. No one understands Anderson like I do. He's a lot more fragile than people realize. I'm not saying he's any less brave, or any less of a badass. It's just that he's got a soft center, and he's a little too good at hiding that.

So I can't tell Andy, and I can't tell the girls, but I also can't bear to be alone. This is crazy, but for a split second, I picture myself running through the rain to Noah's house.

Which is a very bad plan.

But somehow the thought gets me moving, and a minute later, I'm on the other end of the hall, knocking on my brother's door. No answer, of course. I let myself in anyway.

Ryan's on his bed, watching a movie with headphones, Camilla's head in his lap. Ryan's never really minded having the dogs in his bed, even on days like today, when they're matted and damp and smell extra doggy. It's his one exception to being a neat freak.

"What are you watching?" I ask.

"Um. *Black Mirror.*"

I gasp. "You like *Black Mirror*?" I sink back onto Ryan's bed, next to Camilla's butt. "Okay, which season?"

He tilts the screen toward me. "This one."

I shriek. "San Junipero!"

"Okay?"

"Ryan. Like. You know that's the official squad favorite, right? I can't believe you're watching this. It's so good."

"Noted."

"I won't spoil it. I'll be quiet." I peer at the screen, hands burrowing into Camilla's fur. "Oh, I love this part."

He flicks his eyes toward me.

"This episode is so romantic," I add.

Which makes it perfect for today. Because, no question: today has been the most romantic day of my life. September tenth. Forever tattooed on my brain and engraved on my heart.

A part of me wants to spill the whole story to Ryan—though I have no idea how he'd react. I guess he'd probably be confused, like, why are you telling me this? I love Ryan, but we're not the kind of siblings who have deep talks, or even how-was-your-day talks.

We used to be. I used to know all the stupid Ryan details, like how he knows every word of "Hey, Soul Sister." Or that he hates insects so much, he used to keep his Weedles and Meta-pods facedown in his Pokémon card binder. I used to know all of that. And Ryan knew all my details, too.

I wonder if that's a thing you can ever get back.

Ryan's texting now, but his texts don't pop up on his laptop like mine do. And Camilla's blocking my view of his phone screen. But maybe if I lean a little closer—

"Wow," Ryan says. "You are so nosy."

"Absolutely not. I'm politely and appropriately interested." I sit up straighter. "Are you texting a girl?"

He flips his phone facedown.

"So, yes."

"Are we done here?"

"Are you kicking me out?"

He scoffs. "I really should."

Camilla cranes her neck up to lick Ryan's chin, which, if you ask me, is just rude. No one asked her to take sides.

But a moment later, with no comment or preamble, Ryan takes his headphones off and unplugs them. Which makes the sound come through his laptop speakers.

And when I glance at him sidelong, he rolls his eyes—but he's smiling.

# SCENE 44

On Friday, Mom calls me an hour before my alarm's set to go off. Which is so unusual, I'm jolted instantly awake, my heart in my throat. "Everything okay? Mom?"

"Everything's fine, sweetie. Good morning!" She sounds chipper. Like. What the fuck, Mom?

"Why are you calling me at six?"

"Well." She pauses, and I hear coffee-grinding noises in the background. "I'd like us to have a family meeting."

"Um. What?"

We're not a family meeting kind of family. I don't even know the protocol for family meetings. Do they have to be scheduled? Apparently they do. Apparently they have to be scheduled at six in the morning on a Friday, out of nowhere.

"Maybe you and your brother could swing home this morning? Whenever you can."

Home. Mom always does that—refers to her house as home, and I never know how to feel about it.

"So . . . you want me to wake up Ryan?"

"No, he's up. I just called him. I just wanted to make sure we're all on the same page. You don't have an algebra test, right? I'm worried we'll be a little late getting you guys back to school."

"Mom." I blink up at my canopy. "What's going on?"

"Nothing bad, sweetie! I just need to talk to you guys about something. Okay, I'm going to let you go get dressed. Love you. See you in a bit!"

Fifteen minutes later, I'm in Ryan's passenger seat. "This is weird," I inform him, stretching the seat belt over my chest. Stellar outfit today: the sweatpants from last night, and the old ringer tee I mostly use for painting sets. "You don't think this is weird?"

"Oh, it's weird." Ryan yawns, checking the rearview.

"I'm so freaked out. I swear, I thought she was going to say she's in the hospital or something. Or that something happened to Charles or Camilla."

"The dogs are at Dad's house."

"I know, but it was like six in the morning. I wasn't think-ing straight. Anyway, what do you think this is about?"

Ryan shrugs.

"It has to be important, right? Like if it had to happen today, right now. That's kind of—and then she says we might be late for first period? She told you that, right?"

"Yeah."

"Do you think—" I cut myself off, cheeks burning, and thankfully, Ryan doesn't press it. It's such a stupid thought, anyway. Doesn't even make sense. If Mom wanted to have some new phase of The Talk, there's literally no reason for this level of urgency. Plus, Mom's always been pointedly casual about sex talks. She's more into the sneak attack, like hey how was school, honey, want to learn about birth control? So calling us at six in the morning on a school day isn't really her MO. But maybe Mom found out about the kiss at rehearsal and it got her thinking about sex and she totally lost her chill. I guess it could happen. Maybe? Except I'd kind of rather that talk didn't happen in front of Ryan.

We park in the driveway but walk in through the garage—and right away, there's Mom at the kitchen table, waiting for us. She looks mostly normal. Maybe a little rattled. I cut right to the chase. "What's going on?"

"Well." Mom gestures to the kitchen chairs. "Why don't you two sit down?"

"Mom! What?" Now my heart's banging all around my rib cage again. Sit down. Isn't that a thing you say when you're about to deliver bad news? I know I'm lucky, because I haven't gotten a lot of why-don't-you-sit-down news in my life. Maybe three times—when my zayde died, the day Mom and Dad announced the divorce, and the day after the 2016 election.

So yeah. This isn't good.

But Mom seems to sense what I'm thinking, because she touches my arm. "Katypie, everyone's fine. I just wanted to fill you both in on something that happened yesterday, and then run something by you." She smiles slightly. "Okay, so I know you both know my friend Ellen."

"Matt's mom."

"Oh, right—and you had your rehearsal yesterday! I heard you had a blackout."

"Ellen told you that?"

My stomach twists, just a little. Like. Uh. What else did Ellen tell her? How much does Matt tell Ellen?

"So, yesterday, the storm knocked down this big tree in Ellen and Matt's backyard, and it went right into Matthew's bedroom, unfortunately. He's okay," Mom adds quickly. "He was actually at rehearsal."

And suddenly, chillingly, I remember the half dozen phone calls Matt missed from his mom.

"Ellen's okay?" I ask, after a moment.

"Oh, yes. They're both absolutely fine. And luckily, there's a deck, which broke the tree's fall a little bit." She demonstrates, flattening her hand horizontally like the deck, and tilting her other arm down at the elbow like the tree. "Like this. Anyway. Could have been a lot worse, and they have renter's insurance. All good. But there's a fairly large hole in Matt's bedroom."

"That's so scary."

"I know. It's so lucky he was at rehearsal."

"Yeah." I exhale. "Yeah."

"Anyway." Mom clasps her hands on the table. "Last night, they stayed in a hotel room, but obviously that's not a long-term solution. So I hope it's okay, I've talked a little bit with Ellen about having them stay here with us. It would just be for a couple of weeks, while they get everything sorted—"

"You mean here?" My voice comes out almost choked. "Like our house?"

I'm sorry, but what? *What?*

"Yes, here." Mom looks vaguely amused. "I've called out of work so I can clear all the junk out of the guest room. So, we have a couple of options. I think we can fit an air mattress onto the floor of the guest room just fine. But Ryan, if you were open to it, maybe Matthew—"

"That's fine," Ryan says simply.

Mom nods. "So you're fine having Matthew in the extra bed."

"He could stay in my room," I suggest.

Mom laughs. "Absolutely not."

"On the air mattress!" I feel the heat rise in my cheeks. "I don't mean. Like. That. I'm just offering."

"Nice try. Not happening. And by the way, the six-inch rule is still six hundred percent in effect."

"That is heteronormative and sexist."

"Anyway," Mom says. "Ry, honey, are you sure?"

"Yeah, it's fine. Matt's cool."

Oh. Ohhhh. Hold up. It hadn't even occurred to me that Ryan and Matt might actually be friends. But why wouldn't they be? They're both seniors, both in AP classes, and the people in Matt's pictures from Alabama definitely look like people

222

Ryan would hang out with. It's not like he's never been to an f-boy party.

I've just never really pictured Matt's world outside of Andy and me. But wow. For all I know, he himself could be an f-boy.

Except, no. Absolutely not. He can't be. F-boys aren't sweet and silly, and they definitely don't do theater. I mean, Noah Kaplan is and does, sort of, but he's always been somewhat of an anomaly among f-boys. Whereas Matt's not an f-boy whatsoever. Would an f-boy hold his diaphragm while singing scales and doing warm-ups? Would an f-boy even give Andy and me the time of day? I don't think so.

"You guys are awesome," says my mom. "The best. Seriously. I'll tell Ellen to check out of the hotel." Her phone's already pressed to her ear, ringing. "Sound good?"

Ryan nods.

But I just quietly combust.

# SCENE 45

"Shut. Up," Anderson says, as soon as he sees me in history.

"I literally said zero words—"

"Matt just told me! Oh my God, Katy. Like, a tree? A fucking tree?"

"Who's fucking trees?" asks Raina, sliding into her usual desk behind Anderson.

"Well," Andy says, putting a hand on his hip. "According to my sources, a tree—an actual tree—fell onto Matt Olsson's house while he was at rehearsal yesterday, so now apparently, he's moving into Kate's bedroom—"

"What? That is absolutely—"

"Damn," says Raina. "Kate. Get yours."

"Okay, first of all, he's staying in Ryan's room—"

"Still!" Anderson slips into his seat but turns right back to face me. "Kate Eliza, you are the luckiest girl on earth, I swear. Between this and the Larken and Harry stuff."

The bell rings before I can reply, bringing the usual flurry of movement—people claiming seats, dropping backpacks, hugging, talking, ignoring Mr. Edelman. Noah walks in wearing a T-shirt featuring—I'm not kidding—the word "Daddy" and a picture of Daniel Tiger's father.

I look up at him. "Really?"

"Just raising awareness."

"Unbelievable."

Anderson nudges my sneaker with his loafer. "Hey," he says, eyeing me meaningfully. "I have to pee."

Our signal. I nod almost imperceptibly, my eyes fixed straight ahead.

Ten minutes later, we're practically skidding down the hallway, each with our own crumpled up hall pass from Mr. Edelman. It's amazing—we didn't even have to stagger our exits. But of course, Edelman's one of those teachers who's always visibly relieved to have fewer students in the classroom. We reach the BTF and assume our usual stall positions immediately.

"So. Kind of crazy, right? Matt's moving into Hotel Garfield."

"Uh, yeah, but more importantly," says Andy. "What's going on with you and Noah?"

For a moment, I'm speechless. "Me and Noah? Noah Kaplan?"

"You're gonna act like there wasn't a major vibe just now? Please."

"Um." I snap a quick, befuddled-looking selfie and text it to Anderson. "Andy, are you high?"

"I'm just saying. You had the look. The mouth."

Anderson swears I do this thing with my mouth, some kind of twitch at the corners. He says it's my tell when I like someone. I happen to think it's bullshit.

"Andy, he's a fuckboy. What are you talking about?"

"He's a misunderstood fuckboy. Barely a fuckboy. He's not exactly Jack Randall."

"Jack Randall literally drew boobs on Noah's cast."

"Eww," Anderson says. "Well, definitely don't start dating him until he gets his cast off."

"Oh, the boobs are gone. He has a replacement cast."

"Well, in that case—"

"Also, what the fuck? I'm not dating Noah Kaplan!"

"Mm-hmm. If you say so."

I can barely form words, I'm so shell-shocked. I just scrunch my legs up onto the side of the toilet and shake my head slowly. Anderson's finally lost it. He has to be kidding, right? Noah? Sorry, but that's clearly wishful thinking. On Anderson's part, not mine. NOT mine. Because if I'm occupied with Noah Kaplan, Andy gets Matt all to himself. How convenient.

"Is this just you being weird because Matt's moving into my house?"

"Pssh. No." There's this tiny rustle from his stall that makes me think he's taking a selfie. Sure enough, within moments, I get a photo of Anderson rolling his eyes. "You know this means you'll be sharing a bathroom with Matt, right?"

"So?"

"So? Kate, excuse me, are you forgetting about *Bring It On*? Kirsten Dunst and Jesse Bradford? The toothbrush scene?"

"Oh my God." My stomach flutters. "Oh my God."

"This is your life now, Kate. Sexually charged dental hygiene. Every single night."

"But just Mom's house nights—"

"You have to, like, check the medicine cabinet or something. It's not creepy if it's your own bathroom. Do you think he'll bring condoms?"

"Why?"

"To have sex," Andy says.

"In Ryan's room?"

"I'm just saying, there are no secrets now. We are about to solve the mystery of Matthew Thomas Olsson." Anderson pauses. "What if you walk in on him showering?"

"What if he walks in on me showering?" My stomach drops. "Or pooping!"

"You can't poop while he's there," Anderson says, matter-of-factly. "You poop at your dad's house now."

"But what if—"

"Or my house. Katypie, I am dead serious. If you have to poop, you walk your stiff little butt out that door and over to my house. I've got you."

"You're an amazing friend. Like. Next-level amazing. You know that?"

"Make it up to me by inviting me over tonight," Andy says.

I grin. "Consider yourself invited."

# SCENE 46

Matt and Ellen combined have just four suitcases of stuff, which is less than the volume of clutter and storage boxes Mom just moved from the guest room.

"Maggie, I can't thank you enough," Ellen says. "And you kids. Honestly—"

"Hush. We're family."

"Are you three still heading out?" Ellen asks. "I'm just so glad Matthew's finally making real friends here. I thought he was going to spend the whole summer just playing that animal island game. I swear, every day, he'd come home from camp and—"

"Mom. Not every day."

"Just the second half of the summer." Ellen winks. "After Jessi left."

"Ooh, who's Jessi?" Mom asks.

"Matthew's ex-girlfriend. Sweet girl, absolutely beautiful. Of course, she doesn't hold a candle to Kate."

"Okay! I think we're heading to dinner," Matt says loudly.

"Have fun! Drive safe," Mom says. "Love you guys. Mwah."

Matt cringes all the way to his car. When we get there, I surrender the passenger seat to Anderson without hesitation. It's not that Anderson's super tall, but I'm easily six inches shorter than he is.

I smile out the open back seat window, replaying the whole conversation in my head. I feel strangely giddy about it. So many fascinating updates. Like the fact that Matt's clearly single. I mean, this Jessi girl is apparently out of the picture, and I doubt Matt replaced her by playing Animal Crossing nonstop like a dork. Like an adorably breathtakingly beautiful dork.

I bet you anything Jessi's the girl in the formal dance photo. Though if Ellen thinks I'm prettier than that girl, she needs to get her eyes checked. If this were a teen movie, Jessi would be the supermodel love interest, and I'd be one of the extras sitting in math class.

"She thinks she's so funny." Matt rolls his eyes. "I didn't play Animal Crossing all summer."

"Mm-hmm." Andy grins at him.

"Don't be jealous I'm a bellionaire." Matt starts backing out of our driveway. "I can't believe I actually know you guys now. You were so funny at camp. I remember you always had ice cream after breakfast."

I nod. "Breakfast dessert."

"You always got mint Oreo," he says to Andy. "I remember that."

"Gay people have to love Oreos now," explains Anderson.

"Yeah, but mint." I rest my hand on the back of Anderson's seat. "That's like eating chocolate with toothpaste."

"Kate, we've been through this. I like toothpaste."

That's true. He used to beg his mom to let him eat it by the spoonful. Even now, he brushes his teeth twenty billion times a day. That's actually the main thing I remember about kissing Anderson: his minty freshness.

Matt smiles at me in the rearview. "And you always turned your cone upside down in a bowl."

I smile back. "I can't believe you noticed that."

It's too early for sunset, but I swear there's a sunset feeling. We're taking Matt to Alessio's pizza, a squad institution. Anderson sets his R&B/hip-hop playlist on shuffle, and thirty seconds later, he's off and running on the topic of Lizzo's genius vocal inflections in "Truth Hurts." I let my mind drift, remembering yesterday's rehearsal and Jessi the ex-girlfriend and the way Anderson actually didn't get into hip-hop until last year. He said he always felt this weird pressure to love it, which made him avoid it, but then he finally gave it a shot and fell hard. I'll never forget the day Anderson played me *Scum Fuck Flower Boy* from start to finish. He kept glancing sideways at me, beaming, and then monologued for a full ten minutes about how Tyler, The Creator is the most underrated storyteller in history.

The song flips to "Old Town Road," and now Matt and Andy are singing along so loudly, they're practically yowling.

It makes me wish you could film a whole entire moment.

Not just the visuals and vocals. I want to hold every piece of this. I want to save the details for later: the breeze ruffling my hair through the open car windows, the soft warmth of my flannel. The feeling of being sixteen on a Friday night in September. The pull of the seat belt over my greased lightning heart.

It's early enough that we land a table right away, and we proceed to order both pizza and fries. I cup my chin into my hand, gazing at our spread. "I read somewhere once that the longest fry is called—"

"The loomster!" Matt smacks his palms on the table.

"Yes, the loomster!"

"Sounds fake," Andy says.

"I know. But they're not fake. Andy, this is like a core piece of life trivia."

"I think I found it." Matt holds up a fry of extraordinary length. "The loomster."

"But what's the point?" asks Andy. "Do you get to make a wish? What do you do with the loomster?"

"We just appreciate its length," says Matt. "And eat it."

The tiniest dimple impresses into Andy's left cheek, and I'm one hundred percent sure he's thinking of a dick joke. But he'd never say it out loud in front of Matt. It's weird how much you have to hold back when you're secretly in love with someone. But then again, the whole point of love is getting close enough that you no longer have to hold back all the dick jokes. Or farts, or all the other gross parts. I'm pretty sure at some point love makes room for the gross parts.

It's finally getting dark out by the time we finish and pay, which means normal teens are just winding up for the night. Mira Reynolds is no doubt practicing her duck face in her selfie cam. And I'm sure Jack Randall's hard at work making sure he's wearing his hat stupidly enough. But we have to wake up early for set design tomorrow—and anyway, none of us are particularly in the mood to be called Fiona by drunk f-boys. So the three of us just head straight home with vague plans to watch *Tangled*, which Matt's never seen.

"Have you been living under a rock?" Andy asks, as we buckle our seat belts. "*Tangled* is one of the top three movies of all time."

"What are the other two?"

"*Anastasia and Clueless*," Andy and I say in unison.

"With an honorable mention for *Pride and Prejudice*," I add. "BBC version."

"It's technically a miniseries, so we couldn't count it," Anderson says. "And obviously *Ella Enchanted* would be right in there, but Kate's got some baggage—"

"Okay!" I say quickly.

Matt smiles at me in the rearview. "I've actually seen *Clueless*. It was—"

"A classic?" Andy says.

Matt pauses. "I'm just going to say yes."

"Right answer."

Twenty minutes later, I'm settled between my two favorite boys in a giant nest of pillows. Anderson traces the lines of my palm like he does sometimes during movies, and my brain doesn't know what to make of that. Just that tiny electric physical contact, and the fact that it's happening in such close proximity to Matt. It almost feels like Matt and I are touching, even though we're not. I'm so hyperaware of him—every time the movie makes him laugh, every time his arm shifts, every time he's concentrating. When the part with the lanterns comes on, Matt just sits there, grinning into his fist. Which makes me grin, too. Because Matt's just like Rapunzel, the way he's leaning forward, fully absorbed.

Those paper lanterns. And the boat. And the song.

It's my favorite part of the movie, the part I most know by heart. It's almost unbearably romantic—and I don't even mean the hand-holding part or the almost-kiss or the massive amounts of mutual eyegasming. It's before that. It's the part when Rapunzel catches that first glimpse of a lantern, and that's it. She's totally lost. She almost knocks the boat over, scrambling to get a better viewpoint. And for the entire first verse of the song, the screen doesn't even cut to Flynn Rider, because she's completely forgotten about him. It's just Rapunzel and the lanterns. She's standing there, clutching the prow of the boat, and at one point, she does this exhale. Like the world's so beautiful, she can't take it.

And then she suddenly remembers Flynn, who's been quietly watching her the whole time. Holding back, not intruding. He's just there for her when she's ready. Anderson thinks it's hilarious that my number one romantic fantasy involves me forgetting the boy exists, but to me, it just shows how safe Rapunzel feels with Flynn. Her brain doesn't even have to remember he's there, because some bone-deep part of her knows it. And there's that beautifully obvious contradiction. The way being wrapped up in someone can make you more free. The wide-open safety of home.

# SCENE 47

Saturday feels like a dream before it even starts. There's birthday dinner for Ryan tonight, but before that is set building, so I throw on my ringer tee and sweats and fight to achieve that perfect messy set-painting ponytail. By the time I make it down to the kitchen, Matt's already there, eating cereal, wearing—oh my goodness—a Camp Wolf Lake T-shirt. The first shirt I ever saw him in.

"Good morning," he says. And I just stand there, frozen to the spot, my mind reeling through the greatest hits of our hypothetical future together. Our first apartment. Drinking coffee side by side on the couch, reading the news on our phones. Matt looking sleepy and scruffy in our bed with his laptop, writing an essay. He'll be getting his PhD in something romantic and nonlucrative like ancient Greek literature, but it's fine, because by then I'll be a successful actress. Not like a starlet or celebrity—just a serious working actress. And every night, I'll play guitar by the fireplace. Basically, our lives will look just like the Crosby, Stills, Nash, and Young song, "Our House," which every single member of my family loves, even Ryan.

"Anderson's awake." Matt holds up his phone. "He's walking over here now. Are we supposed to bring anything?"

"I don't think so. Just paint clothes. I love your shirt."

"Aww, thank you." He smiles.

Matt drives, which means we get to park in the senior lot, which is mostly just a status symbol—and I don't usually buy into status symbols, but the lemon-sour look on Lana Bennett's face makes it all worth it. Anyway, there's something so sweet about walking into set painting day with Matt and Anderson, knowing I'll be leaving with them, too.

It's early—just a little past eight in the morning—but lots of the tech people are already here. There are newspapers and giant half-painted sheets of foam spread out over the entire floor of the auditorium lobby. "Should we just . . ." I glance back at Matt and Andy before squatting down across from these sophomores named Suman and Bess. Now that I'm closer, I can see the foam is lined with masking tape in a brick pattern.

"Just paint them gray for now," says Bess, handing me a paintbrush. "We're going to add shading later."

Andy and Matt settle right in beside me, and we fall into a comfortable rhythm. Painting sets is so soothing—I love the hum of the air conditioner and the even back and forth of my brush strokes. Someone's playing music in the auditorium nearby, and every so often, it leaks faintly through the auditorium doors. Andy's cross-legged, leaning carefully forward, his bright white T-shirt completely paint-free. But Matt's bangs keep falling into his eyes, so he keeps pushing them back, and now his hair's adorably streaked with castle-stone gray.

"Hey. You missed a spot." Andy nudges Matt sideways. "That's supposed to be my house. Don't fuck it up."

Matt swipes sideways with his paintbrush, leaving a gray streak on the back of Andy's hand. "Oops." His eyes are still fixed on the foam board, but he's grinning. "Missed a spot." He plants another streak on Andy's wrist. "Missed another spot."

Anderson gasps. "Matthew Olsson, don't you dare."

I don't know quite what to make of it. On the one hand, this is starting to feel a little like a rom-com moment, the kind that begins with flirtatious paint slinging and ends with Andy and Matt making out in front of the dramaturgy display. But on the other hand, I can't imagine having a boyfriend who doesn't get along this well with Anderson. It would be like having a boyfriend who doesn't like my face.

Suddenly, the auditorium doors burst open, revealing Noah. I'm surprised he's here. First of all, it's not even nine in the morning. Plus, Saturday set building is optional, and Noah seems like a bare-minimum kind of guy. He stands in the doorway for a moment, watching us paint, and I swear, Anderson Walker's about to get murdered. Because I don't know how Andy managed to get in my head about this, but Noah definitely looks . . . passable. I don't even get it. He's wearing gym shorts and an RHHS baseball T-shirt, his dark hair winging out messily in all directions, but he looks so soft-lipped and sleepy, I feel almost personally attacked. He shuffles over, plop-ping down beside me without hesitation. "Zhao won't let me use the drill," he complains.

"Because you're wearing a cast? Or because you're you?"

"Mmm. Both."

Anderson coughs loudly, pursing his lips out in kiss for-mation, and I shoot him a lightly homicidal glare. I don't even know what the worst offense is here—the fact that he actually thinks Noah could distract me from Matt, or the fact that he's broadcasting it all over his face.

"You should paint," I say quickly, shoving a brush at Noah. "It's really relaxing. See? I'm relaxed." I glob some gray onto the foam backdrop, whirling my brush around frantically.

Noah settles in. "So this is my castle, huh?"

"My castle," says Andy.

"Not till I die," Noah says happily. "I'm your father."

"I am your father," echoes Matt, in a Darth Vader voice.

Andy looks at Matt and laughs. "You're cute."

My heart leaps into my throat. Okay. That was more bla-tantly flirtatious than I expected. And a part of me's like, wow, Andy, step up that game. Get yours.

But yeah. A part of me wants to stab him with a paintbrush.

Anyway, Matt's blushing, but I can't tell if it's a swoony blush or an awkwardly-flattered-straight-guy blush. Either way, it looks good on him. And obviously Anderson thinks so too, because now he's dead silent, grinning down at his hands.

I feel this twinge of—something. Maybe restlessness. It's

hard to pinpoint. But I have this sudden urge to put the world on fast-forward. "We need music," I say, and Noah's lips fall open like he's about to start singing. I clamp a hand over his mouth. "No."

So Matt starts singing instead—the first verse of "In a Little While." But he's singing it as Matt, without Sir Harry's round knightly vowels. It's soft and light and actually really lovely. I take my hand off Noah's mouth and point to Matt. "Yes." Then I pat Noah on the shoulder, and Anderson bursts out laughing.

Matt only sings four lines—just the first verse—but it makes the whole room go still. It's just something about his earnestness, or the casual sweetness of his voice. He finishes, and there's this pause that feels practically electric. But then Noah nudges me with his elbow, breaking the spell. "Kate. That's you."

"What?"

"That's your cue!"

I shake my head.

"I'll sing it," he offers.

"NO." I look up to find Matt, Anderson, Suman, Bess, and Noah all watching me with a range of vaguely amused facial expressions. Then Anderson tilts his head and goes full puppy dog face. I roll my eyes. "Stopppp it."

Andy starts humming my part of the song.

"Okay, fine."

I start singing. And I feel weirdly self-conscious about it, even though no one outside our little circle is even paying attention.

And it's not like my singing voice is big news to any of the boys. Matt practically got a whole private concert at Thursday's rehearsal.

But it's one thing to sing for a musical, at rehearsals or auditions or even onstage in front of an audience. Singing without structure is another thing entirely. It's like my heart keeps trying to slide out of my sleeve, and I keep shoving it under the cuff. In a play, everything's planned out and controlled, even the dramatic parts. But nothing in real life is like that. Real life is chaos. You always end up lurching the wrong way, yelling the wrong thing, and drowning in all the wrong emotions.

And, of course, sometimes you end up on Mira Reynolds's Instagram.

I shake the thought away and keep singing. And my voice is startlingly crystal clear.

"Pretty," says Anderson, as soon as I finish, and I flash him a smile. But then, without hesitation, Matt picks it up with Sir Harry's next verse, and after that, we're singing straight through the harmonies without any accompaniment. Andy leans toward Suman to brag. "Perfect pitch. Isn't she amazing?"

I'm not actually amazing, and I don't have perfect pitch, but there's something magical about the way my voice blends with Matt's. A few more people wander over, like there's some invisible string yanking them toward us. I catch Noah watching me with a face that looks so much like Flynn Rider, I full-on blush and turn away.

When the song ends, Matt shoots me this tiny wink, and I pretty much melt all over the auditorium lobby floor.

"Hey." Noah hugs me sideways. "That was really good."

I bite back a smile. "Thanks, Noah."

I swear, I can feel Anderson beaming mental cupid arrows down on me, which is insanely annoying. Like, I get it. The communal crush isn't fun anymore. But that doesn't mean I'm about to force some Noah thing to materialize.

Anyway, it all turns to mush when I look at Matt. I shoot him a tiny smile, like *hey, not bad*, which makes his eyes crinkle at the corners. And suddenly the world feels ten steps away. Like we made a force field somehow, with our beaming, locked eyes.

Anderson gets weird after that. It's not that he seems angry, or even grumpy. He's just quiet, and it lasts the whole afternoon. We leave around four, and Andy asks Matt to just drop him off at home. So I spend half the ride in silence, feeling strange and unsettled but not wanting to probe in front of Matt. Finally, I just text him. **Are you coming to Ryan's birthday?**

A moment later: **Ehh . . . I need a break. You'll be fine.**

**Wait really?? You're not coming?** 😞

Anderson's always there on Ryan's birthday, at least for birthday dinner. Otherwise, it's just my family—Ryan, Mom, Dad, and me—which is the most awkward combination of people in existence. But when Andy's there, at least there's a buffer. And he's just so good at managing that kind of situation. He knows how to derail all the weird, tense parts and keep a conversation funny and airy.

241

You've got Matt. And then, a moment later: He lives at your house now, remember?

Idk what M&E are even up to tonight!

"Hey, are you guys doing Ryan's birthday dinner tonight?" Andy asks out loud.

Matt glances up at the rearview. "Oh, yeah—I think my mom mentioned it. Taco Mac, right?"

"You should go," Andy says matter-of-factly. "Taco Mac's really good."

There, you're welcome, he texts a moment later, and it's so frosty and curt, I get a pit in my stomach. I've seen this sharp-edged, walls-up version of Anderson before, but that's for other people. Andy's never put up the fortress against me.

I hate that I'm sitting directly behind him. If I could just see his face, even in profile, maybe I could figure out what he's thinking.

But I can't. So I just stare at my phone.

Nothing.

Nothing. Okay, ELLIPSES! Wait for it, wait for it . . .

More nothing.

Oof.

# SCENE 48

Dad's meeting us at Taco Mac, but Mom insists on driving the rest of us in Ryan's Altima. It's a real kids-in-the-back ride, with Ellen in the passenger seat. Ryan spends the whole time texting, probably coordinating logistics for whatever party he's going to tonight. And sure enough, just as we pull into the parking lot, Ryan asks, "Oh hey, is it cool if I hang out with some people tonight?"

The classic request. First we have *oh hey*, spoken with carefully calibrated nonchalance. Then we have *hang out*, which is obviously code for get drunk, and *some people*, aka f-boys. Ryan's timing is smart, because even though Mom's obviously going to say yes either way, she's distracted enough that she won't remember to ask awkward questions. Mom gets a little scatterbrained when we're about to have dinner with Dad. Like, she drops things and forgets things and sometimes turns left when the GPS says right. Once I heard her say on the phone, "Every time I see Neil, I'm all the bad parts of being twenty-one again."

Anyway, Taco Mac is one of those sports bar places with TVs hanging down in all directions and a multitiered chicken wing classification system. No surprise that it's my brother's favorite restaurant of all time. It's always slammed on Saturdays, though, so Mom and Ellen head inside to get on the wait list for a table. We're about twenty minutes early to meet Dad, which is most certainly an Awkward Time Pocket—an ATP, as Ryan used to call them. Too long to stand around waiting, but too short to go anywhere. So, Ryan, Matt, and I end up walking across the shopping center parking lot, toward Walgreens. And of course, my troll self can't resist asking Ryan if he's going to buy condoms.

Ryan's eyes widen. "What?"

He's blushing, which makes me blush, because I'm a terrible troll, and that makes Matt blush, and THIS IS WHY WE NEED ANDERSON. "Because you're eighteen," I say quickly. "That's a thing."

"You don't have to be eighteen to buy condoms," Ryan says.

"You don't?" By now I'm blushing so hard, my cheeks are the ones that should have their own multitiered classification system: mild, medium, hot, habanero, death. I don't dare look at Matt. He's probably pity-wincing hard, because I pretty much admitted that I've never even tried to buy condoms. Yup. Here I am. Wide-eyed virgin with all the sophistication of Rapunzel. *I die a little. I die a little. I die a little.*

But Matt just says, "You could buy cigarettes."

Ryan shakes his head. "That's twenty-one now."

"Which doesn't matter," I add, "because he doesn't smoke. Right?" Ryan shakes his head, but I stare him down anyway. "Don't you dare start in college, either. I'm serious, I will drive to your dorm and smell your clothes every single day, and you better believe I'll tell Mom."

Ryan nods. "I believe you."

"Good," I say firmly.

"Do you know where you're headed?" Matt asks.

Ryan pauses. "Not sure yet. What about you?"

"Definitely somewhere in-state," Matt says. "Or maybe somewhere back in Alabama."

"Well, I personally think Ryan should pick Kennesaw," I say, "because A, it's the closest, and B, they have not one, but two Pokémon leagues."

"And you know this . . . how?"

"It's this totally obscure site called Google," I say. "You should check it out sometime."

"Noted." Ryan smiles, but his eyes seem to snag on some point in the distance. Then he looks back at me suddenly. "Hey, do you guys want to come out tonight?"

I stare at him, gobsmacked. "To your party?"

"It's not my party. It's just people hanging out at Michelle's house. You can bring your squad if you want."

"Michelle McConnell?" I raise my eyebrows. She's an f-girl from the soccer team, Ryan's grade. I've never actually inter-acted with her, but she's lowkey famous for snorting Ritalin in French class and getting away with it, even after getting caught in the act. Andy says her parents made a massive PTA donation, and therefore, Michelle McConnell is the reason the math department has new SMART Boards. Anyway, Ryan hanging out with Michelle is weird, but not that weird, because they're both athletes. But Ryan inviting me to join him is absolutely unprecedented. He's usually great at keeping his cool friends and his dorky family very firmly separate. I mean the only f-boy who ever really comes over anymore is Noah, which barely even counts—he's our neighbor. But suddenly I'm on the guest list?

I mean, I'm obviously not going. Not in a million bazillion years. Michelle McConnell's house? That's practically Fuckforce Headquarters.

But here's the weirdest thing of all: I kind of like that Ryan asked.

# SCENE 49

By the time we head back to Taco Mac, Mom, Dad, and Ellen are just kind of hovering around the hostess stand. Dad hugs us and gives Ryan a card that no doubt contains money, and then he shakes Matt's hand and says, "You don't look like Anderson, so I'm guessing you're Matthew."

"Anderson's not coming," I inform Dad. "He flaked out."

"Oh, that's too bad! I had a great bank robber story to tell him." Once in ninth grade, Anderson dutifully nodded along while Dad yammered about criminals who screwed up and got caught, so now Dad thinks Anderson's really into incompetent criminals. He's not.

"I'll fill him in," I say.

We end up at a table, not a booth, which is a good thing in this case. But I'm smack-dab between my parents, who have Ryan in their crosshairs. "So baseball's keeping you busy, huh?"

"Neil, it's the off-season."

Dad laughs. "Then, Ry, I'd like to know where you're running off to every afternoon."

"To the gym."

"It's part of their training," Mom chimes in. "Ryan and his teammates are doing a sixteen-week program. From what I've seen, it's very challenging."

"Matt, do you train as well?" Dad asks.

"Do play rehearsals count?"

"Ah, you're a thespian," Dad says. "So you and Kate probably spend a lot of time together."

Matt nods.

"Now tell me, how do you balance that? Theater and baseball. I bet that gets busy."

Mom and Ellen exchange totally unsubtle weary glances.

"Dad, Matt doesn't do baseball. He just said that."

"Well, he said he wasn't training—"

"You have to train. If you do baseball, you have to train," I say, like I know anything about sports. But Ryan just smiles wryly and nods. I smile back at him, looking quickly away. It's funny. I always forget how extra close I feel with my brother at family dinners. Like our parents are an event we have to cringe through together.

Luckily, Dad saves the biggest cringe for after dinner, sidling up as we head out to the parking lot. He waits until everyone's a few yards ahead before lowering his voice. "Now, are you and Matt an item?"

I freeze in my tracks. "Dad."

"Just asking." He tips his palms up. "Since you brought him to family dinner—"

"Okay, first of all, not a date. Second of all, definitely not a date. Third of all, his mom is literally right there." I shake my head. "Dad, they're staying with us. I told you that."

"You did? Oh, that's right, the tree."

"Yes."

"So you're not officially dating? He seems like a good kid."

"We're not officially dating or unofficially dating or any kind of—"

"Kate! You coming?" Matt calls. He's standing next to Mom's car, waving me down.

I don't even realize I'm smiling until Dad raises his eyebrows. "Not dating," I repeat firmly.

But then again, the way I feel sliding into the back seat next to Matt, maybe my heart never got the memo.

# SCENE 50

Mom and Ellen head out to a movie around eight, and then a Jeep full of f-boys swings by to pick Ryan up at nine. It's not that I'm trying to keep tabs on the household or anything. I'm just messing around with my guitar, and I happen to be on my bed, facing the window, and the blinds happen to be open.

And it just so happens I'm alone in the house now with Matt.

Except fifteen minutes later, Matt leaves, too, without even trying to talk me into coming. Maybe I shouldn't have shot Ryan down so forcefully about that party. I mean, Matt's taking his own car, so he's clearly planning to stay sober. We could have been the token sober people together. I can just picture it. Matt and I, tucked onto a couch somewhere, drinking plain orange juice and taking bets on which f-boy will be the first to puke. Just a couple of wry outsiders.

Unless Matt's not actually an outsider.

Who knows? Maybe he and Michelle McConnell are actually friends. Maybe they're "friends" in the way Noah and that girl Madison are "friends." I'm sure Noah will hook up again at this party, too. And maybe Matt and Noah will do that dudebro fist-bump-hug thing when they see each other. Maybe Noah will change into a crisp, preppy button-down like Matt did, and neither of them will mention the fact that they spent their whole day painting sets for the school musical.

It just bugs me. So much that I whip my phone out to whine about it to Anderson. I even type out a text, **OMG guess where our boy is going right this second**, except—

Something stops me from hitting send.

Maybe it's the fact that Anderson's been so weird about Matt staying here. It's hard to know where his head is with it. Literally, one day he's making gleeful declarations about sexy toothbrush encounters, and the next day, he's sending passive-aggressive texts. **He lives at your house now, remember?**

I shove my phone under my pillow. I know I'm being cowardly and avoidant. But thinking about Anderson hits me in this weird, guilty place, and I need a break from that now. I just want to play guitar and sing, and I have the house to myself, so why not. I start with "On My Own" from *Les Mis*, because it's the ultimate pining crush song. But it ends up reminding me too much of Anderson—go figure—so I switch to a slow, acoustic version of Abba's "Super Trouper." And then "Our House," which I privately dedicate to Ryan in honor of his birthday, even though he's generally unimpressed these days by anything involving me and guitars. It's actually one of the first songs I taught myself, back in eighth grade.

But now I just feel odd, almost disconnected. I finally give up halfway through, my left hand still pressing the frets for an F chord.

I can't stop thinking about Anderson.

It's like one of those flashback montages from a movie, the way my mind cycles back through every little moment from set painting. How wistful Andy looked when Matt and I were singing, even though he's the one who practically begged me to sing in the first place. The way he bragged about me to the set crew girls anyway. And how Matt and I had that eye-lock moment. Anderson sort of folded into himself after that. I've never seen him look so heartbroken and depleted.

And I'm the one doing that. I'm breaking his heart.

I mean, I'm following the ground rules. I am. And if it turns out that Matt likes me, I'm sure Andy will follow them, too. He'll be happy for me. At least he'll act like he is. But then what? What happens when it starts to hurt too badly? He'll stop texting me? Or he'll text me, but it'll be formal and obligatory. He'll stop spending the night and inviting me over. We'll lose our language. Our inside jokes will just vanish.

And what about me? The ground rules say I have to be honest. But I know I won't be. It's not that I'll want to lie. But I'd never gush to Anderson about what kissing Matt feels like. I couldn't. Not when I know how deeply that would cut. But the thing is, the minute we start holding stuff back, we're done for. The Andy-and-Kate who share everything are done for.

It can't happen. I can't let it happen. But how on earth do I stop it?

I could step away. Dial back the chemistry. Snuff out my feelings, or at least try to contain them. But say Matt asked me out tomorrow. Could I say no? I don't think I have that kind of willpower. I don't think anyone does.

If I could stop this crush, I would. I'd slam that brake so hard, with the full force of my brain. It's just that I know it won't work. I don't think my brain's in the driver's seat.

# SCENE 51

Wednesday's the second Harry/Larken intensive rehearsal, and I think Ms. Zhao might be trolling me. "Okeydokey," she says, after we run through both songs a few times. "Let's get this kiss fine-tuned. It's still looking a little bit stagey. And do let me know if this feels too weird for you. If you'd like, we can rework the blocking so there's no actual kiss."

"You don't have to—" Matt starts to say, but then he cuts himself off. "I mean, whatever Kate thinks."

"It's fine," I say quickly. My heart's beating so loudly, I swear the whole room probably hears it.

"Fine like let's keep the kiss, or fine like let's rework it?" Ms. Zhao asks.

"We can keep it. Unless Matt—"

"Let's keep it," Matt says, wrapping his arm around my shoulders.

So I spend the next twenty minutes kissing Matt. Which is

easily my new favorite pastime. That is, as long as I don't think about Anderson.

I'm not a monster, right? I'm an actress. I'm just doing what the script says. This is me being professional. Blissfully, euphorically professional.

Anyway, it's not continuous kissing. It's all very dry and quick and stylized, with Ms. Zhao pausing periodically to have us move our hands or tilt our heads differently. "Try not to hunch your shoulders up, Kate. We want this to look really natural, like you've been meeting in secret for a while now. Yes! There you go. Much better. Hands just a touch lower on her waist, Matt. Good, hold that pose for a second—let me just make a few notes."

"Okay, question," Matt whispers. "How are you getting home after this?"

"Oh! I guess—"

"Because Andy was going to help me find those Oxford character shoes. But we can drop you home first, or leave from here, or—"

"Wait, Andy's still at school?"

Matt looks like he's biting back a laugh.

I narrow my eyes at him, smiling. "What am I missing?"

"Ooh, I love that glance you guys just did," Ms. Zhao says. "That felt very real."

"Well," Matt says, "don't look now, but I think there's someone in the lighting booth."

I whip my head toward the back of the auditorium, and sure enough, there's Andy, waving through the glass partition. He smiles widely, and shoots us a double thumbs-up.

"Oops!" says Zhao. "Stick with me, you two. Okay, Kate, you're facing him. Let's get that head tilt again."

I turn back to Matt, flabbergasted. "How long has he been here?"

He grins. "Literally this whole time."

All the air rushes out of my lungs. "What?"

"And . . . great," Ms. Zhao says, clapping her hands a few times. "You guys are great. The chemistry is A-plus. Just keep doing what you're doing."

But her words barely land. I hardly even feel Matt's high five. My eyes home straight in on Andy, who's now making his way through the auditorium aisles, toward the stage. I don't think he's upset. I mean, the house lights are pretty dim, so maybe I'm missing some facial nuance. But he really just seems normal. Even after all those head tilts and glances and Matt's hands on my waist. All that kissing.

It just doesn't compute. Andy wasn't even on the call list. Why on earth is he here? And why on earth didn't he tell me?

Matt and I step down from the stage, joining Anderson in front of the orchestra pit. He hugs me as soon as he sees me.

"You watched our rehearsal?" I blurt.

"Well I was trying to work on my chem homework. But y'all were more interesting."

"I mean." Matt's eyes twinkle. "If you're looking for chemistry, I'm pretty sure Kate and I delivered."

"Right. A-plus chemistry. Teacher-approved," Andy says, with this goofy little eye roll.

And okay, that just bugs me. Like, Matt and I can't even have one fairy-tale moment without Andy jumping in to trivialize it.

But even as I think that, I know it's desperately unfair. If I'd had to watch Andy and Matt kiss for twenty minutes, I'd definitely be scrambling to rewrite that scene in my head.

So, that's me: Lady Kate, Queen of Hypocrites. Shittiest friend in all the land.

# SCENE 52

Ms. Zhao dismisses us early—funny how it's starting to feel weird leaving school before six. Matt keeps saying he's happy to drive me home, but I turn him down. I just can't stomach the idea of riding with Matt and Andy right now—not when I feel this edgy and guilty and strange. So I hit up my brother, figuring I can always catch the late bus if he doesn't answer. But to my amazement, he texts me back instantly. No prob, on our way.

He shows up five minutes later with Noah, who immediately hops out to offer me the passenger seat. "Little Garfield, your chariot awaits."

"You know, you don't have to switch—"

But then Ryan rolls down the back window, and out pops Camilla's giant floofy head.

"Actually, yeah, you take the back," I say, practically dive-bombing the passenger seat. Within minutes, Noah's got Charles perched on his shoulder and Camilla sprawled in his lap, both of them determinedly licking either side of his face.

"Okay. Wow. Yup. Thank you." He twists his face away from Camilla.

I grin. "You okay?"

"Good. Great. Never been better."

I turn back to Ryan. "Thanks for picking me up."

"Sure—worked out great. We were just heading to Dad's house."

"Okay. Camilla. Blech. That's my mouth."

I glance up at the rearview. "Getting some action, Noah?"

"Don't be jealous, Little G."

"Jealous of you or the dogs?"

"Well, this just got weird," says Ryan.

"Don't look at me. I'm not the one getting to first base with Camilla."

Noah sighs. "And second base."

"Wow." I twist around in my seat. "If you and Camilla need some privacy, let us know. Wouldn't want to block any touchdowns."

"Okay, first of all, gross," says Noah. "Second of all, please tell me you know touchdowns aren't what comes after second base."

I wave my hand dismissively. "Obviously. You've got to get through third base and fourth base first—"

"KATE. NO. That's not—"

"But if you get to fifth base, that's, what, a three-point touchdown? So by now, the point guard's pretty much begging you to join the MLB—"

"Kate?" Noah says. "You're a disaster."

"Says the guy making out with a Labrador retriever."

"And a dachshund," chimes Ryan, and we exchange a quick fist-bump.

Noah splutters. "Whose side are you on?"

"Oh, he's definitely on my team," I say. "He plays quarterback and outfield—"

"Okay, you know what, hot shot? Your reign of ignorance is over." Noah leans forward, reaching past Camilla to rest his hand on my seat. "You're going to the game. This Friday—" I open my mouth to protest, but he cuts me off, grinning. "Nope, this is happening. Just you wait, Little G. You're gonna know so much about football."

"Yeah, no. I'm not going." I shrug. "No way in hell."

# SCENE 53

"So, why are we going to a fuckball game?" Raina asks on Friday, peering up from my bed.

We're at Dad's house—just the girls, since Andy's got a voice lesson. But even Andy keeps sneaking texts in. **Outfit updates please!!**

Funny how Andy's squad FOMO flares up right when Matt's heading out of town. According to Andy, Matt's visiting his dad in Alabama. Not gonna lie, the thought of Andy being so casually, intimately looped into Matt's plans stings a little. Maybe more than a little.

"So how did Noah Kaplan talk you into this?" asks Raina.

"He didn't," I say loftily. "I decided completely independently of Noah. I don't even know if he's going to be there."

"Of course he'll be there. Fuckboys always go to fuckball games." Raina leans flat on her back, resting my teddy bear Ember on her stomach.

"Okay." Brandie emerges from my closet, holding my brown

ankle boots in one hand, and an armload of my shortest skirts in the other. "So, Kate, for you, I'm thinking skirt, boots, tights, and a jacket?"

"No shirt?" Raina asks. "Nude on top?"

"And a shirt," Brandie says. She starts laying clothes out on the edge of my bed. "All right, what about this combination with your jean jacket?"

Raina sits up halfway, surveys the outfit, and then collapses back down again, raising two thumbs. "I dig it."

"Put it on so I can take pictures," says Brandie. "Andy needs to approve this."

"He did not say that. Approve my outfit?" I snatch Ember away from Raina. "No. Text him right now and tell him we are not acting out some Gay Best Friend teen movie nonsense."

"Okay, but he's gay . . . and he's our best friend," Brandie says.

"He's our best friend who's gay, not our Gay Best Friend. And we don't do outfit approval." I give Ember an emphatic head squish.

"Hey, you know what else we don't do?" Raina counters. "Sports games."

"I know! I know. But don't you think it could be interesting?" I say. "Anthropologically speaking."

Brandie laughs. "So it's research?"

"Roswell Hill High School football," says Raina. "A groundbreaking exploration of fuckboys in their natural habitat."

"We should take field notes," I say. "Oh my God. I should

put a bodycam on Ryan tomorrow—I think Chris Wrigley's having a keg party. With two kegs. Imagine that cursed footage."

"I just love how up-to-date you are," says Raina. "Queen of the f-boy party scene."

Brandie plops down beside me. "Speaking of tomorrow. Are you around, like, morning-ish? I was thinking maybe we could run through 'Normandy' before next week."

Raina bites back a smile. "Y'all are so cute, planning a rehearsal for your rehearsal."

"Works for me," I say. "Hey, are you guys getting dressed or what?"

Brandie and Raina have their own duffel bags of clothes, which is how we generally handle group fashion consultations. We're not the kind of friends who share clothes. For one thing, our shapes are all totally different. Raina's drapey tank tops would be corsets on me, and, like, bras on Brandie. And we have totally different aesthetics. Raina's so minimalistic and casual, and Brandie basically lives in boho sundresses. As for me, I'm wearing a flippy blue skater skirt, black tights, brown ankle boots, and a gray sweater cropped right at the waist of my skirt. If I were an f-girl, or even Raina, I'd be all in with that crop top. But since I'm me, I've got a white T-shirt tucked in underneath. Raina says that's acceptable and I look hot and I should let my hair down.

But I think I want to pin the sides back.

The doorbell rings. And a few seconds later, my dad yells, "Peapod!"

Weirdly, my first thought is Noah. Even though he's been letting himself into our house and up to Ryan's room for years. I mean, if it weren't for the formality of the doorbell, I'd just assume it was Andy getting out of his voice lesson early.

No matter who it is, I better intervene before Dad hits some new great height of awkward dadness. I race downstairs, my boots clapping on the hardwoods. Entering the foyer, I feel strangely winded. Maybe just breathless.

Maybe some part of me knew.

Matt Olsson's supposed to be in Alabama, but he's not in Alabama.

He's in my doorway.

# SCENE 54

He's nervous. I can tell from the way he's pacing. And the way he keeps smiling and then unsmiling and then resmiling. "Do you have a minute?" he asks.

"Oh! Um. Brandie and Raina—" I start to say, but when he looks over my shoulder, I realize they've started following me down.

"Hi," Raina pats Brandie's elbow. "We were heading right back up to Kate's room, weren't we, B?"

"Right," says Brandie.

"Uh. So. Brandie and Raina are here." I smile sheepishly, and then turn back to Matt. "But what's up?"

Matt starts to step toward me—but he seems to change his mind partway through, leaning back against the doorframe. "I should go," he says finally.

"Wait. What?"

"I don't want to intrude on your girl night."

"You're not intruding! We're just getting ready for the

fuck—the football game. The football game. Sorry." I blush. "You're totally invited. I thought you were going to be in Alabama for some reason."

"No, I am." He pauses. "I'm driving there now, but I just thought—I have to tell you something."

My heart's thudding like crazy. Matt has to tell me something? Something worth derailing his trip to Alabama? This couldn't—

This couldn't be a love declaration, right?

I mean. Wow. Wow. I kind of thought that was more of a movie thing than a real-life thing. In real life, you just kind of flirt and touch and keep maneuvering to be together, until you're either drunk or sleepy enough to hook up, and then you sort the terms out later. But I could almost swear Matt's about to flip that script completely. He's got that Fitzwilliam Darcy look on his face. Or even that Eugene Fitzherbert look. Definitely a Fitz look.

My hands are shaking. Maybe my whole body's shaking.

"Okay, so—"

Something crashes in my room, followed by Raina's voice through my door. "Oh my God, ignore us! Brandie, you—" The rest is muffled with giggles, but Matt's already reaching for the knob. "I don't want to keep you from the game," he says quickly.

"What? No. You're not—"

"We'll talk later. I should head out anyway." He hugs me tightly. "I'll see you on Tuesday, okay?"

I nod, dumbfounded. I can't quite catch my breath. I don't know what's more astonishing—the fact that he left so abruptly, or the fact that he was here in the first place. I can hardly wrap my mind around it. Matt Olsson was here, and he wanted to tell me something. He *had* to tell me something.

But then he yanked it right back.

# SCENE 55

Andy picks us up for the game after his voice lesson, and he's got this jittery, backstage-on-opening-night sort of energy. He keeps glancing sideways at me in the passenger seat like he's trying to read my face. I don't quite know what to make of it. Anderson knows Matt came over—Brandie and Raina didn't hesitate to blurt that out. But the whole Matt encounter was so quick and confusing that it's hard to pinpoint how I feel about it—much less how Anderson feels about it.

We pull in around seven, about a half hour before the game starts, and the parking lot's already packed. Even though the sun hasn't quite started setting, the air's crisp, almost chilly. It's sort of nice, because it gives an excuse to huddle up. Always best to maximize body contact with your friends to fend off the terror of walking into a football stadium.

It's not that football games are strictly f-boy dominated zones. There are a lot of little kids here, too, and old people, and teachers, and pretty much everyone. I used to come to the Roswell Hill home games all the time when I was younger. We even used to have bake sales here for middle school honor chorus, and once they did this whole bouncy house community fundraiser thing with professional Elsa and Anna character actors. Raina still has a selfie with Elsa as her phone background, Harold be damned.

Still, there's no denying the very real f-charge in the air.

"I guess we're playing Lassiter," says Brandie, taking note of the bold letter signs in the away section.

"I hate Lassiter," Andy says, so emphatically that Raina bursts out laughing.

"Since when do you have sports opinions?"

"It's not a sports opinion. They fucked us over in the one-act competition freshman year. Remember?" Andy shakes his fist. "I will never forgive."

"So it's a revenge thing. You want our fuckboys to beat their fuckboys."

"Our fuckboys are gonna destroy their fuckboys."

We head up into the stands, settling in near the marching band, a verified safe space for theater kids. There's a pregame performance by the color guard, which Brandie actually joined for a year until it conflicted too much with play rehearsal. She's still friends with a lot of the guard girls though. I always feel like drama club, marching band, and color guard are secret allies, who will one day join together and overthrow the f-force.

"Hey," Anderson says, scooting so our bodies are flush together. He hooks his arm around my shoulders. "You look really pretty tonight."

I smile. "So do you."

And somehow, even though we're at a fuckball game, I feel completely at home. Which is a feeling I only really ever get when I'm with Anderson. It's one of those things I can't say out loud, because people will just think I'm in love with him or something. But it's not a romantic feeling at all. I think it's more like how some people feel about their parents. Not that there's anything wrong with my parents. It's just hard to feel like home with them when everything's split in two. But Andy's like this little island between them.

Which makes the Matt thing so much harder.

I keep expecting Andy to bring the topic up somehow, at least to ask about Matt's visit to Dad's house. It's kind of weird that he hasn't. A month ago, we'd be sitting here obsessively analyzing every detail of an encounter like that. I'd be diving deep into the nuances of Matt's facial expressions, so we could breathlessly decode them. But all of that feels so far away. I can't imagine mentioning Matt right now, rubbing the whole encounter in Anderson's face. But you'd think Andy would at least be curious about it. Especially with the weird vibe he's been giving me all night. I mean, I know he's curious. But it's like he's pretending it never happened.

"Little G, you made it!" I glance up, and there's Noah, looking so pleased, I can't help but smile a little.

"I guess my reign of ignorance is over."

"Oh, well, let's not get ahead of ourselves." He plops down on the bleachers, hugging me sideways. Then he leans forward, beaming down at the squad. "Sup, my buds?"

"Your buds?" Anderson says, but Noah's already turned back to the center aisle, waving down my brother.

"Hey," Ryan says, scooting in next to Noah.

"Okay, eyes on the field, Katy. I'm gonna walk you through the rules."

"Nah, I'm good." I tilt my head. "You sure you don't want to sit with those guys?" I gesture across the aisle, where a group of boys have taken over. It's not even that many of them—maybe a dozen or so—but the manspreading's so intense, they practically take up a whole section.

Noah shakes his head vehemently, without even sparing them a glance. "No, I hate them. I hate those guys."

"Pshh. You don't even know who I'm talking about."

"I don't need to know."

Raina snorts. "I officially like him," she says, leaning forward. She points to Noah. "You're the only f-boy I accept."

"Thank you!" says Noah.

Ryan squints. "Did you just say f-boy?"

"It means fuckboy," says Raina.

Brandie freezes, eyes comically huge, while Andy and I clap our hands over our mouths. F-boys can't know that they're f-boys. It's like the fundamental rule of being an f-boy. But Raina just did that. She made the f-boys self-aware, and I have no idea how I'm supposed to feel about it.

It's f-ception.

"I'm a fuckboy?" Noah asks.

"Eh." Anderson tilts his hand back and forth the way French teachers do when they say *comme ci, comme ça*.

Raina leans over and points to Noah's phone screen. "Are you or are you not about to Instagram a grainy-ass picture of the field with the hashtag 'FNL'?"

"Um—"

"Caption: 'whatta night.'"

Noah turns his phone facedown.

"Fuckboy," says Raina. "I rest my case."

# SCENE 56

Ryan's up early on Saturday, zoned out with his phone and a literal mixing bowl of Frosted Flakes. But as soon as I settle in across from him, he looks up.

"So." He sets his phone down and stretches. "I guess your friends think I'm a fuckboy."

My mouth falls open. "No! Absolutely not."

He shoots me a look that's equal parts skeptical and amused.

"You really think I'd let anyone call you an f-boy?"

He leans back in his chair. "So they don't think I'm a fuckboy? Or you won't let them call me a fuckboy?"

"Both. Because you're not one." I bite back a smile. "Not exactly."

He takes a bite of cereal. "So how do you know if you're a fuckboy? What are the fuckboy identifiers?"

"Okay, no." I blush. "You're taking this too seriously. It just means someone's a jock. It's not personal. It's like a shorthand we use. It's dumb."

"So fuckboys are just jocks."

"Yes."

"And all my friends are fuckboys."

"Well, sometimes we call them f-boys if we're feeling classy."

"Whoa, that is classy," says Ryan. He pauses for a moment. "But I'm not sure I get it."

"Okay . . ."

"Like, how am I not a fuckboy?"

I narrow my eyes. "Do you want to be one?"

"It's just a question."

"I think the real question is, why are you friends with fuck-boys," I say breezily.

Except it doesn't come out breezy. It lands like an anvil.

Ryan just looks at me.

My cheeks go warm. "Sorry. Yeah, that was a shitty thing to say. I shouldn't police your friends."

"No, I get it—"

The doorbell rings, and I practically leap from my chair. "Oh! That's Brandie."

"Just Brandie? Where's the rest of the geek squad?"

"Geek squad?"

He tilts his palms up, spoon in hand. "What about g-squad? Is that classier?"


Normally Ryan's got this magic trick where he vanishes into thin air whenever my friends show up. But when Brandie and I swing back through the kitchen, he's right where I left him.

274

"Okay, Tony Tiger," I say, "we're heading up to rehearse."

Ryan points his spoon at me. "You mean Tony the Tiger."

I scowl at him, but Brandie smiles as sweetly as ever. "Want to come be our Minstrel?"

"Your what?" He looks horrified.

"Not the racist kind," Brandie says quickly. "Like those medieval musicians who walk around playing the mandolin."

"Hashtag: jammin'," I add.

Ryan side-eyes me intensely.

I pat his head and turn back to Brandie. "You ready?"

"Okay, wait, what do you need me to do?" Ryan starts to stand.

I stare at him, stunned. He's not . . . serious. Right?

But Brandie just nods, like this is just some normal occurrence. Ryan. My brother. Filling in for Lana freaking Bennett. "Yeah. I mean, if you want to give us our cues, that would be great. You don't have to sing or anything."

Ryan shrugs. "Okay, sure."

Nope. This is too weird to be real. Either Ryan's trolling us, or I'm dreaming. Unless—

It hits me with the force of a volcano. Holy shit. Holy holy HOLY shit.

I have to text Andy. Right now. Right this second.

I don't even wait until we're upstairs. I trail behind Brandie and Ryan, frantically typing.

**ANDY YOU'RE NOT GOING TO BELIEVE THIS.**

I'm just 😲 😲 😲

I think Ryan has an actual crush

ON BRANDIE

This is not a drill

Brandie and Ryan head into my room, but I pause in the doorway, peering down at my phone. No response. Which is fine. It's not like I'm about to explode all over Mom's hardwood floors. You just take your sweet everloving time, Anderson Walker.

Brandie takes her usual spot on my bed, but Ryan wimps out and goes for the desk chair. So I stick my phone in my pocket and settle in next to Brandie—but I barely last a minute before I whip it out again to check. Nothing.

I scoot out of Brandie's screen-reading range.

Anderson where are you???

Andy he's helping us rehearse. And hanging out with us

voluntarily. RYAN!!!

Like THIS MAKES SO MUCH SENSE. He's been hanging

out with me so much more than usual and NOW I GET

IT

He's IN LOVE.

Are you getting these??

No response. No ellipses. Just nothing. A giant box of nothing.

# SCENE 57

Anderson doesn't write back for hours, and even then, it's just a halfhearted lol. Not even an LOL with exclamation points. I'm sorry, but that has to be the most severe underreaction in all of human history. It makes me feel like I'm being punched in the face every time I look at my phone.

It's just so totally not like him. It's the antithesis of Anderson.

Unless, of course, he's mad at me. But why? I keep reading and reading the whole series of texts, trying to crack the code. Like, did I say something creepy? Or problematic? Is he just opposed to the Good Ship Bryan? Maybe Andy's got Ryan pegged as a fuckboy. Maybe he loathes Ryan the way I loathe Eric Graves.

So I try to steer us back to neutral with a link to some irresistible content about Disney prince hotness rankings. But Anderson never writes back, and I honestly feel a little sick about it. I spend all of Sunday on tenterhooks, practically magnetized to my phone.

I text him again after dinner, and I swear, I actually feel shy. Which is more than weird. It's unnerving. I spend ten minutes tweaking the wording to make it sound extra chill and casual.

**Hey, am I still riding with you tomorrow?**

He writes back instantly. **Of course!!**

Followed by a full line of emojis.

So gloriously normal, I could weep.

Matt's not quite back from Alabama, so it's just Andy and me this morning. The OG duo. My triumphant return to the passenger seat. And maybe Anderson's a little subdued, but at least I don't get a vibe that he hates me.

So we're good. Normal ride, normal Monday, normal us. I mean, it's approximately normal. Round-up normal, at least as long as I keep doing most of the talking. By the time we reach Hardscrabble Road, I've already walked Anderson through my theory that Ryan and Brandie have been secretly texting for weeks.

"I'm getting to the bottom of this." I press my lips together, nodding. "Maybe if I photograph Ryan's phone screen and zoom in, I could make out the name—"

"Or you could just ask him," says Andy.

"He'll deny it."

My phone buzzes, and the sound alone makes my heart flip. I guess I spent so long obsessing over texts yesterday, my brain got stuck there. But then again, maybe the heart flip is justified. Because the text is from Matt.

Hey, I'm so sorry if that was weird on Friday. I shouldn't
    have just shown up.

I grin down at my screen. There are ellipses. He's still
typing.

A moment later: I feel so bad!

OMG, don't feel bad! I write back. You're fine. How's Alabama??

Ehh. It's 🗑️ 🔥

Oh no! I'm so sorry!!! You okay?

I look back up at Andy. "Yikes. Sounds like Matt's not having the best weekend."

"Yeah . . ."

My phone buzzes again. I'm fine. My dad's just a lot. One
more night. 💪 I'll be back by rehearsal tomorrow. We'll talk
this week, okay?


As promised, Matt arrives around dismissal on Tuesday, just in
time for rehearsal. He plops into the seat beside me. "Hi."

I smile up at him. "You made it."

"So glad to be home." Home. I like that when he says that,
he means Roswell. He means us.

"Did things get any better with your dad?"

"I mean, not really? My dad's kind of . . ." He trails off,
smiling, like he always does when he talks about his dad. Over
Matt's shoulder, I see Anderson enter through the far side auditorium door, cutting straight to the front row of seats.

Which is weird. I'm sure he saw us. It's not like we're hidden.

So maybe Anderson really is mad at me. I've been going back and forth about it all day. In history class, he just seemed quiet. He didn't show up to lunch. And now this.

My eyes keep drifting toward him, but he seems to be pointedly ignoring us, thumbing through his script like he's practicing his lines. Even though we all know Anderson's had the whole play memorized since the first week of rehearsal.

"—missed the game," Matt says—and only then do I realize he's been speaking this whole time. I look back at him with a start. "But it is what it is," Matt says, and I nod my head vaguely.

My brain's on a loop. Anderson's mad at me, Anderson's mad at me, Anderson's mad at me. He's not supposed to be mad at me, per the ground rules. But I think he is. I'm almost positive. And it's giving me that verge-of-explosion feeling in my throat.

I guess if I were a perfect friend, I'd nip the Matt issue in the bud. I could end the whole thing right now. He'd have to understand, right? Matt would never want to come between my friendship with Andy. Though if I even mention Andy, that's basically telling Matt to his face that Andy has a crush on him. Which would be an earth-shattering, almost unspeakable betrayal, a full and flagrant violation of the Code of Secrecy. Putting Anderson's heart on the line, opening him to the full humiliation of publicly confirmed unrequited love.

I'm not a perfect friend, but I'm a better friend than that.

# SCENE 58

But Wednesday morning, something finally shifts.

We're all pretty quiet on the ride to school, but the silence feels softer somehow. Then, when Matt's a few steps ahead in the parking lot, Anderson holds me back with a tiny elbow grab. "Hey. Can we talk?"

I look up at him, startled. "Sure."

"Kate." He exhales, looking me right in the eye. "I'm so sorry." And then, before I can even process it, he gives me this massive, tight hug—so sudden and forceful, we almost bang into Matt's car. "I love you so much," he says. "I've been so weird. I'm sorry. I'm so sorry." He disentangles, peering closely at my face. I feel my eyes start to prickle. "Are we okay?"

"Of course." My voice breaks, just slightly. "I hate the weirdness. It's the Matt thing, right?"

Andy nods, and for a minute, I swear he might burst into tears. "I'm not handling stuff well."

"No, I'm the one who's not handling stuff well!"

He does this choked little laugh. "Katy, how does anyone ever fight with you?"

"I love you so much," I say, and now I'm crying for real. I don't deserve Anderson. I honestly don't. He could hate my guts right now, and under the circumstances, I'd understand it. Anyone would understand. He's too good. "You're the most important person to me, okay? I'm not going to let anyone come between us." I hug him again, burying my face in his chest, and he wraps his arms around me tightly.

"Same. Oh, Kate." He releases me, then wipes his cheeks with the heels of both hands. "You're the most important to me too." He exhales. "I love you so much. More than anything."

And I know it's stupid, needing that validation, but I'm almost giddy with relief.

# SCENE 59

Andy's got an intensive rehearsal today, so it's just Matt for the ride home from school. My heart does this little jolt as soon as I shut the car door. It's officially our first moment alone together since he showed up on Dad's doorstep, and I just feel so larger-than-life about it. I feel like a verse in a poem.

We haven't even left the school lot when he asks me if I want to grab ice cream. "Wasn't there a place near Taco Mac?"

"Bruster's."

"Okay, cool." He does this quick, eager nod, and it's so cute, I feel dizzy.

It's about a five-minute ride from school. Neither of us says much on the way there. I keep glancing sideways at Matt without meaning to. He's staring dutifully at the road, but his jaw keeps clenching. It's so hard to know what he's thinking.

The lot's almost entirely empty. There's only one other customer hanging out on the benches—an older white guy working on a giant rainbow waffle cone. We follow the old guy's lead on the cone, but Matt gets chocolate, and I get cake batter. And a bowl to put my cone in.

"Want to sit by the tree?" Matt asks, pointing to a little bench on the other side of the parking lot.

"Sure."

The minute we sit down, I get the same anticipatory feeling you get when you step onto a stage. That little heart palpitation chest hiccup.

"So I know we never really got to talk after last weekend," Matt says.

"Right." My heart beats another notch faster. "What's up?"

"Okay. Here I go." He nods, smile flickering. "Sorry. You can probably tell I haven't done this a lot."

"Take your time," I say, trying to sound calm.

He keeps fidgeting with his napkin, wrapping and unwrapping his cone.

"I know we haven't been friends for that long," he says. "Which is crazy to me, because it really feels like we have. I feel like I knew you in a past life or something."

"Me too."

"I don't even know why I'm nervous. I'm just going to say it." He blinks and then inhales and then looks right into my eyes. "So I'm sure you already guessed this, but. I'm gay."

I freeze. My whole body. Heart, lungs, every cell, every organ.

"Oh," I say simply.

"Okay." He grips his ice-cream cone with both hands, smiling hugely. "I did it."

"Wow." I nod. Really fast. Like maybe if I nod quickly enough, my eyes will stop prickling. "Yeah! Wow. I'm just— wow. Thanks for trusting me."

"I mean, of course. You're best friends with Anderson. Obviously I knew you weren't, like, a homophobe." He's still smiling. "I feel so—" He sighs. "Wow. I can't even tell you how good this feels."

"So you haven't told a lot of people?" I ask, and Matt shakes his head.

"I'm telling my mom tonight. And your mom, I guess."

"What about your dad?"

"Oh, God no." He does this choked little laugh.

"I'm really sorry. That's so shitty."

"I'm just glad I don't live there anymore. Last weekend was just . . . unbearable."

"Did something happen?"

"Oh, no. Yeah, nothing in particular." Matt pauses, swallowing a bite of his cone. "It's just so much better here, which made it hard to go back, even for the weekend. I hated my old school so much. Like, I didn't know a single queer person there. Or maybe I did, but no one was out. And then I came here, and there are so many of us. And you've got Andy, who's just, like, almost nonchalant about it, you know?"

I take the last bite of my cone, and set my bowl on the

bench. "I don't think people usually describe Andy as nonchalant."

Matt laughs. "Okay, true. But you know what I mean. He's so sure of himself, and he's out to everyone, and I'm just in awe of that. I didn't even know I could want that."

"Yeah. I mean, I think it took him a minute, but, you know. He's had time to figure it out. You will too."

"Thanks, Kate." He smiles at me.

It makes my throat catch.

"You know what's funny?" he says. "That whole time at camp, I thought you and Andy were dating." He studies my face for a moment. "Okay, you've got a little bit of ice cream . . . here, I'll just—"

He swipes the corner of my mouth with two fingers.

I think my brain just derailed.

I just can't wrap my head around it. He's touching my face. But he's gay. And he was gay when he asked for my number. All those secret smiles and locked eyes, all the moments I stacked in my head like they meant something. All that snowballing romantic tension. All that kissing.

All that choreographed, staged kissing.

"Have you ever just been so totally wrong about someone?" Matt says.

"Yup," I say softly.

I think I might burst into tears.

One day, I'll tell him. In a year or two, maybe. Whenever the thought of it stops making me want to sink into the floorboards. I'll tell him over cocktails when we're twenty-five. Hey, remember when you came out to me at Bruster's? And I was shocked? Because I thought you were in love with me? Me and my fine-ass observational skills. Queen Kate the Clueless strikes again and again and again.

# SCENE 60

The next morning, Andy's waiting outside my algebra class, looking frantic. "Hey! I have to pee."

"Isn't the bell about to ring?"

"Just check in with Ms. Whatshername—"

"Evans."

"Ms. Evans! Great. Just tell her you have to puke or something." He grabs my hand. "Come on."

"You have Senior D—"

"Kate. It's fine. Come on." And the next thing I know, I'm trailing behind him through the arts wing, all the way back to the BTF. I can't quite read his expression. He seems happy. I think? I don't know why he wouldn't be, because clearly Matt just came out to him on the ride to school. And he must know I know. He's probably bursting to talk about it.

It is kind of exciting, if you look at it from Andy's perspective. I don't want to say Andy's only ever had crushes on straight boys, but there have been quite a few straight boys. And obviously Matt being gay doesn't automatically mean he's into Anderson, but there's still that possibility. I actually think I wouldn't mind it, down the line. Once all the dust settles.

"So Matt talked to you," Andy says, settling in on his toilet.

"Yes," I say, but then I hesitate. Because maybe Andy thinks this conversation is about something else entirely. I don't want to say more than I should.

"Yes, about him being gay, Kate," Andy says, apparently reading my mind. I can tell from his voice that he's smiling. "I like that you were careful not to out him, though."

"I just—"

"I'm not being sarcastic. For real. Like, he's not really out. So you're right to be careful. I think we're the only ones who know. Period."

"So he told you this morning?"

Anderson's silent for a moment.

"He literally just told me yesterday," I add. "I promise."

"Katy, Matt and I are dating," Anderson says.

And that's when the world stops. Not just me. Not just my body. It's like the whole entire world just went still on its axis. "I thought . . ." He pauses. "I don't know. We thought you'd kind of guessed."

"We?" I say faintly.

"Me and—"

"You and Matt. I get it. I know who the we is." I stare at

289

my jeans, tucking two fingers into the scraggly denim around my knees. My voice falls. "You're dating? He's your—like your boyfriend?"

"We haven't said boyfriend. I don't know," Andy says.

"So when?" I feel like my chest is caving in on itself. "When did this happen?"

"A while ago."

My voice cracks. "A while ago."

"Kate."

"What do you mean, a while ago? We've known him for like a month."

"Like . . . two weeks ago? Just under. He picked me up after you got back from your brother's birthday dinner."

The memory lands like a punch. Watching from my bedroom window as Matt left right after my brother did. I'd assumed he was going to Michelle McConnell's party. He'd even changed his shirt.

"Katy."

I don't reply.

"Kate, say something. Please be happy for me." His voice breaks. "Please."

"I—"

"I swear, I really thought you knew. Like when we were talking about it in the parking lot, and you said you weren't handling it well—"

"Yeah, because I'm an idiot. I thought you were jealous. I felt so guilty. I thought I was breaking your heart."

"That's ridiculous—"

"That Matt would like me? Yeah—"

"No!" Anderson's voice quakes. "You shouldn't have felt guilty, Kate, we talked about this. The ground rules—"

"The ground rules weren't working."

Anderson sputters. "Since when?"

"Well, let's see. What was that second rule? Oh right. Be honest with each other. Yeah, how'd that go for you?"

"Are you serious right now?" I hear Andy step out of his stall, slamming the door behind him. "What was I supposed to do? Matt wasn't out! How could I have told you?"

"You said you thought I knew!"

"I did! But I wasn't sure. And, Katy, it wasn't my thing to tell."

My cheeks flush. "Yeah, well, you could have waited until he was ready to tell before you decided to hook up—"

Anderson laughs incredulously. "Are you listening to yourself? So you're saying I should have told my boyfriend, hey, I'll kiss you, but we're going to have to loop in Kate first. Just FYI—"

"So now he is your boyfriend!"

"Wow, you really can't be happy for me, can you?"

"I am happy for you." I stand up, yanking the stall door open. "Okay? There you go. You win, Andy. You get the guy. You get the guy we were both half in love with all summer—"

"We barely knew him this summer!" Andy's crying now. We both are.

"Well I know him now. I like him just as much as you do, okay? Just as much." I can't catch my breath. "But I'm supposed to be happy for you? So if it were reversed, if he were my boyfriend, you wouldn't feel any sort of way about that?"

Andy's face crumples. "Of course I would."

"Then congratulations! Your ground rules are bullshit." I storm over to the sinks, trying to scrub my face clean of tears. But they just keep coming. "So, what, you didn't think this would break my heart? Or you just didn't care?"

"Of course I care! But—God. I thought we talked about this—"

"You could have gone for any other guy, Andy. Any other guy."

"That's not how it works—"

"Oh believe me, I know." I laugh harshly.

"I mean that's not how it works when you're me, okay?" Andy's voice comes out choked. "Do you even get that? I'm gay and I'm Black, and, Kate, we live in the deep fucking South. You think we're treated the same? You think we're playing the same odds?"

"This isn't a game—"

"I know! I know it's not a game. Can you just listen—"

"No, you listen." I whirl back around to face him. I look him right in the eyes. "I was a wreck when I thought I was hurting you. Okay? I agonized over how I was gonna break the news to you. And you? You don't even give a shit. Just drop that bomb before algebra, right? Cool, I'll take the whole day to savor it." For a moment, I just stare at him, shaking my head. "So, thanks for that."

Then I burst out of the bathroom, leaving Anderson tear-soaked in my wake.

# SCENE 61

I don't know how I'm ever going to look Matt in the eye again.

I mean, if Matt and Andy tiptoeing around my oblivious self for two weeks wasn't humiliating enough, Andy's about to walk right back into Senior D looking like Niagara Falls hit his face. I can just picture it. Matt will wrap his arms around him and kiss his forehead until he stops crying. Deep breaths, deep breaths. Tell me what happened.

The crazy thing is, I don't even think Matt will be mad at me for yelling at his boyfriend. He'll just pity me. Stupid Kate and her pointless, pathetic crush. Maybe Matt and Andy will even hash out the issue with everyone in Senior D. Circle of trust, right? They can all just sit there discussing what an absolute steaming-hot desperate mess of a human being I am. It'll be like the real-life version of the Kate Garfield Singing Instagram page.

I mean, it's seriously the longest school day of my life. Hands down. I can't bear to go to history. I'll start crying if I see Anderson. So I tell Mr. Edelman I have a meeting to discuss college applications, and then I walk straight past the guidance office and spend all of second period hiding in an empty locker room shower. And then I spend lunch there, too.

But even eavesdropping on Genny Hedlund's locker room conversations is barely a distraction. The mortification comes in waves. Every time I catch my breath, an even worse thought smacks me down.

Like all those rides I took with Andy and Matt. I was so unbearably naïve. The way I curled up smugly in the back seat, thinking I was just a good friend for giving Anderson the front. Letting him pretend he was the center of the story.

Guess there wasn't much pretending involved after all.

By eighth period, I'm downright spiraling. I can't stop thinking about how terribly sorry Matt must feel for me now. And how sorry he's felt for me for weeks. How he and Anderson must have talked about me. I bet every time I was away, every night I spent at Dad's house, they were wincingly speculating that I'd lose my shit when they told me. And then, lo and behold, here I am proving them right.

I want to run away. I just want to walk out the atrium door, break into my brother's car, and drive all the way home. Or I could walk home. Andy and I used to walk to and from football games when we were in middle school. Two and a half miles. I could be at Mom's house in less than an hour.

But in the world's greatest example of laughably ironic bullshit, I'm stuck here for an intensive rehearsal. For the song "Normandy." Which is literally about Lady Larken trying to run away from the castle.

The dismissal bell rings, and I lurch toward the auditorium like a zombie. I can't make eye contact with anyone in the hallways. Because everyone must know the whole story by now. Everyone. The whole school. Kate Garfield? Yeah, isn't she that girl who constantly deludes herself into thinking gay guys are in love with her?

Except—okay.

Maybe a handful of people have missed the memo that I'm a pathetic shameball loser. Everyone in rehearsal's acting so normal, I could weep. Lana's being snotty with the tech kids about stage left versus stage right. Brandie plops into the chair next to me, all excited about some viral video about baby wombats, so we watch that for a while. And then, the minute she gets up to pee, Noah steals her seat and starts babbling about some little kid's YouTube channel.

"That's all he does. They send him new toys every day, and he films his reactions. I'm not even kidding. The kid's like eight. What a lifestyle. I stan."

I smile, but it feels rigid and forced, like a marionette dummy. It's been six hours since Andy's bombshell, and I barely know what smiles feel like anymore. "You have so many opinions about children's media," I say.

"To be fair, I have a younger sister." He pokes me. "Question. Madison's having, like, a very lowkey party tomorrow."

"That's not a question."

He just smiles. "Want to come?"

"I don't even know Madison. Why would I go to her party?"

"Because it's going to be fun. And because you'd be going with me. And," he says emphatically, "you have no excuse not to go, because it's right in our neighborhood."

"I'll be at my mom's house."

And as soon as I say it, it hits me. Mom's house. Which is where Matt lives. That's going to be a fucking joyride. Just a fun weekend at home with a boy who knows all about my former sad, pathetic crush on him. Oh wait, let's make it even more fun by adding a Saturday all-day run-through rehearsal where I get to kiss the boy I had a sad, pathetic crush on. Wow. This won't be awkward at all. And then tech week. And then opening night next Friday. Can't wait to see how many times Matt pulls me aside this week with gentle pitying eyes because he just wants to make sure I'm okay.

Thankfully Noah—oblivious Noah—doesn't even seem to realize I'm on the edge of a meltdown. He's still talking. "—this Tuesday. Finally—"

"Hey, Noah?" I squeeze my eyes shut. "Sorry. When's this party again? Tomorrow?"

"You're coming? Oh, sweet!" And he looks so genuinely psyched that I feel bad for every mean thought I've ever had about f-girls and partying and about Noah. Especially about Noah. "It's gonna be really chill. You'll love it."

"Good. Chill sounds good," I say, trying to ignore my ricocheting heart.

# SCENE 62

I don't know why telling my brother I'm going to a party feels weird, but it does. It feels—kind of thirsty, I guess? Like I'm trying to weasel my way into the f-force. But when I bring it up on the way home from school on Friday, he doesn't even blink. "Yeah, I was thinking about going to that. It's supposed to be chill."

"So I hear."

"Who are you going with?" Ryan asks, which makes me melt a little, because I know he wants me to say Brandie. But then I mostly just feel awful, since I totally could invite Brandie if I wanted to. And I do want to. Of course I do. But it's just complicated.

I bite my lip. "Um. I think just Noah."

Here's the thing: if I invite Brandie, I have to invite Raina, and if I'm inviting the girls, I have to invite Anderson, and at that point I'd definitely have to invite Matt, and avoiding Anderson and Matt is the whole reason I'm even going.

I mean, it's most of the reason.

As soon as we're home, I make a beeline for my room. Matt's not home yet, if he's even coming home tonight. It's highly possible he has better plans. But I shut the door just in case. Ryan doesn't want to leave for Dad's house until eight, and he says we should shower and get ready before we go.

There's nothing lonelier than getting dressed without the squad—if nothing else, we've usually got the group text chain going. But it's that weird squad thing again, where if I text Raina and Brandie, they'll wonder why Anderson's not on the thread. And if I tell them Andy and I are fighting, they'll want to know why. Of course, it's possible Andy and Matt have already told them, in which case I'm sure they think I'm pathetic and problematic. But if they haven't, there's no way to even talk about the situation without outing Matt. And that flat out can't happen. I won't let it.

So I just have to keep my distance. Just like how last weekend, Anderson kept his distance from me.

The thing is, I really do get it. I do. I get why Andy was so weird and restrained. And I know it's downright ridiculous to want him to wait until they had my blessing. The more I think about it, the more I'm embarrassed I said that. I guess in the moment, it felt like every single choice Anderson made was designed to destroy me.

But I know that's not true. And if I didn't already know that, I now have a wall of texts to prove it.

**Katy I'm so sorry. I never expected this to happen.**

I never wanted to hurt you

Please say something

Kate I love you. You know that right?

I know you were blindsided. I feel awful about that.

I hate that we're fighting

Please text me

It's so Anderson. He's a monster about grudges. He really is. Except when it comes to me. Whereas I'm just awful at staying mad at anybody, ever.

But every time I start to type a reply, I fall short. It just feels insurmountable. I keep picturing Andy receiving my apology text. He'll show Matt, of course. And Matt will scoot closer, resting his chin on Andy's shoulder. "Told you she'd come around," he'll say. I'm sure I'm a regular topic of discussion between them. I wonder if they bonded over pitying me, and if my rage brought them even closer. All my inconvenient feelings.

Every time I think about it, it stings even harder.

Whatever. I'm a grown girl. I can dress myself for a party, even an f-boy party. But when I thumb through my closet, all my clothes feel cringingly overdone. Everything feels like I wore it just yesterday. But I don't have the energy to be creative. God forbid I attempt to layer things and end up looking like a toddler. Maybe I should just wear jeans and a T-shirt and a flannel. Probably the whole f-force would faint from the sheer underwhelmingness.

In the end, I go for a dress—one I've never worn, even

though I saved all of last year's birthday money to buy it. I always feel like it looks really try-hard, which is ironic, because it's probably the lowest-effort clothing item I own. I mean, you don't even have to zip it. It wraps and ties around you. But it's just a little more fitted than what I usually wear, mostly under the boobs, with all these dainty-looking printed flowers. And it's red, which can feel very WHOA. But maybe whoa is a good thing. Who knows?

I throw a jacket on over it and hope for the best.

# SCENE 63

By the time Ryan and I get to Dad's house, Noah's already waiting, stiff-backed on our living room couch. It's not weird that he's here; the only weird thing is that he's sitting, not sprawled. But then I realize Dad's there too, sipping bourbon in his recliner like he and Noah are having an old-timey meeting of gentlemen.

We chat with Dad for a bit, and the boys tell him about the party—how it's just a few streets down, near the clubhouse, and how Madison and her sisters are fine, upstanding girls. I mostly just nod along, trying not to think about Madison and Noah being upstanding together against Sean Sanders's refrigerator.

By nine or so, we step out into the September evening stillness. Just like the block party, it's a little bit surreal to be spending a Saturday night with Noah and Ryan. Especially Ryan. By the time we reach the end of our block, the boys are already deep into a conversation about sports. I drift a few steps behind them. My mind keeps circling back to Andy and

Matt, and whether they're together, and what they're up to, and whether they're talking about me, and how much they pity me, and—

"Hey, space cadet, we're here," Noah says.

I realize with a start that ten minutes have passed.

Madison really does live just a few blocks from us, in the kind of house you always see here—overly large, with stucco exteriors, big windows, and potted plants on the doorstep. But there are absolutely none of the usual party trappings. No plastic cups littering the yard, no loud music, no one spilling out of the driveway. Not even a line of parked Jeeps on Madison's street—that classic f-boy calling card. There's just a handful of cars parked in her driveway. I squint at Noah and Ryan. "Are you sure this is her house?"

"Told you it was going to be chill," Noah says. Then he opens the door without knocking. "Hello?" he calls out. "Madison?"

"She's in the basement," someone calls back—and her voice, though muffled through a wall, is familiar. I try to place it, with no luck—but then there's a toilet flush, followed by hand-washing noises, and then the bathroom door opens. It's Mira Reynolds.

"Oh, hey, y'all!" she says, her voice obnoxiously musical. She's wearing high-waisted shorts and a shirt so cropped it could legit be a bra, dark hair softly wavy. She leans forward to hug Noah, which feels wrong, and then Ryan, which feels wronger, and then me, which is straight-up nonsensical. I mean, Mira

Reynolds. The worst and meanest f-girl of all. Is she trolling me right now? Ella-gate wasn't even three full years ago, and it was one of the worst days of my life. Does she even remember who I am?

"Maddie's downstairs. Y'all are kind of early, but no biggie. I just talked to Sean and everyone, and I think people are coming around eleven?"

Gotta love f-girls. Three sentences, and Mira's already managed to make me feel like the world's most overeager, irrelevant loser.

"Hey." Noah grabs my hand. "Should we head down?"

I freeze in place. Because this isn't the maybe-accidental backswipe hand contact from the block party. This is my hand. Being held by Noah Kaplan's hand. But in a way that can't possibly mean anything, seeing as we're standing inside the house of a girl Noah sometimes makes out with against refrigerators. But still. I like the way his fingers look, curved around mine. It's our cast-free hands. I mean, all my hands are cast-free. Both. Both my hands. Anyway, it's Noah's right hand. And my left hand, which is the one with all the guitar calluses. Great. That's just great. I bet Noah's super into calluses.

And just like that, he lets go, and I don't know what to make of any of it. On the bright side, obsessing over the presence and absence of Noah's hands makes for a more than decent distraction. I make it all the way down Madison's staircase without a single thought about Matt and Andy. So props to Noah, I guess, for that.

I follow the boys into the party, which turns out to be . . . legitimately very chill. Besides us, there are only about a dozen people here. Everyone's tucked onto this curved, wraparound couch, drinking from plastic cups and calmly watching two f-boys play a video game. No grinding or puking or staggering around drunk. Just a quiet, poignant f-boy moment. I really am like an anthropologist. The secret life of fuckboys. Fuckboys: they're just like us! I honestly should collect field notes. I could get a PhD in Fuckboy Studies.

A moment later, Madison appears, looking unicorn-level gorgeous in one of those tight bodycon dresses. She's curled her hair for the occasion, and it swings around like a shampoo commercial when she moves in to hug us. Up close, that per-fumey floral smell is even stronger than I remember. With girls like Madison, that flowery scent always feels somehow essen-tial, like it's part of their very humanity. I'm sure I smell like Mom's laundry detergent.

"Drinks are back there on the table," Madison says. "We're low on mixers, but I think my sister just restocked."

She has this proud-hostess gleam that's kind of endearing. I don't think she's particularly relaxed, or even enjoying her-self, but she looks pleased and satisfied. Like a wedding planner surveying her perfectly executed reception. I think Madison's actually the only one not drinking.

Of course, Ryan and Noah head straight to the booze table. "Little G, Katy Kate, do you want something?" asks Noah.

I shake my head dazedly, watching Ryan throw back a shot,

like he's some teen movie frat bro. Which somehow seems to summon Chris Wrigley, who appears out of the ether to give Ryan a fist bump.

Noah steps closer. "You sure you don't want anything? Water even? Or OJ—I think Maddie said her sister's bringing some more." He pours some rum into a red plastic cup, and then empties the end of a Coke bottle on top. He takes a sip then gasps. "You know what we should do? Right now?"

Leave. We should leave. We should go drink herbal tea with my dad and watch eighties movies on Netflix.

"We should sing!" Noah claps my shoulder emphatically. "Not me. Just you. Like at set design."

I stare straight in his face. I might actually be speechless.

"Come onnnn." He takes a big gulp of his drink. "I know, I know, Sir Harry's not here. But you don't need him. I'm telling you. We can find background tracks on YouTube. Wait, doesn't your dad have a karaoke machine—"

"Noah, I literally can't tell if you're making fun of me, or if you're actually that clueless—"

"What? Kate! I just like your voice. Hold on. I need a refill."

I can't do this. I can't be here. I'm so far out of my depth, I don't even know how I'm still breathing. I need Andy. I can't do this without Andy. God knows Noah's not helping. I don't even know what he's thinking. Me, singing along to YouTube karaoke tracks at an f-boy party. I mean, why stop there, right? How about I climb on top of the booze table and belt "Somebody to Love"?

And to make the moment that much more perfect, Mira Reynolds bursts in, cradling a carton of orange juice and a two-liter Coke bottle. She promptly steps on my foot. "Oops, sorry, boo," she says.

I blink up at her, speechless.

"You're probably looking for these, huh? Ohhhh boy." She lifts up the carton.

I feel almost dizzy. Mira Reynolds with the mixers.

I knew Mira lived in my neighborhood. And I knew she had sisters. But those sisters are twelve, right? Maybe the older one's thirteen or fourteen.

But then again, that might have been a thing that got locked into my head freshman year. Which was two years ago. Which would make the middle sister—

Madison. Madison Reynolds, who sent her sister to pick up mixers. Her sister Mira.

I'm in Mira Reynolds's house.

"There you are." Noah sidles up, flushed and smiling. "You sure you don't want anything? You know drunk karaoke is a thing, right?"

I shake my head slowly. Mira's house. Noah wants me to sing in Mira's house.

"Okay, but Ryan wants me to tell you that if you want to drink, it's fine, and he has your back, and also he'd rather you drink while he's here to, like, keep an eye on you. So if you did want to drunk anything, I mean drink, ha—"

"Where's Ryan?"

"Playing Fortnite." He shrugs toward the couch. "But he said—"

"Okay, well. I'm leaving."

"What? We just got here."

"You don't have to come with me. Stay with Ryan."

"I don't want to stay with Ryan. I want to stay with you." There's this fluid softness to Noah's voice I've never heard before. "Kate, don't leave. I'm sorry. I shouldn't have—oh man. Little Garfield. I shouldn't have had anything to drink. I made you uncomf—"

"Noah, you didn't make me uncomfortable, okay? You're fine. Drink whatever you want."

He takes my hand. "But you're leaving? Are you okay?"

"I'm fine! Noah, I'm fine. I just don't want to be here."

"Because of all the fuckboys, right?" Noah says. "Too many fuckboys."

He's smiling expectantly, and yeah, I get it. There's nothing my squad loves more than ranting about f-boys. We observe them and categorize them and quietly mock them, and we don't care what they think of us. Why would we care? The f-force is basic and awful and we don't play by their rules.

But it's all bullshit.

The realization hits me so suddenly and forcefully, I almost lose my breath.

I say I don't care what they think of me—and yet, their faces pop into my head every time I press post on Instagram. Every time I walk down the hallway at school.

Every time I sing.

Especially when I sing.

It's a reflex, seeing your dorky, cringey life through their eyes, picking it apart to try to anticipate where they'll cut you. It's like having a tiny Greek chorus of people who hate you. Except they never shut up, and they live in your brain.

*yikes lol*

*this is so embarrassing, I literally can't watch*

*I die a little*

The truth is, fuckboys terrify me. Mira Reynolds terrifies me. And I'm not strong enough to withstand it without Anderson.

"I know Mira's awful," Noah says, tilting his head. "But I just think of it as Madison's house, and Madison's a cinnamon sweetheart. A roll. A cinnamon roll. I mean, if you want to leave, we can leave, but I'm just saying. Madison's—"

"She's amazing. I know. Got it. You guys are friends."

"What? What's that supposed to mean?"

"What?"

"Friends. With air quotes."

"I didn't do air quotes."

"You did them with your voice."

"Noah." I squeeze my eyes shut. "It's nothing. Just—forget it. I have nothing against Madison, okay? I just want to go."

"Oh," says Noah, eyes softening. "Then we should go."

"I've been trying to make this point for the last five minutes."

"Come on." He grins. "I'll walk you."

"Pretty sure I'm the one walking your drunk butt home, but okay." I bite back a smile. "Should we tell my brother we're leaving?"

"He's fine," Noah says quickly. "Look at him. Look at our boy. Playing Fortnite. So happy. Come on." He tugs my hand. "Let's go."

# SCENE 64

Walking home with Tipsy Noah is an experience. He swears he only had four drinks, even though four doesn't feel very only to me. And he's clearly feeling every drop of them. It's not that he's staggering around or falling on his face or anything. He's kind of like Regular Noah, only more so. The main thing about Tipsy Noah is that he doesn't. Stop. Talking.

"I'm serious," he says, veering closer. "This fucker is a land fish. It can walk—"

"Absolutely not. Doesn't exist."

"It does exist, and it's a cursed demon hellspawn." He lights up. "Okay, marry, bury, or fuck? The snakehead fish—"

"Bury."

"Okay. A cockroach—"

"Also bury—"

"And the naked mole rat."

"Peaceful, platonic coexistence."

"Okay, I feel like you're stretching the rules a little bit, but

I'll allow it." Noah pauses. "Hey, speaking of naked mole rats, what's the deal with you and Matt Olsson?"

"Do I even want to know how you went from naked mole rats to Matt?"

"Because Matt rhymes with rat, and Olsson half rhymes with Mole. Anyway, I'm just asking," he says, "if you and Matt Olsson twins are bf-gf."

He actually says bf-gf. Not even the whole words.

"We're not bf-gf," I say flatly.

Noah's face lights up. "Has anyone ever told you about your initials?"

"I know my initials."

"Kate Eliza Garfield," he says. "Keg!"

"Very exciting."

"But," he says, leaning so close our arms are touching. "The ironic thing is, you don't drink. That's what's ironic. And iconic."

I just look at him, shaking my head slightly. I should be so annoyed right now. I mean, Noah's being objectively annoying. Those are just the facts. But I find him so weirdly charming, it's almost infuriating.

"I'm not really that drunk, Kate. Katypie. Hey, why do people keep calling you Katypie?" He turns toward me, wide-eyed. "Is it because you like pie?"

"Do you actually want to know?"

"Yes!" He turns to face me head-on, his face gleaming in

the lamplight. We're almost home, just a few houses away from our cul-de-sac.

"Okay, well. My mom's name is—"

"Maggie," he says. "Maggie Garfield. She never changed her last name back, did she? Why not? Is that weird of me to ask? Garfield's a good name, though. It reminds me of the cat."

"It reminds everyone of the cat. Do you want to hear this or not?"

"Yes! Yes, I'm ready." He frowns solemnly. "Go."

"You don't have to make that face. It's not a sad story."

He beams. "It's a happy story?"

"It's not even a story. It's just that people used to call my mom Magpie, so I made everyone call me Katypie. I was like five."

"So it's a cute story."

"If you say so."

"I say so." He smiles down at me. And then before I can entirely process what's happening, he reaches forward with his right hand, trailing his fingertips along my cheekbone.

Like a Disney movie. Like Rapunzel.

His fingertips fall still, and he stares at me, smile faltering. It's wild. He doesn't look like Drunk Noah the fuckboy. He looks like an earnest-eyed geek with his heart on his sleeve.

"Hey, Kate?" he says softly, and my cheek burns hot beneath his fingers. I open my mouth to reply, but I think my lungs have stopped working.

He smiles slightly. "I'm really glad we're friends again."

Friends. He's standing here cupping my cheek, but we're friends. Then again, friend was his word to describe Madison Reynolds, and that was definitely more than fingertips on cheekbones. So maybe that's just how Noah operates. Maybe it's how f-boys operate in general. A little bit of eyegasm and some calculated face touching, and suddenly you're expressing your friendship all over Sean Sanders's refrigerator.

I take a step back, and Noah's face falls. He pulls his hand back, letting it drop to his side.

"Sorry." He swallows. "Kate—"

"You're good. We're good." For a minute, I just stand there with my arms crossed while my heart dials slowly back down to normal.

"Kate. I'm so sorry."

My mind's spinning. He's got this wide-open, purely smitten, totally un-Noah look on his face. But who am I to say he's smitten? It's not like you can actually know how a person's feeling just from their face. Because for one thing, they could always be acting. And acting itself is kind of bullshit. It all comes back to the idea that certain gestures show certain feelings. Ms. Zhao's always saying how the emotion of the scene should be readily apparent, even without dialogue. But it's all a fucking joke. It's a bunch of stupid associations we make because we've always made them, and because everyone else makes them.

I mean, just the idea that you could read on someone's face that they're in love with you? That's ridiculous. In real life, we're a bunch of fucking messes who have no idea what our own faces are telegraphing, much less anyone else's. I could stand here right now and convince myself Noah's in love with me. And then, watch, he'll turn around and announce he's been dating Madison for a month.

Not to mention—

"And what about Mira?" I blurt.

Noah's brow furrows. "Mira? What do you mean?"

"You want to be friends again? Why'd you bring me to Mira's house, Noah?"

"Kate, seriously. I wasn't thinking—"

"And then you tried to pressure me to sing in front of her? After what she did?"

He looks down at his feet, before meeting my eyes again. "You mean the variety show thing?"

"The variety show thing." I laugh flatly. "You mean, when she posted a video to mock me? And then took screenshots and made a whole new account just to mock me even more?"

"Kate. I'm sorry. I'm so sorry. I wasn't thinking—"

"Whatever. It was a long time ago." My throat goes tight, and I start walking again, quickly. I feel—God. I feel so stupid already.

He rushes to catch up. "Wait—"

"Forget I said anything."

"It's not fine." He rakes his hand through his hair. "Kate, I swear. I swear to God, I wasn't—"

"Just stop! Okay?" I try to swallow, and it hurts. "I get it.

315

You were just drunk and trying to be funny."

"Kate—"

"Can we just stop talking? Please?"

He snaps his mouth shut and nods.

And all the rest of the way home, there's this silence, hanging like a force field between us. Noah lingers for a moment when we reach my door, and it strikes me all over again how uncertain he looks. He's half hugging himself, right arm crossing his body to his shoulder.

"So I guess I'll see you at rehearsal tomorrow?" He glances down at me nervously. "Sorry I made things weird—"

"No, I'm—"

"Seriously, I'm so fucking sorry."

"Okay."

"Okay." He bites his lip. "I'm . . . gonna go." He takes a few steps back, toward the cul-de-sac.

A part of me wants to watch him go, just to fully absorb this weirdly off-brand, off-his-game version of Noah. But even more than that, I want to lock myself in my room and forget this whole week ever happened.

# SCENE 65

By the time I wander downstairs in my sweatpants, Dad's already camped out at the kitchen table, sipping coffee and reading his iPad. "Hiya, Peapod. How was the party?"

"Fine," I say. "Ish."

"Fine-ish?" Dad says.

"Yup."

"Well, your brother got in late," Dad adds, obviously grasping around to keep the conversational ball in the air. He can be cringey like that when it comes to human interaction. When you meet my dad, you no longer have to wonder what all the nervous, chatty boys you know from Hebrew school will be like when they're older. "Sounds like it was a real rager."

"It was mostly just people playing video games."

I join him at the table with a bowl of dry Honey Nut Cheerios, watching a whole stream of apologetic Noah texts come in. He seems convinced I'm mad at him. Luckily, Dad's already sucked back into his iPad and therefore not asking me more questions about the party. Or why I keep rereading the same texts over and over without replying to them. Not because I'm trying to make a statement or anything by not replying. I just need to come up with something appropriately casual, because this is a deeply casual texting situation. One that happens to be occurring at eight a.m. on a Saturday morning.

How are you even awake? I write finally.

He writes back immediately: Sleep is for the week.

Then, a moment later: WEAK. It's for the weak. Followed by a whole stream of face-palm emojis. Maybe I should get more sleep or something???

Better hurry, rehearsal starts in two hours. I add a snoring emoji, press send, and retreat to my room for some quality guitar time. But the minute my fingers touch the frets, there's a knock. Then the door creaks open, revealing a sleepy, bed-headed Ryan. "Hey." He yawns.

"You're up early."

"So are you. You have fun last night?" He settles onto the edge of my bed, rubbing his eyes. "Wish you'd told me you were leaving."

I press my fingertips hard against the frets, without strumming. "You seemed like you were fine."

"I was. I just didn't know where you were. You know I would have walked you home, right?"

"It's fine. I had Noah."

"I know." Ryan pauses. "He's kind of freaking out about it. You guys okay?"

"What? Of course." My face goes warm.

"He feels so shitty about bringing you to Mira's house. I don't think he made the connection. I didn't either, and I should have. I'm sorry—"

"No, seriously, you're fine. You didn't do anything wrong. I'm the one who needs to learn how to stop obsessing over drama from eighth grade. I'm sure Mira's super nice now. I know she's your friend—"

"She's not my friend." Ryan shakes his head slowly. "You think I'd be friends with Mira Reynolds after what she did to you?"

"Ryan, we were at her house. I watched her hug you."

"She hugged you, too. She was just drunk. Trust me, we're not friends."

"You don't have to boycott Mira Reynolds for me. Just don't, like, start dating her or anything."

"Not a problem." Ryan yawns. "You know, she's not exactly my biggest fan either. I kind of . . . lost my shit at her after the variety show thing. And Eric."

I almost drop my guitar. "Wait, you fought them?"

"No. God. No. I don't fight little kids—"

"They're one year younger than you."

"They were in middle school. And come on. I don't fight people. I just . . . sent a few strongly worded DMs."

"Wait, really?" He nods, and I just stare at him, flabbergasted. "Did they write back?"

"Well, Mira blocked me."

"No she did *not*." I set my guitar down. "Are you serious?"

"I'm still blocked." He rubs his neck. "And I guess Eric kind of came after me."

"What do you mean, came after you?"

"I mean." He leans back on his hands. "I'll tell you, but you have to promise you won't tell Mom."

"Promise."

Ryan glances up at my door, like he's worried Mom might just happen to be hanging out at Dad's house for the first time in four years. "Okay, remember that neck thing I had for a while in ninth grade?"

"The one Mom thought was a hickey?"

"Wasn't a hickey."

I smile slightly. "And it wasn't a curling wand injury?"

"Um. What?" Ryan looks at me like I'm speaking Martian. "No, it wasn't a curling wand injury. Is that a thing?"

"You'd be surprised." I nod soberly. "So what was it?"

Ryan bites his lip. "Seriously, you can't tell Mom—"

"I won't. I promise. I double promise."

Ryan takes a deep breath. "Okay, so. Eric Graves shot me—"

"WHAT?"

"—with a paintball. Kate, chill. A paintball."

"In the neck?" I cover my throat. "Is that allowed? That can't be allowed!"

"It's not."

"I'm just." I blink. "When were you playing paintball?"

"I crashed the eighth-grade trip—"

"What? Aren't there chaperones? And the coaches? Ryan, those were Mom's coworkers—"

"My whole face was covered. You have to wear this helmet thing—"

"So you just showed up with a blatant paintball bruise the day after the eighth-grade paintball trip, which Mom obviously knows about—"

Ryan nods. "Yup."

"Nope. There's no way Mom wouldn't have put that together. I don't buy it—"

"I know. I couldn't believe it. But I guess she was distracted."

"Distracted?"

Ryan looks at me. "Do you even remember that week?"

"The variety show?"

"Kate, you couldn't stop crying. It was brutal. And Mom's there thinking it's all her fault for talking you into it, and you wouldn't even talk to her. And then you dyed your hair that toilet bowl color. I mean, you were a wreck, she was a wreck . . . so I took advantage of you being wrecks."

"I mean, it's not like you knew Eric was going to shoot you." I exhale. "God, Ryan. Eric shot you! Because of me!"

"No. Kate. Not because of you. Because he's an asshole." Ryan straightens up and slides off the bed. "Anyway, you good here? I'm going back to bed—"

"Wait!"

He turns to me, yawning, his eyebrows raised. "Yup?"

"So. Um." I rub my cheek. "I'm not really on speaking terms with Andy right now."

Ryan winces. "Oh! Okay. Wow. Are you—"

"I don't want to talk about it," I say quickly. "But I have one of those Saturday rehearsals today. So . . ."

"Let me guess. You need a ride."

I shoot him my best pleading smile.

# SCENE 66

Half an hour later, we're parked in Noah's driveway, waiting for King Sextimus the Slowpoke to finish brushing his teeth.

I check the dashboard clock, glancing back up at Noah's window. "What's taking him so long?"

"I mean. He's in a cast—"

"Nope. Brushing your teeth isn't a two-handed job."

Ryan shrugs. "I'm just telling you what he said."

I bite my lip, feeling instantly guilty. Because Ryan's a saint to drive me to rehearsal, and the last thing he deserves is me being a grouchy little butt. "Seriously, thanks again for driving us," I say.

He yawns. "Don't worry about it. It's fine."

"You know . . ." I turn to face him, an idea dawning. "If you want, you could come hang out at rehearsal."

"Um. I'm good."

"I'm just saying. Brandie will be there."

"Okay . . ." Ryan's phone buzzes in the cupholder, and he grabs it. "All right, Noah says he'll be down in—"

"Also, Brandie's a Capricorn," I inform him.

Ryan looks slightly bewildered.

"For real! Her birthday's on Christmas, which sucks, because she gets half the amount of presents, and someone always forgets—I mean, not me, obviously. Not the Jews. We remember." I thump my chest. "But I think it all evens out, because her two-in-one presents are so epic. Like, multiple American Girl dolls. Okay, not multiple per year—"

"I'm . . . not sure where you're going with this," says Ryan.

"Where I'm going with this is that Brandie's a Capricorn and you're a Virgo, which is perfect!" I give a chef's kiss.

"I truly have no idea—"

"I'm just saying, I approve of this crush. And I can actually help you with this. I'll be your wingwoman."

"You think I have a crush on Brandie?"

I look at him. "Come on. Why else would you be suddenly up for hanging out with me all the time?"

"So let me get this straight. You think the only reason I could possibly want to spend time with you is to get with Brandie."

I tilt my palms up. "Literally what else could it be?"

The back door behind me yanks open, and I whip my head around, startled.

"Hi!" Noah grins back at me, scooting across the seat to Ryan's side. "Sorry I'm late."

I stare at his face. There's something strange about the skin below his eyes. "Are you . . . wearing makeup?"

"There's nothing wrong with guys wearing makeup," Noah says loftily.

"Agreed. It's just . . ." I bite back a laugh. "Normally, people try to match their skin tone a little bit?"

"It matches!" He leans forward, checking himself out in the rearview mirror.

"Mmm." I shut one eye.

"It's a little . . . pale," says Ryan.

I nod. "You look like a reverse racoon."

"Oh, well, excuse me for trying to look a little more awake." He pokes at his undereye. "I think it looks good."

"Great. You do you."

He pauses. "Okay, if you happen to have—"

"Here you go." I pass him a makeup wipe.

Ryan turns the car on, but then he looks at me. "You want to drive?"

I side-eye him. "Uh. What?"

"Do you want to drive? I'll sit in the passenger seat." He shrugs. "You should practice."

"You have to be twenty-one to drive with me."

"Kind of like how I'm supposed to be twenty-one to drink?"

"Boom," chimes Noah from the back seat. He pantomimes a mic drop with his makeup wipe.

"Ryan, no—I'm not getting arrested less than a week before opening night."

"We're not going to get arrested. Come on. We can run back home for your permit."

"You think my permit's going to help when they arrest us? Or when I crash your car? Are you crazy?"

"Kate, you've taken Driver's Ed. You're not a bad driver. You just need practice. I'm telling you, you could have your license—"

"Okay!" says Noah, poking around his eyes again in the rearview mirror. "How'd I do?"

Ryan looks up at the mirror and shoots him a thumbs-up. "All clear."

"And I promise I'll get my license, okay? I'm just busy."

"You've been busy since March."

"Ryan. The play opens Friday. It's literally tech week."

"Okay. But it ends on, what, Sunday? Then what?"

"The cast party," says Noah. "No fuckboys allowed."

"Okay, that's accurate." I turn back to Ryan. "So what, you're sick of driving me around or something?"

"No." Ryan shoots me an eye-rolling half smile. "I just need to know you'll be able to get around next year."

He checks the mirrors and starts reversing slowly, and weirdly, I find myself taking mental notes of where he's looking, where his hands are. Backing out of places is my least favorite part of driving, but Ryan makes it look effortless.

Maybe it will be effortless for me one day, too.

# SCENE 67

"All right. You know the drill," says Ms. Zhao. "The whole thing, twice. Start to finish. First run-through, I may stop you with notes. Second time, you're on your own. And tech week starts tomorrow." A few people groan. "I know. I know. But we're going to suck it up and whip this monster into shape. Who's with me?"

"Me!" yells Mr. D from the piano. He starts playing football fight music, because, you know. We're all big sports fans here. I catch Noah's eye and quickly look away, grinning.

"We've got costumes hung up in the dressing rooms in alphabetical order. You'll find a tag on the hanger with your name on it. If you'd like extra practice in your costume, go ahead and wear it. But please—please—put it back on your own hanger, in the exact spot you found it. And do not, I repeat, do not eat in your costume." Ms. Zhao exhales. "How are we feeling?"

"We're feeling great," says Emma, looking around the circle fiercely.

"Then bring it in," says Ms. Zhao, and we all scoot into a huddle. "One, two, three . . . WE ARE ROSWELL HILL, AND WE ARE ONE."

"Woo-hoo!" Lindsay Ward does a cheerleading kick, landing with her hands on her hips. "Go team! Go us!"

Luckily, Anderson's in practically every scene—and even when he's backstage, he's usually blocked to enter from stage left. So he spends most of his backstage time on a completely different side of the stage from me. Kind of a lucky break.

Of course, Matt's a different story. I honestly can't believe this is my life. My love interest in the musical is my real-life unrequited crush. Who's now dating my best friend.

Though, now that the shock has worn off, I think I'm fine with Matt not liking me. I mean, he's gay—it's not even personal. It's just another Éponine situation, right? He was never mine to lose.

I'm even warming up to the idea of Matt and Anderson dating. But the thought of Matt knowing I liked him—I can't shake that. I can't stop thinking about how it all must look to Matt. My sad, misdirected thirst. I hate being pitied. It makes me feel like such a loser. When someone feels sorry for you, you can't help but become that sorry person, at least a little bit.

It's enough to make a person want to lock herself inside a dressing room forever.

To be fair, the dressing rooms are party central. I always forget how much I love these backstage moments. Someone took the gender signs off the doors years ago, and we use both rooms interchangeably. There are tiny bathroom stalls for when you're actually changing, but for the most part, people just lounge around in folding chairs and eat pretzels and listen to the Official *Once Upon a Mattress* Playlist, curated by Lana Bennett. Admittedly, full of bops.

There's just something to be said for the fact that I'm sitting in a circle, smack-dab between Margaret Daskin and Emma McLeod, whom I suddenly trust with my life, even though I never really hang out with them outside of theater. It's this strange way of knowing someone. I never think of it as true friendship, because how could it be if we don't know each other's secrets. But when you can sit in a room with someone and feel totally at home, what else would you call it?

Devon Blackwell appears in the doorway with his binder. "Okay, Minstrel's starting the prologue. We need Aggravain, Sextimus, Dauntless, Wizard, Lady Larken, Lady Rowena, Lady Merrill, Lady Lucille, Princess Number Twelve, and"— he turns the page—"any other knights and ladies for Act One, Scene One. In the wings, please."

"Raina, Noah, and Anderson are already in the wings, stage left," Emma says, rotating her wheelchair toward the door. "But Colin and Pierra are, uh. In the lighting booth."

"Of course they are." Devon double blinks, shaking his head slowly.

# SCENE 68

"Zhao's going to quit," I murmur to Raina and Brandie two and a half hours later, as we settle onto the various platforms and set pieces for our first round of notes. "She's gonna be like, nope, y'all are hot messes, and I'm out."

"You say that every single show," Brandie says.

"I know, but this is going to be the one. I can feel it." I scoot back against the stack of mattresses, tucking my legs up into triangles. "See, it's because we lost a Saturday rehearsal because of Rosh Hashanah. So now everyone's going to blame us Jews if this sucks."

"No one's blaming anyone," Brandie says, scooting up beside me—and then she sniffs the air suddenly. "Hey, pizza's here."

"Which means Zhao needs to hurry up and give us notes. I'm hungry," says Raina.

"And, Kate, it's not going to suck," Brandie says. "This happens every time, remember? We run through it, it's rough, we keep going, it gets better, and by opening night, it's great. Every time, Kate."

"I just want to fast-forward," I say. "Let's just skip to the part where it's great."

"She's just hangry," Raina tells Brandie. "Watch. She'll have one slice of pizza, and she'll be a brand-new person."

"Shut up." I shove Raina's arm.

"Am I wrong?"

I sigh heavily. "You're not wrong."

Pizza's forbidden onstage near the set pieces, so we all trickle out into the auditorium seats and the lobby. Anderson and Matt disappear pretty much immediately, which doesn't hurt anywhere near as much as I thought it would. Maybe one quick pang, but mostly relief that I can just settle in with Brandie and Raina and Colin and Pierra and whoever, and not worry about avoiding them.

But I've barely had time to grab my pizza and a water bottle when Noah materializes beside me. "Hey, want to eat outside?"

I nod. "Should I grab Raina and Brandie?"

"Oh." He presses his lips together. "I was thinking just us."

"Oh."

"Is that . . ."

"Okay." There's this pinprick feeling, just below my rib cage. "Yeah, that's fine."

"Okay, great," he says, smiling, and the next thing I know, I'm cutting through a row of seats behind him, out through the side door of the auditorium. It feels strangely rebellious, stepping out here in the middle of rehearsal even though we're on break until two thirty. Noah stakes out a spot around the back of the auditorium, and we settle in for a curb picnic. He sets his pizza on the ground beside him and leans back against the school's brick exterior. "This is perfect."

"Better than the lobby," I agree. "Hey, you were great this morning."

He looks both startled and pleased. "Me?"

"I don't think I've seen you guys do 'Man to Man Talk' since the read-through. Y'all are hilarious."

"Well, so were you."

I laugh. "I don't think my character's supposed to be hilarious."

"It just makes it even more impressive."

"I don't know if that's how it works." I shake my head, smiling.

"Well, you were really good. Matt too. Are you sure you're not dating him?"

"Ha ha."

"You're not bf-gf?" Noah glances at me sidelong, and for one stomach-plummeting moment, I'm sure he knows the whole story. Maybe Andy and Matt really did spill the beans in Senior D. But then again, something about the way Noah's looking at me makes me think he's really asking. It's as if he's trying to read between the lines of my expression.

"We're not bf-gf. I already told you that."

"On our walk home," he says, nodding. "Hey."

I turn to face him, head-on, but he doesn't elaborate. "Hey what?" I ask finally.

He nods, opens his mouth, shuts it, grins nervously, and then shuts it again, and I almost laugh from the pure Noah-ness of the sequence. But something stops me. Maybe it's the strange flicker of uncertainty in his eyes. Or maybe it's the way my own heart won't stop pounding. "Hey. Okay," he says finally. "I owe you an apology. A couple of apologies."

"For what?"

He looks like he's not sure if I'm kidding. "For last night. For bringing you to Mira's house. For drinking and being weird."

"Noah, you already apologized like twenty times. And you're fine! I'm not—"

"I know, I know. You're not mad. But I still feel really gross about it. I feel like I'm giving you the wrong idea about me—"

"You know I've known you since we were eleven, right?"

"I know, but you think I'm a fuckboy."

I bite back a laugh. "Okay. So . . ."

"So I'm mad at myself for proving you right."

He looks so serious about it that I have to hug him. "Noah, you're not that kind of f-boy."

"What do you mean that kind of f-boy?"

"You're not a jerk. You're barely a dudebro. You're not even that slutty—"

He snorts. "Thanks."

"I mean it." I nudge him sideways with my shoulder. "After all, I've only actually seen you sloppily make out with one girl—"

"Okay, just so you know, that started out as a dare. Madison and I are friends. It's totally, totally not like that."

"It's fine—"

"Also, I'm a way better kisser than that. Way better. That was not representative."

"I don't know. Maybe I should ask Camilla—"

"Kate, I'm serious."

"Noah." I tilt my palms up. "I don't care, okay? You can kiss whoever you want, however you want."

"I wish you did care," Noah says.

My breath hitches. "What?"

"I don't know." He shakes his head. "I'm not saying—okay. I want to tell you something, but I don't want you to think I'm, like, a total dumbass—"

"I'm not going to think that," I say.

God, my heart is just—not keeping its cool right now. Not even a little bit. It's beating ten miles a minute, and Noah keeps inhaling but not speaking, and I swear I'm not—

"I broke my wrist during training," Noah says finally. He's staring at his feet. "But I didn't break it playing baseball. It was the dumbest thing."

He pauses, but I don't speak. I have this sudden feeling that I'll shatter the moment somehow if I move or breathe or anything.

Finally, Noah continues. "We were spending the weekend at this campground place. Kind of like an ensemble building exercise." He grins, eyes flicking toward me like he wants to make sure I didn't miss him whipping out the theater terminology. I grin back.

"Anyway, Jack and a couple of the guys met these girls staying at this other campsite, and so they made this whole plan, where we were all going to sneak out after curfew and meet up in the woods outside the campground. Just drink and hang out. And it actually worked. Coach Franklin went to bed early, and Jack was texting with this one girl, and finally we all crept out super quietly. And it was totally pitch-black out. This was like way, way outside of Atlanta. I don't know if Ryan's ever told you about this place. He hates it. It's crawling with insects."

I bite back a smile.

"Anyway, it's like twelve of us, and we're really deep in the forest, and then I just—freaked out." He pauses, taking a deep breath. "It wasn't even the curfew thing or getting into trouble or being in the woods with bears—"

I gasp. "There were bears?"

"I don't know," Noah says. "I kind of wish there were, because then I could just be like, yeah, I broke my arm running from a giant fucking bear. But no—I was just, like, overwhelmed. It was just the whole situation and the random girls and thinking, what am I even going to talk to these girls about, and not knowing if it was supposed to be like a hookup thing or a chill thing, or what. And anyway, we were basically all the way at the meeting point, but I just, like, bolted."

"Which is when the bear started chasing you."

"Right." He smiles. "Then the bear—ha ha. Anyway, I

tripped over a root and landed like this." He demonstrates on his cast-free arm, pressing his hand flat on the concrete. "So yeah. I broke my wrist running away from hot girls. Voilà."

I grin into my fist. "Oh, Noah."

"I know." He exhales. "So here's the thing, and I'm just going to say it. And it kind of ties back to last night." He shuts his eyes. "I don't really tell people this, but I'm kind of . . . not good in social situations? I just get really weird and overwhelmed and I don't feel that comfortable, which is why I drink sometimes. And I know that's bad—"

"It's not bad."

He smiles slightly but doesn't speak.

"It's not, like, necessarily healthy, but it doesn't make you a bad person. It just sounds like social anxiety. Also, anyone would be overwhelmed by that party. A bunch of hot girls and bears in the middle of the woods?"

"Good point."

"And don't even get me started on whether the bears were wearing pants."

He nods soberly. "They weren't."

"Didn't think so. Pervs."

Noah laughs. "So you think I have social anxiety, huh?"

"It's not a bad thing." I shrug. "I think I'm like that, too."

"But I don't see you drinking and making an ass of yourself."

"Yeah, because I'm not a fuckgirl," I say, and he bursts out laughing. "But seriously, why do you think I do theater?"

"Because you suck at sports?"

"Shut up." I swat him, smiling. "Because I like having a script. I like being told where to stand and what to do with my hands. Like—I don't know. I would have run from those girls, too. Because it's the ambiguousness of it, right? No one gives you lines. No one even tells you what show you're in." I sigh. "Theater's so much better than real life."

"Theater is pretty great," he says. And then he looks at me so intently, I feel like I've swallowed a sunburst.

"Anyway, now you know why I was acting like a drunk fuckboy last night."

"It's okay. Seriously."

"I just don't like that I was so focused on making myself feel comfortable that I made you uncomfortable. Like. That's not cool." He shakes his head. "I need to learn how to be cool around you."

I bite back a smile. "Please don't be cool around me."

"Deal." His eyes catch mine. And suddenly our faces are inches apart.

It feels like stepping onto a stage. It feels like every cell in my body waking up all at once. He leans forward.

"Kate? Hello? Noah?"

Noah jolts up straight, eyes huge, shooting me a quick, awkward smile.

"Guys, it's 2:28. Where are you?" Devon Blackwell's voice carries faintly from around the corner.

"Hey! Sorry." I jump up, scrambling to collect our pizza

plates and bottles. "We're right here. We're ready. I'm so sorry." I speed walk back around the perimeter of the school, Noah drifting behind me. When I glance back, he looks like he's about to burst out laughing.

I try to glare at him, but it's hopeless.

For the rest of the afternoon, every time I look at him, I get goose bumps.

# SCENE 69

Naturally, Ryan's ignoring my texts. Which is great. Because Brandie's riding with Raina, and Raina's only allowed to drive one person. And it's not like I can call Mom, because she'll want to know why I'm not just riding home with Matt and Anderson.

Looks like I'm riding home with Matt and Anderson.

We all leave through the auditorium side door, so Ms. Zhao and Mr. D can lock up behind us, and I end up falling into step beside Noah. I smile up at him. "So."

"So." He flicks his cast. "Guess how much I hate not being allowed to drive right now." His voice is light, but there's this glint in his eyes, and I feel achy and warm all the way to my toes.

I mean. That was real, right? Noah Kaplan almost kissed me, right there. Right outside the auditorium. Completely unscripted.

"I guess I'll see you Monday?"

"Kate?" Matt appears behind me, lifting his key ring. "You ready?"

"Yes! Sorry." I shoot a quick smile at Noah.

He does a tiny salute with his cast-free hand and then trails off toward the carpool circle.

And now I can't stop thinking about the fact that I'd probably be kissing Noah Kaplan this very minute if I had my license right now.

I mean. I'm sixteen years old, I have access to a car, and I've already taken Driver's Ed. There's literally no reason for me not to have my license. This isn't a glitch or bad luck or sucky timing. This is me choosing to rely on my friends for rides. Or my brother. Or my parents. And something tells me none of them are dying to deliver me to Noah's house so we can make out in his bedroom.

I've said it a million times: I have no game. I'm my own cockblock. But, like, it's an actual measurable fact now. I myself am the reason I am not kissing Noah Kaplan on this fine September afternoon.

Instead, I'm third-wheeling it with Andy and Matt. It's especially great, seeing as Andy and I haven't spoken since our super-fun talk in the bathroom on Thursday. Which—I'm startled to realize—was only two days ago. It feels like centuries. I think it's the longest Andy and I have ever gone without speaking since we met.

As for Matt, I'm just too mortified to even look at him.

I stay a foot or two behind the boys all the way across the

parking lot and slip straight into the back seat, before Andy can even think of offering me shotgun. And for the first minute or two of the drive, it's total silence.

"Thanks for the ride," I say finally.

"No problem." Matt shoots me a smile in the rearview mirror. "What are you up to the rest of today?"

"Probably homework," I say.

Or, you know. Sitting in my room, replaying every single second of the forty-five minutes I spent outside with Noah. Especially the moment there at the end where I swear—I swear—he would have kissed me if Devon hadn't shown up.

Except it's not the almost-kiss I keep circling back to. And it's not the closeness or his electric-bright eyes or even his laugh—which just might be my favorite song on earth.

It's the conversation.

I just keep thinking about the secret anxious Noah—the one who gets overwhelmed by human interaction but goes to parties anyway. The one who literally breaks bones running away from ambiguous social situations. I think I might be the only person in the whole world who knows that Noah.

I kind of can't wait to know more.

"—if you want," Matt's saying, and I look up with a start to find him glancing back at me again in the mirror.

I blush. "Sorry, will you say that one more time? I was just . . ."

"Sure, I was just saying Andy and I were gonna watch *Anastasia* back at his place. You should come."

"Oh. Uh. I'm sorry. I don't think that's . . ." But I catch a glimpse of Matt's wrinkled brow and quickly change course. "I have a lot of algebra to catch up on."

"Okay," he says quietly.

Andy shifts in his seat, directly in front of me. He hasn't said a word this whole trip, and of course I'm sitting in the one spot where I can't see his face.

I feel this pang of missing him, so sharp I almost lose my breath. Two days of not speaking. I was smart to avoid him. Sitting this close to him is practically unbearable.

It feels like standing on the doorstep without a key to your own home.

# SCENE 70

Matt stays at Anderson's house until well after dinner, which is more than fine by me. It just makes it that much easier to avoid him. Of course, he clearly knows I'm avoiding him, which I feel a little sick about. He hasn't really been pushing the issue, though.

Until tonight. When he knocks on my door.

For a second, I consider waiting him out. Pretending I went to bed early or something. I'm sure he sees the lights on under my door, but maybe I could pretend I fell asleep doing algebra homework. But I can't bring myself to lie, at least not so directly. "What's up?" I ask softly. Probably too softly. Probably he won't even hear me through the door. Probably—

"Hey!" Matt cracks the door open. "Can I come in?"

"Sure. Everything okay?"

"I'm okay," he says quickly, stepping inside. He shuts the door carefully behind him. "Are you okay?"

I scoot back against the headboard of my bed, lips twitching into a smile. Matt's just such a world-class bean. He's so fundamentally nice. And listen. I may be unbearably clueless and an all-around hopeless case of a girl, but at least I didn't fall for someone terrible. I have excellent taste in guys I can't have.

Matt plops right down beside me. "Can we talk?"

"Sure." I feel strange and unsteady. Mom and Ellen are already in their respective rooms, and I don't even know where Ryan is. So we really are very much alone together, for the first time since Bruster's.

"So," Matt says, leaning back on his hands.

"I know you think I'm avoiding you because you're gay," I say quickly.

"Wait, what?" He sits back up, peering at my face. "Why would I think that?"

"I mean. I've been a shitty friend, and I haven't been there for you at all, and—"

"No, no, no, no, no." He shakes his head firmly. "Nope. Don't you dare steal my apology moment."

"What could you possibly have to apologize for?"

"Because." He blushes. "Kate, I'm so sorry. I know Andy told you about—"

My heart leaps into my throat. "You don't have to apologize for that."

"I know, but I feel bad. I do."

"No. Matt!" I'm so panicked, I can't even think straight. My brain feels fuzzy and my stomach won't stop flipping and I swear, I don't know how people do this. How do people admit this kind of thing and say it out loud and have it not be a big deal? Someone knowing you like them. Or even liked them. I can't make it not a big deal. "Matt, you can't—"

"I feel awful, Kate. That ride home today? You and Andy mean everything to each other." He sniffs—so quietly, I barely even hear it.

I swallow, trying desperately not to cry. "Matt, I don't even know what you think you did wrong. I'm happy for you guys. I am."

And it's funny. In this heartbeat of a moment, I really am. I'm so happy for them, I'm almost speechless. Andy's first real kiss, and it's with a boy he's crazy about. With a boy who actually deserves him. And I get to be here to see it happen. I get to watch my best friend fall in love.

Suddenly, I'm crying.

Matt grabs my hand. "Kate—"

"You know I'm not mad, right?"

"I know," Matt says, with that bright smile he does when he's sad. "But I get it. It's new territory for you guys. Andy told me this is the first time there's ever been a guy in the picture for either of you." He blushes suddenly, like he's worried he said too much. "I don't mean—"

I wipe my eyes, laughing. "It's okay. I have no game. You can say it."

"Okay, that's totally not what I mean." His laugh joins mine, just for a moment—but then his voice grows soft and serious. "All I'm saying is that I know it's different. I know it's always been the two of you, and now I'm here, and it's this whole new kind of competition for his time and attention and—I don't know, I'm not saying this right. I just want to make sure you know that I never, ever want to come between you guys."

"No, I know," I say slowly. And a thought starts edging into my brain. But I can't quite catch it. "And you aren't! I'm the one who's been—"

"Nope. No taking blame. I just wanted to put that out there. You're Anderson's best friend, and I completely respect that. I never want to usurp that."

"Usurp." I smile. "SAT word?"

"SAT word."

Then it hits me.

This conversation isn't about my crush on Matt.

I replay the whole thing in my head, heart pounding. New territory. Competition for time and attention. Not wanting to come between us.

Holy shit.

Matt doesn't know I had a crush on him.

Which means Anderson kept my secret. Here I was yelling at him in the bathroom and ignoring his texts and calling him a shitty friend, but still. He hid that entire piece of himself from Matt, just to keep from embarrassing me.

And I punished him anyway.

# SCENE 71

Now I'm desperate to talk to Anderson. It's all I can think about. But the chances of me getting him alone during tech week are hovering somewhere between Nope and Not Happening.

Monday's cue-to-cue lasts until eight, and except for when we're onstage, Andy and I barely even see each other. Even after we finish, Andy's stuck staying an extra hour to troubleshoot "Song of Love." I honestly think we'd have a better shot at a private conversation in the middle of history class.

Maybe we should leave campus.

I've never done that. Not being able to drive does tend to interfere with that school-skipping lifestyle. But f-boys do it constantly. I mean, on any given day, at least two or three f-boy desks are empty. Even Noah's absent from history class on Tuesday, though I happen to know he's not living the lifestyle. Not today.

Here's the thing. If I'm going to skip class, today's the day for it. Mr. Edelman's lecturing on the Founding Fathers, and

God knows we have that info locked down. I keep glancing sideways at Anderson to see if he's thinking the same *Hamilton* thoughts that I am. And sure enough, there he is, barely suppressing a smile. Dimples and all. And even though his eyes are glued to his notes, I think he knows I'm watching him.

But I can't quite work up the nerve to poke him or pass a note or whisper his name. Which is crazy. This is Anderson. Not a crush. But there's this awkwardness that comes with knowing I messed up. It makes me shy. And it makes every interaction feel wrong. Every move feels so loaded—too obnoxiously casual, too cringingly formal.

I can't wimp out, though. Not anymore. And I've got to go big.

Mr. Edelman's eyes drift back down to his lecture notes, and I stop thinking.

I just go for it.

I heave my whole body sideways, tipping my desk closer and closer toward Anderson's, until it crashes down into the aisle between us. And for a minute, I sit there, startled. Yeah, okay, it was premeditated, but I didn't actually think I'd go through with it. I can't even do a trust fall. And now everyone in the whole class is looking at me.

I wonder if this is what it's like to be Noah.

Raina gasps. "Holy fuck." Brandie leaps out of her seat to help me up.

"Guys, can we please be more careful? Please?" asks Mr. Edelman, rubbing his chin wearily. "Kate, are you okay?"

348

"Absolutely," I say quickly. "Totally fine. Can I go to the infirmary?"

Lana Bennett eyes me suspiciously from across the room. "You just said you're totally fine."

"I am. Totally fine. But you never know, right? Internal bleeding and stuff?" I pick my desk back up and slide it into its place. "I think I better get checked out, just to be on the safe side."

Mr. Edelman sighs. "I'll write you a hall pass."

"Thanks! Would you mind writing one for Anderson, too? I might need some help."

I can practically feel Anderson's surprised gaze, but I force myself to stare straight ahead. Mr. Edelman closes his eyes briefly. "Why not? Anything else? Should we call an ambulance?"

"Hey," says Jack Randall, "how about a whaaaaaaaaaambulance—"

Raina kicks his chair leg. "Shut up."

"You okay?" Brandie whispers, brows knitted.

"I'll text you," I mouth.

"Okay, here you go. Hall passes for Kate and Anderson."

I jump up—and then catch myself, forcing a wince, like I stepped on my ankle wrong. It's such obvious bullshit—at least I think it's obvious—but maybe I'm a better actress than I thought. Because Anderson hooks his arm around my waist and says, "Try not to put weight on it."

I smile up at him. "Got it."

"Why are you making that face?" he asks.

"I'll tell you in juuuuuuust a second."

He side-eyes me. "I'm intrigued."

We make slow progress out of Mr. Edelman's room, but the minute we're out of sight distance, I wriggle out of Anderson's arm. "Okay, you know I'm totally fine, right?"

"I was getting there." He raises his eyebrows. "What's up?"

"I had to break us out of there."

Anderson looks like he's trying not to smile. "It's Mr. Edelman. You can just leave."

"I know," I say. "But I wanted you to come with me."

"To the BTF?"

"No." I shake my head. "I just—I want to talk where I can see your face."

"It's a good face."

I push him lightly, and then clutch my arm, yelping, "Ouch!"

Anderson's eyes get huge. "Oh shit. Are you actually hurt?"

"Just kidding." I smile. "Hey. Okay. Do you want to leave campus?"

"Leave campus? Wow, Garfield."

"I know, I know. But hear me out. What if we go to Target to grab party supplies—"

"Party supplies?"

"For your birthday, dummy." I grab his hand. "Come on, side door."

He shakes his head, smiling. "I'm not having a party."

"Excuse me?" I gape at him. "Why not?"

"Because it's the second night of the play. There's no way we'll even be home before eleven."

"It's your seventeenth birthday!"

"We'll celebrate at the cast party on Sunday."

"What? No. We're having a party. I don't care if we have to start at midnight. We'll live like f-boys. And we're going to Target." I pause by the door, peering around. "All clear."

Anderson slips through the side door behind me. "Why are you so dead set on us going to Target?"

"To get supplies," I remind him.

"Right now? During history? And this was worth knocking over a desk?"

I nod. "Yes. Because I'm about to apologize to you—like majorly apologize to you, before I totally wimp out." I exhale. "And I need to do that in the car."

Andy looks at me, opens his mouth, and then shuts it again. Then he smiles, just barely. "I thought you wanted us to talk in a place where we could look at each other's faces."

"Well, I want to be able to see your face so I can read your reaction," I say, following him through the parking lot, "but yeah, no—I don't want you to see my face. In case I start crying. So that means you're driving or I'm wearing a mask."

"Ooh, I liked that giant unicorn mask head we saw at—"

"Don't you dare. You shut up. I don't want to talk about that unicorn head."

For a minute, Andy just looks at me smiling, one hand on the hood of his car.

"It was alive," I remind him.

And it's only when we're tucked into our usual seats that it hits me: we haven't done this for ages. Just Andy and me in the car. My passenger seat. My little home. Andy doesn't say a word as we pull out of school, and at first I think he's worried we'll get caught. But even when we pull onto Hardscrabble Road, he's silent. It takes a minute before I realize he's waiting for me to speak.

It's like a spotlight blinking on. My heart flips, and then beats faster. I just need to spit it out. The apology I've been dancing around for days. I don't even know why I'm nervous. It's not like I have to beg for Anderson's forgiveness. He's clearly not mad at me. At least not anymore. I know exactly where he stands. But just because someone forgives you doesn't mean you don't have to apologize.

Okay, now. Right now. I'm just going to—

"I can't believe you aren't going to have a birthday party," I blurt.

Baby steps.

Andy laughs, but it's the kind of laugh that snags on itself. "I mean, I'd only be inviting you guys, and Brandie and Raina don't know my boyfriend is my boyfriend, so it's not like Matt and I really get to relax. And you." He pauses. "You were mad at me."

"I'm not mad at you." There's this tug in my chest. "So he really is your boyfriend. The official b-word."

"Yeah." Anderson smiles faintly.

I look at him. "Cool."

"Kate, it's fine. I get it. I really, really do—"

"No, it's fine. I promise." I squeeze my eyes shut. "Andy, I'm so sorry."

"Kate—"

"No, hear me out. I'm so sorry. I was awful to you. And you didn't do anything wrong. We had ground rules, and you followed them, and I'm the one who—"

"The ground rules were bullshit, though. Katy, you're right. You can't force yourself to be happy for someone. That's not how joy works." His voice cracks. "That's not how anything works. But it just felt like the whole thing was getting so big and so messy, and we were both half in love with him, and Kate. I'm so sorry. I'm so—"

"Okay, can you stop?"

"Sure." The car stops.

"Andy, no, I don't mean stop the car—"

"But we're at Target."

"I meant stop apologizing."

"Kate, you just gave me this whole thing about wanting to see my face, and now you're sitting here with your eyes closed."

"I know." I laugh shortly.

"Don't you want to see my reaction?"

"I don't know!"

"Kate." Anderson grabs my hand, threading our fingers together over the gearshift. "Look at my face."

I crack my eyes open tentatively.

"I love you," he mouths. And then, faintly audible, "That's my reaction."

I smile, just barely. "But I'm not done yet."

"Okay—"

"I thought he liked me. And it's stupid. It was all in my head. There was never anything—and I get it now, but it made me feel like I couldn't even trust my own perception. I just kept thinking, wow, I'm like the worst kind of loser, and everyone knows it."

"Excuse me? No. You're the best kind of loser, and only I know it, which is why I'm your best friend in the whole world, and always will be."

"I know. I know." Suddenly, my eyes fill with tears. "God. I'm so sorry. I was just—Andy, I swear to God, five minutes after you told me, I was like, okay, fine. Andy and Matt, great. Okay, not totally fine."

Andy squeezes my hand.

"I was starting to get fine with it, though." I sniff. "But I couldn't stop picturing you guys talking about me and feeling sorry for me, and Matt thinking I was so pathetic for liking him—"

"But, Katy, I didn't—"

"I know. You didn't tell him. Code of Secrecy. I know."

"I would never do that to you," he says. "Ever. Believe me, I fucked up like that once, and I still feel—"

"What? You never did that."

He's quiet for a moment. "Don't you ever wonder why Vivian Yang stopped talking to me?"

"I mean." I wipe my eyes. "I just figured she ditched you for the track team. She became an f-girl."

"She's not an f-girl," Andy says.

"Okay, but—"

"And we stopped being friends because of me. I fucked up." He exhales. "I violated the Code. I'm the one who told Jeffrey Jacobs she liked him."

"Wait." I pause. "Really? I feel like that was common knowledge though."

"Yeah, because Jeffrey told the whole track team." Andy looks distraught. "It was such a dumb thing to do. I don't even remember what I was thinking. I guess I just didn't get it, you know? I'd never really liked anyone like that. I didn't get what a big deal it was."

"To be fair, that was freshman year—"

"So what? It was still shitty. The Code of Secrecy exists for a reason."

"You're being way too hard on yourself."

"I'm just saying. I've regretted that for years." Andy shakes his head. "I'm never going to sell you out to Matt like that. Kate, I promise—"

"Andy, no." I twist around in my seat, suddenly desperate to face him. "You can tell him. It's fine. You can tell him I used to like him—the whole story."

"Um. Are you high?"

"You shouldn't have to hide that. You should be able to tell each other everything."

Andy wrinkles his brow. "I don't need to tell Matt everything."

"You can't keep secrets from each other if you're in a relationship. That doesn't work."

He turns to face me. "You really think that?"

"Everyone thinks that."

"What? No! Not everyone thinks that. You really think two people can't be close unless they know everything about each other?"

I shrug.

He tilts his head. "Okay, so what about all that time before I came out to you. Right? My big secret. You think we weren't close before that?"

"I know we were closer after."

"Your mom had just moved next door! Come on. I'm not saying it wasn't cool to be able to talk about boy stuff with you, but are you seriously gonna write off everything before seventh grade? None of that counts, because I didn't tell you this one thing about me that I didn't even totally understand myself?"

"That's different. You were figuring it out. You weren't trying to keep anything from me—"

"But so what if I was! Are you kidding me? You can be close with people who aren't out. I wasn't out! And I was close with people! You can keep whatever secrets you want." He smiles, shaking his head. "I swear, it's like you think there's only one way to do relationships."

"I don't know how to do relationships. I've never had a relationship."

"Hello? You have me."

"We're not in a relationship."

"We're not in a romantic relationship. That doesn't mean we're not in a relationship."

My heart tugs. "I know."

"And maybe we're going to have boyfriends sometimes, and yeah, we probably won't tell each other everything. But that doesn't mean you and I are less close. It just means we're separate people and our lives are separate sometimes. And that's good! You don't need to know what happened in your brother's room when you were at your dad's house—"

"Oh. My God."

"Not that. Kate. Come on. Your mom was like ten feet away. I would never."

"Yeah, blame your lack of game on my mom."

"Touché. But you know what I mean, right? I'm going to have secrets, and so are you. I don't want to hear about you and Noah Kaplan and your sloppy f-boy fridge makeouts—"

"Okay, first of all, I've been informed that the fridge makeout was not representative of Noah's abilities."

"Wait." Andy's jaw drops. "Did you kiss—"

"No! What? No."

"Not yet. And listen up." Andy presses his palm to my forehead. "You better not do your Kate thing and stop liking him just because I'm not trying to jump his bones too. We are gonna let this ball keep rolling, okay?"

"Who said the ball was rolling?"

He stares me down.

"Okay, the ball's rolling," I say. "Maybe. Almost."

"Yeah, well." Andy's eyes are gleaming. "Seeing as he's texting you pictures of his body parts right now—"

"Stop looking at my phone." I swipe it away, tapping into my texts. "Oh my God!" I press my hand to my heart. "Look, he did it! He got his cast off!"

"Wow, if you're swooning over an arm—"

"I'm not swooning!"

"I'm inviting him to my nonexistent birthday party."

"Good for you."

"Tell him to bring his cute little arm. It's so pale. Hope you weren't pinning your hopes on having a jock boyfriend, Katypie, because this boy is not playing baseball this season."

"You're not funny." I lean back against the seat, head tilting toward Anderson.

"Yeah I am."

"Shut up."

"Hey, Kate?" He smiles. "This fight is officially adjourned."

# SCENE 72

Noah's driving again, and the car selfie he texts me Wednesday morning (reunited and it feels so good!!!!!!!!!!!!!!!!!!!!!!!!!!!!!!!!!!!!!!! !!!!!!!!!) has more exclamation points than letters.

So of course I spend the whole day just about bursting, because I'm pretty sure this means I'm getting a ride home after our tech run-through. And all sorts of things can happen on a car ride. Things that involve mouths.

Okay, but not like the sexual kind of mouth involvement. Just mouths on mouths. Just kissing.

Not that kissing is ever just.

*I need to learn how to be cool around you.* I can't stop thinking about Noah's face when he said that. Also, his face in general. Also, the possibility of his face against my face.

I'm so distracted in all my classes, I can barely string two words together. And rehearsal's even worse. By the end of Act Two, I'm practically floating. Noah and I can't even look at each other without grinning. "Why are you so giddy?" Raina asks me in the dressing room, and I just tip my palms up. She narrows her eyes and stares at me for a full minute.

Every time I'm offstage, I check the time on my phone, sometimes more than once—even though there's no set end time for tech week rehearsals. But I try to will the clock forward anyway. Thank God I know this musical well enough to put it on autopilot, because today my brain lives in Noah Kaplan's car.

Ms. Zhao finally calls everyone onto the stage for notes, and the anticipation is almost unbearable. It's like I have to hug myself to keep from exploding.

Almost time. We're almost dismissed.

"Moving to Act Two, Scene Nine," says Ms. Zhao. "Quick note. Dauntless, when you go to Winnifred, let's have you cross in front of the Queen."

Andy nods.

"Also, just a reminder that tomorrow's our official dress rehearsal, so please make sure your costume components are all together, labeled—shoes, everything. I don't want to see any sneakers poking out under anyone's gowns. Got it?"

Okay. Okay. Here we go.

"And I think that's it. Very good, guys." Zhao starts to stand up—but then she pauses. "Oh wait. Noah."

No. NO.

"If you can just hang back for a few minutes, I want to rework a few more of your pantomimes. We really want to get that hand back in play."

NO. NO. NO. I puff my cheeks out, sighing.

"Kate, come on." Andy tugs my flannel. "Stop death-glaring Zhao. Matt can drive you."

"You guys don't have to go out of your way," I say heavily. "I'll just call my dad."

"We're your dads now," says Matt.

Raina and Brandie burst out laughing. Meanwhile, Anderson just looks at Matt, wide-eyed, with this twisty little smile. "Wait. Do they know?" He gestures between Raina and Brandie. Matt grins, cheeks flushed, nodding.

"Mazel tov, you two." Raina sidles up between them.

"So when was this big talk?" He's smiling at Matt, shaking his head.

"During your father-son scene with Noah," Raina says. "Right during the part about the boy flowers and girl flowers. Beautiful timing."

"Why, thank you," Matt says.

"Kate, I'll drive you," says Brandie. "I'm taking Raina, so you're on the way."

We all drift toward the parking lot, and even though my Noah ride fell through, I can't help but give in to that electric fall-evening feeling. Even the sports teams have gone home, so it feels like the whole world is ours. Just us theater kids, actors and tech crew. Andy and Matt are walking side by side, just a little closer than usual, and Raina's got her phone out, Face-Timing Harold. "Don't judge me," she says to Brandie and me, with the cutest, most self-conscious smile.

"Couples," I say, shrugging at Brandie.

"I know. Did you hear Pierra and Colin were in the lighting booth earlier?"

"Again?"

"They're insatiable."

"Kate! Hold up." Noah sprints from the auditorium side door to catch up to Brandie and me. "Hey," he says, breathlessly, pressing a hand to his forehead. "I can drive you."

"Oh, hey, look who got his car back," says Anderson, circling back to meet us.

"This guy did. Back in business." Noah grins, and then takes a big, gulping breath. "Anyway, guys, sorry. I have to steal your passenger, because it's Wednesday, which means Dad's house night, which means she lives across the street from me and I just think I should—"

"Okay," I say, smiling.

When I turn back to face Noah, he's fidgeting with the zipper of his hoodie. But his eyes are bright and twinkly.

"Okay. Cool," he says. "Let's do this."

# SCENE 73

"So, aren't you impressed I know your custody schedule by now?" Noah says, once we're all buckled in.

"So impressed." I lean back into my seat, smiling. I've seen Noah's car from the outside probably fifty million times. After all, it's lived in the driveway across the street from my dad's house for years. But this is actually the first time I've been inside it. It's an old Ford Fusion, inherited from his sisters, and it's cluttered but not smelly. Hardly an f-boy car at all. I kind of love it. "So is it weird to be driving again?"

"Nah, not really. It's like—"

"Don't say riding a bike."

"What are you, the cliché police?"

"Something like that." I turn toward him. "I can't believe you got out. I totally thought Zhao was going to keep you for like an hour."

"No, she and Mr. D just wanted me to change a few things now that I have my hand back. It's so weird. It feels like—I don't know. Kind of like when I got my braces off. Oh! Shit. Oops!" He shoots me a sheepish smile. "Forgot to turn my headlights on."

"How do you forget to turn your headlights on when it's dark out?"

"Because I'm out of practice." He swallows. "And I'm nervous."

I lose every ounce of air in my lungs. I can't even explain it. It's just Noah. Noah, with his rumpled brown hair and too-wide eyes, looking way too much like Flynn Rider. Regular Noah in a regular hoodie, and he's so cute, I can hardly stand it. And the closer we get to Dad's house, the worse it gets. I just stare out the window, one hand pressed to my chest, like I'm holding my heart in.

Meanwhile, Noah keeps driving, and he's just as silent as I am.

When he parks in my driveway at last, I stay seated. "Thanks for the ride," I say shyly.

"Anytime. Hey." He turns all the way toward me, and I feel clumsy and tongue-tied and weak with anticipation. God. There's something downright surreal about the fact that I just spent my whole entire day picturing this exact moment, and now it's happening. It's like I conjured it. "So . . . ," he says— and then his eyes flick up to my house. "Your dad's watching us."

"You're kidding me."

But sure enough, there's Dad, holding Charles, fully lit and framed by his bedroom window. He waves hi with Charles's paw.

Noah waves back. "Listen," he says. "I'm not going to kiss you in front of your dad, and, like, your dog, but I'm just going to say this, because otherwise I might explode. Okay?"

I nod, heart pounding.

He exhales. "I really like you."

"Me too. I really like you, too."

He shakes his head. "Let me try again. I have been," he says, "I have had the biggest, most ridiculous crush on you, Kate. For so long." He catches my eye for the barest split second, and then looks away. I realize his hands are shaking. "Since middle school. Since the bread balls at Temple. Since the variety show. I don't need you to say anything. I just want you to know." He covers his face with both hands.

"Noah," I say.

"You can leave. If you want. I'll just." He swallows. "I'm going to go park in my driveway. I can drive you to school tomorrow, but if that's too weird, I totally get it—"

"Noah."

He slides his hands off his eyes and looks at me.

"My dad closed the blinds."

"What?" he says. "Oh."

"Can I kiss you?" I ask, knowing perfectly well he'll say yes.

The look in Noah's eyes makes me feel like Rapunzel.

He unbuckles his seat belt and scoots toward me, and that alone makes my heart swoop. This is actually about to happen. Noah Kaplan's about to kiss me. Strange how it feels both preposterous and inevitable. He takes my head in both his hands, thumb tapping my lip for the barest split second. Then his lips are on mine, and I'm not Rapunzel at all.

I'm a paper lantern.

I'm floating, lit up from the inside.

# SCENE 74

Okay, thank God I'm in a musical that has mattresses for set pieces, and I mean that in a completely nonsexual way.

Almost completely.

Okay, seriously, I'm not going to have sex with Noah on a set piece during dress rehearsal.

Or ever.

On a set piece.

I JUST MEAN I NEED A NAP.

Because last night was . . . not a sleeping kind of night. Not because Noah and I stayed up late kissing. I mean. Maybe we stayed up slightly late kissing. Maybe we kissed until my lips felt like they were buzzing, and maybe I was so breathless by the end that I could barely say good night.

Afterward, I lay in bed, staring up at my canopy, thinking about how I'll be thirty, I'll be fifty, I'll be a grandma, and still. I'll never forget the look on Noah's face as he leaned closer, that breath of anticipation right before our lips met. And I especially thought about the last thing Noah said when I got out of the car. *See you tomorrow, Kate.* So ordinary, and so full of possibility. So completely drenched in magic. He'd texted me a heart emoji about ten minutes later, and I hugged my phone upside down to my chest, thinking: even that is a thing I'll never forget. Even the emoji.

Meanwhile, I've started and deleted about a hundred texts to Anderson, which is its own shot of joy. Just knowing I can text him again. I can text him anything I want to, full giddy ramblings, with nothing held back. There's a part of me that thinks Andy's the reason Noah and I kept getting interrupted. Because the world wouldn't give me a moment like last night if I couldn't share it with Andy.

Maybe I wouldn't give myself a moment like last night until I could share it with Andy.

But in the end, I don't text him. I want to tell him in person. I want to squeal and hug and freak out and obsess over details and field intrusive questions.

And it occurs to me suddenly: I want to do that for Andy. About Matt.

# SCENE 75

The whole day feels like a dream. Noah kisses me twice in the morning, quickly and softly—once when I get in his car, and once in the school parking lot, right before we get out. After that, I immediately find Anderson, sweeping him into the BTF before the first period bell.

When I tell him, he shrieks.

"You did WHAT?" He bursts out of his stall, and the next thing I know, we're jumping up and down next to the urinals. He flings his arms around me, kissing my cheek over and over. "Holy shit, yes!" He presses his forehead to mine. "Is it, like, a thing? Are you telling people? Have you told Raina and Brandie? Can I tell Raina and Brandie?"

I beam up at him. "Go for it."

Turns out, he doesn't even have to. "So, Kate," Raina says, "What was up with all that face sex in history?"

"Whaaaaat?"

"You and Noah. Not even eye-fucking, Kate, you had this little smile—"

"The lip thing!" Andy says triumphantly. "Raina, yes! I've been telling her this for years."

"And Noah's face, Kate. Like, when you leaned forward and your hair did that curtain thing?" Raina says. "He was not okay."

"He should sit with us at lunch," Brandie says.

But before we even step into the cafeteria, we're interrupted by a breathless Devon Blackwell. "Hey." He blinks twice. "Zhao just called for a double dress rehearsal, so we need you to head to the auditorium."

"Now?" Raina asks.

"Right now. You can bring your food—she'll fill you in while you eat." He pauses, catching his breath. "Sorry, I just had to track down every single one of your afternoon teachers. For the whole cast. And crew." He shuts his eyes briefly. "It's a theatrical emergency."

# SCENE 76

As it turns out, Ms. Zhao's freaking out about hats. Many of which are bulky or tall or conical. "This is totally on me," Zhao says, rubbing her forehead. "We need to make sure they don't interfere with your dancing."

Naturally, Mr. D serenades us with a song called "You Can Leave Your Hat On" while we finish scarfing down our lunches, picnic-style, in front of the stage. This is followed by a chaotic twenty minutes in the dressing room—hangers flying, fabric flapping in every direction. Only the hardest-core people, like Lana, have performed in their costumes so far, so it's the first time we're all competing for space to change clothes. It's disastrous.

I end up sharing the little bathroom stall with Raina, standing back to back as we wriggle into our gowns. "It sounds like *Geostorm* out there. Like not even one natural disaster. It sounds like every natural disaster."

"Right? Who knew getting dressed was so violent?" I say—

and right on cue, something crashes, and everyone goes, ooooooooooh.

"We're okay!" shouts Colin.

I grin down at the tiles. Someone bangs on the door. "Hurry up!"

"Don't you dare rush the queen," Raina yells back, and maybe normally I'd feel a tiny twinge of eek-hurry-up. But not today. Today I don't feel rushed in the slightest.

Stepping out of the bathroom, my eyes cut straight through the pandemonium, instantly finding Noah in the doorway. For a moment, we just stand there, at opposite ends of the room, smiling. He's dressed like a king, in the same gold tunic and crown Colin wore two years ago as Prince Charming in *Into the Woods*.

"Wow," Noah mouths, pressing his hand to his forehead.

I look down at my gown and shrug.

Truthfully, I don't know how I ended up with one of the tiny handful of rented costumes this year, but I did, and I love it. It's the palest pink silk, drapey and expensive feeling, high waisted with gold rope accents, and no hat. Just the subtlest tiara. I don't want to say it's exactly like Rapunzel's costume in *Tangled*, but I mean. It's pretty damn close.

And even though it's just the dress rehearsal for the dress rehearsal, I have this opening night, center stage sort of feeling. I can't seem to wind my heart down.

For the next few hours, I barely see Noah—even when we're both backstage, someone's constantly pulling one of us aside for hair or costume adjustments. In the end, I mostly stick with Matt, who's in basically every scene with me anyway. We settle in with our backs against the iconic mattress pile—in our case, twenty pre-stacked mattresses that roll in on tiny wheels. There's a ladder attached to one side, and at this point, I think half the cast has climbed up there to test it out. It's actually super comfortable, but Bess and Suman would murder us if we messed around with it during a run-through.

Either way, it's nice just leaning against it—and I guess we must look cute in our costumes, with the mattresses stacked behind us, because people keep Instagramming us. At one point, during a lull between our scenes, Devon Blackwell dumps a stack of unfolded programs and a stapler beside us.

"We got this," Matt says, carefully creasing a bundle of papers into booklet form. Then he hands them to me, and I staple. "Hey, so, what's the game plan for Saturday?"

I glance around before responding—and even though Anderson is, of course, onstage at this very moment, I keep my voice low. "Okay. He's still saying he doesn't want a party, but obviously we can't have no party."

"Obviously."

"So I was thinking we'll just set up the cake and stuff in one of the dressing rooms between the matinee and evening shows."

"Excellent."

"And maybe a sleepover after the cast party, but that's just us and the squad. And Noah," I add, blushing. Matt opens his mouth like he's about to ask something, but I cut him off quickly. "Oh, and Raina got those giant number balloons. Did you know they don't make seventeen? So she's getting one and seven."

"He's totally gonna swap them around and tell everyone he's seventy-one," Matt says.

"To be fair, seventy-one-year-old Anderson's going to be a next-level badass."

I can already picture it. He'll have a full set of perfect teeth, which he'll brush every five minutes. And he and I will spend every day chilling on the porch with our husbands, texting memes and selfies to our grandkids—who, let's face it, will probably rebel and be fuckboys. But we'll double down and keep trolling them with videos of us singing "Somebody to Love." We're going to Ella our grandkids into submission.

Full-throttle Kate and Anderson, forever and ever and ever.

# SCENE 77

Three hours until we open, and I'm hiding in the lighting booth with Noah.

And, okay, we're not really all that hidden—Audrey, the lighting director, could wander back here any minute, not to mention Colin and Pierra. But it's tiny and cozy and a few steps removed from the usual disarray of opening night. Obviously, we don't go near the computer or switchboard. But it's nice, just sitting side by side, out of view of the window, with Noah's arm tucked around my shoulders. Even nicer is the cloudspun feeling I get when he threads his fingers through the ends of my hair.

"Are you nervous?" I ask. "I panicked so hard before my first show, I almost threw up."

"Weren't you, like, a townsperson?"

"Yup." I grin into his shoulder. "But townspeople can still screw up. Not having lines didn't mean I wasn't going to fart into a microphone or something."

His laugh is so startled and genuine, it makes me laugh too. "Is that supposed to make me less nervous?" he asks.

"Well, I didn't fart into a microphone. Or at all," I add quickly.

He hugs me closer. "Are you nervous?"

"Sort of. But I can't tell if I'm nervous because it's opening night, or just . . . other stuff."

He turns to face me, mouth twitching upward. "Other stuff?"

"Other stuff." I smile slightly.

"I'm up for other stuff," he says, leaning toward me.

And suddenly we're kissing. We are honest-to-God kissing in the lighting booth on opening night. It's not exactly a body-meld embrace—Noah's knee sort of tucks over mine, and my hands end up pressed flat on the ground. But I kind of love the awkwardness of kissing side by side. It gives me this off-kilter sort of nostalgia—a rush of longing for moments I've never even lived through, like handsy middle school makeouts and first summer kisses on moonlit wooden docks.

"Do you have any idea"—Noah's voice is low and breathless—"how long I've pictured this?"

"This in particular? In the school theater lighting booth?"

"Yup." He kisses me again softly. "And everywhere. Lighting booths, airplanes, bathrooms, airplane bathrooms. You name it."

I can barely wrap my head around it. The way we keep sliding between joking and talking and kissing, like it's the most normal thing in the world. I guess I always had this idea of kissing as this moment of transformation—with swelling music and faded backgrounds and your brain filled with nothing but the kiss itself.

But it's not like that at all.

It's Noah's lips, and the way they move softly against mine, and the fluttery ache in my stomach. It's the way Noah can't go ten seconds without talking, even when we're actively kissing, and I keep erupting into giggles, and every so often one of us gets paranoid and checks our phones so we don't miss call time.

But I like that.

I like that when we're kissing, we never once stop being us.

# SCENE 78

An hour later, Raina and I attempt to sit still while Brandie does our makeup.

"We'll be fine," Raina says, "we're just gonna get out there and do our thing, same as we've always done it, and then no one has to be nervous anymore. It's smooth sailing. Brandie, why are you putting lipstick on my cheeks?"

"Just trust me," says Brandie.

In all honesty, Brandie's the only person on earth I do trust for the job, because she never tries to talk me into globbing on more than I want to wear. And I get it: stage lights wash you out, you need extra definition, etcetera, etcetera. But listen. If the boys don't have to wear bright lipstick, I'm not wearing bright lipstick. Except on my cheeks, apparently.

I don't know. I just want to look like me.

Once everyone's in costume, Ms. Zhao herds us out to the secret teacher parking lot for the ceremonial burning of the program. "We are Roswell Hill," she says, "and we are one."

We all chant it over and over. "WE ARE ROSWELL HILL, AND WE ARE ONE. WE ARE ROSWELL HILL, AND WE ARE ONE."

I wish I could bottle up this moment and keep it for the rest of my life. Tucked up close between Anderson and Raina. Holding hands in a circle in the crisp fall evening air, feeling so flooded with love and belonging.

"Bring it in!" Ms. Zhao says, stomping out the last few flames of the freshly charred program. We all rush to the center for the group hug of the century.

And the next thing I know, it's six thirty, and Ms. Zhao's out there in front of the curtain, telling people to turn off their cell phones for the duration of the play.

"Musical," mutters Lana Bennett from the wings.

The orchestra glides through the overture, and just like always, I lose my breath for a minute. But Noah hugs me. "You've got this."

"Noah, Andy, Raina—stage left please!" Devon whispers sharply.

Noah hugs me again. "Break a wrist."

And we're off.

# SCENE 79

So, once upon a time in eleventh grade, Lady Kate the Starlet steered herself right to center stage.

It's all so beautifully uneventful. No one forgets to push the mattresses out, no one's voice cracks. Brandie's flawless on the soft-shoe, the mics don't go out, and Matt and I manage not to laugh during our kiss, even with our moms heckling us from the front row.

Raina peeks through the curtains when the house lights come on. "Aww," she says. "Look who brought flowers."

I follow her gaze downward, where people are making their way down the aisles, to the exits. Ellen and my parents are gone, which means they're probably in the lobby, but my brother and some of his teammates are still camped out near the stage. Ryan's holding a bouquet of blue and purple flowers.

Whoa. Okay. I'm definitely supposed to be changing out of my costume right now. But also, I'm definitely too nosy to resist this.

It takes some major skirt maneuvering for me to properly settle onto the side steps off the stage. Once I do, though, I beckon him over. "Ryan Kevin Garfield," I say, beaming. "Wow. Holy grand gesture."

He looks taken aback. "Wait. What?"

"No, don't worry. Grand gesture in a good way!" I press my hands to my heart. "Do you want me to go see if she's in the dressing room?"

"Kate, oh my God." Ryan rolls his eyes and shoves the bouquet into my arms. "These are for you, doofus. Here."

I shoot him a puzzled half smile. "You don't have to give me Brandie's flowers."

"They're not Brandie's flowers. Kate, I don't even know where you're getting this." He rubs his temples. "I don't have a crush on Brandie—"

"Right. So when you decided to rehearse with us the other day, it's because you're such a fan of musicals—"

"I decided to rehearse with you the other day because you'd literally just called me out for only hanging with fuckboys."

I hug the bouquet to my chest. "Okay, but what about the texting?"

"I'm . . . eighteen. I have a phone. I text people sometimes?"

"But you're shady about it now! Like, I get within a mile of you, and you yank your phone away so fast—"

"Because I'm secretly texting with Brandie?" Ryan shakes his head, grinning. "Kate, ninety-nine percent of the time, I'm talking to Noah."

"Ohhh."

"And most of the time, he's talking about you."

"Got it." I'm beaming.

"Kate, I like Brandie a lot, but I'm not looking for a girl-friend. It's senior year. I'm leaving in a few months—"

"Right. Totally." I nod quickly, a lump rising into my throat. "But you liked Kennesaw, right? And some of the other local schools—"

"Yeah, definitely, but." He sighs. "Okay, scoot over."

He squeezes in beside me on the steps. Just about everyone's left the auditorium by now, which makes the whole space seem weirdly huge and majestic. For a moment, neither of us speaks.

"I don't know where I'll end up," Ryan says finally. "Might be Tech. Might be Kennesaw. Might be California. I don't know what scholarships are going to look like. I don't even know where I'll get in. But it's definitely starting to feel real."

I nod mutely.

"So, it's like, suddenly this big change that seemed really far away is right there. And I'm excited, yeah, but it's also kind of freaking me out. So if I seemed a little, I don't know, clingy—"

"Clingy?" I laugh, startled. "I can't even imagine you being clingy."

"Okay, well." He smiles. "If it seemed like I was around more—Kate, I'm really sorry if it seemed like I was just trying to hook up with one of your friends."

"It's fine! I was all for it!"

"Yeah, you made that pretty clear." He laughs. "But, Katy,

that was never a thing. I just feel weird about the fact that I'm leaving you."

I just stare at him. "Oh."

"Kate!" I look up with a start, to find Andy peeking out from the side of the curtain. "Where have you been? Come on! Almost everyone's changed already."

"Oops—coming!" I scramble up, biting my lip. "Sorry—"

"It's fine. Go do your thing."

"I did." I step back onstage, grinning. "And I am."

# SCENE 80

"You know what just hit me?" I say, as I follow Andy to the dressing room. "You're going to be seventeen in, like, two hours."

"I know! Did you ever think we'd have boyfriends on our seventeenth birthdays? We're like movie teens."

"Um. Slow your roll, Walker. No one's used the b-word yet."

"Yeah, whatever." He grins. "I give it a week."

It's so strange. Two months ago, when it came to my friends' collective love lives, Harold was the whole story. But now my whole squad's gone Shakespearean. Okay, Brandie's still saving herself for Harry Styles, but it's barely October. At the rate we're all going, she'll probably be married by homecoming.

I open the dressing room door, and there's Noah.

"So here's the thing," he says promptly. "I want to be your b-word."

"Wow. You're here. Hi." I can't quite catch my breath. "I guess you heard us—"

"Yeah. Yup." He grabs my hand.

"That's my exit cue," says Andy, already backtracking. He pulls the door shut behind him. No six inches. No inches whatsoever.

Noah's back in his hoodie and gym shorts, face scrubbed clean, cheeks still pink from the washcloth. He presses my hand to his chest, and his heart's thudding.

I stare at him. "Noah, I'm—"

"God. I'm sorry. I don't mean to ambush you. Did I ambush you?"

"Maybe?" I drop his hand, stepping nearer. "I kind of liked it."

"Kind of. Okay. So is that like—"

"Noah!" I grab his face in my hands and kiss him.

He exhales, startled. But then he tugs me closer, walking me backward until his back's flush with the vanity, his face framed with lights. And there's me in the mirror, in my gown and tiara, but I shut my eyes quickly.

I don't want to watch this like a movie. I don't want to save the details for later.

I want—

Noah's lips, an inch from mine. "Happy opening night," he says, smiling.

But it feels so much less like a night, and so much more like an opening.

# ★ CURTAIN CALL

Ryan says driver's license pictures are always garbage, but then again, he didn't have an entourage. Brandie keeps straightening my collar and blotting my nose with a tissue, and Raina's physically tucked my hair behind my ears three times. And that's just since we walked into the DDS. But all Anderson cares about is the smile.

"Katy, they're going to tell you not to smile, and you have to—are you listening to me? You have to ignore them. Or it will look like a mug shot."

"I can't decide if you sound like an f-boy or a pageant mom."

"I'm just saying. Don't let them intimidate you," Andy says. "Smiling's not illegal in Georgia."

Noah leans toward Matt. "Is smiling illegal in states that are not Georgia?"

"I guess so?" Matt shrugs.

I love my hype team: the full squad, including Matt. And my brother. And my boyfriend.

I've even got my guitar. I mean, it's in the trunk of Ryan's car.

Our car. Mine and Ryan's. Officially.

I felt nervous this morning—but it was a manageable kind of nervous. Kind of like theater nerves. Like stepping onto a stage when you know every line by heart. In the weeks since the play, I've practiced driving every single day, with both my parents. Which definitely paid off, seeing as I got a perfect score on the driver's test.

So it's official: I'm a driver's seat person. All that's left is the picture.

"Look into the bottom lens, please," the woman says. "Eyes open, neutral expression."

Anderson shakes his head frantically, poking the corners of his mouth up with his fingers. "Ignore her," he mouths.

Like I could ever—in a million years—make it through this moment without smiling.


THE END

# THE PART WHERE YOU MAKE THE SUNDAY MATINEE AUDIENCE WATCH YOU PRESENT YOUR DRAMA TEACHER WITH FLOWERS AND AN ENLARGED FRAMED PRINT OF THE PROGRAM ART SIGNED BY THE CAST AND CREW AND YOU'RE ALL CRYING BUT NO ONE'S CRYING HARDER THAN THE FUCKBOYS WHO CAN'T LEAVE THE THEATER AND ARE THEREFORE MISSING CRUCIAL TELEVISED SPORTING EVENTS BECAUSE THEY LIVE BY YOUR RULES NOW AND IT'S VERY SAD OF COURSE BUT THE CURTAIN SPEECHES MUST GO ON

Hi! Can you all hear me? Good! Okay, first of all, on behalf of the entire cast and crew, I want to thank you all so much for being here. I'm Becky, the author, and this production has truly been one of the most rewarding experiences of my career so far. I'd like to take a minute to acknowledge the people whose work and support behind the scenes brought this story to life.

First, I'd like to present this giant unicorn head mask to my editor, Donna Bray, who deserves top billing for her wisdom, humor, and utter mercilessness toward fuckboys. And on behalf of the RHHS theater department, enormous thanks to every member of my team at HarperCollins/Balzer+Bray, including Tiara Kittrell, Patty Rosati, Suzanne Murphy, Jacquelynn Burke, Sam Benson, Ebony LaDelle, Sabrina Abballe, Shannon Cox, Kristin Eckhardt, Mark Rifkin, Shona McCarthy, Jill Amack, Nellie Kurtzman, and Alessandra Balzer. It's my honor to present each of you with your very own medieval costume (yours to keep for two years).

Thanks to Jenna Stempel-Lobell, Alison Donalty, and Pepco Studios for this showstopper of a book cover. I hereby present each of you with your own name in lights (maybe even floating paper lanterns).

At the special request of Noah Kaplan, I'd like this sawed-off cast (signed and illustrated by Jack Randall) to go to my agent, Holly Root, along with Alyssa Moore, Heather Baror, and my entire team at Root Literary—with infinite thanks for keeping me together behind the curtains.

Next, I'd like to present Devon Blackwell's heavily annotated copy of *Once Upon a Mattress* to Mary Pender-Coplan, Orly Greenberg, Julia Brownell, Julie Waters, Isaac Klausner, Laura Quicksilver, and my teams at UTA and Temple Hill (without whom the show would simply not go on).

For Brooks Sherman, Roma Panganiban, and the wonderful team at Janklow & Nesbit, I'm thrilled to present you with this baseball signed by the entire MLB.

For my standing-ovation-worthy international publishing teams, I'd like to present official hall passes to Senior D (signed with extra flourish for Leo Teti, Anthea Townsend, Ben Horslen, Ruth Bennett, and Mathilde Tamae-Bouhon).

Top volume thanks go to Bebe Wood, for an audiobook that sings. It's my pleasure to present you with Kate's guitar.

To thank my earliest readers for sharing their wisdom and knowledge, I'm presenting a bound copy of my full doctoral dissertation in the field of Fuckboy Studies: Julian Winters, Mark O'Brien, David Arnold, Aisha Saeed, and Nani Borges.

With heartfelt gratitude for keeping me from losing my everloving mind, I'd like to present each and every one of my friends, in and outside the book community, with a pair of Cotton Mather's cotton trousers. In addition, I'd like the following people to join me onstage to receive limited edition RHHS baseball hats, each one signed by all eight of Sean Sanders's abs (please hold your applause until the end): Adam Silvera, Adib Khorram, Aisha Saeed, Amy Austin, Angie Thomas, Arvin Ahmadi, Ashley Woodfolk, Becky Kilimnik, Chris Negron, Clark Moore, Dahlia Adler, David Arnold, David Levithan, Diane Blumenfeld, Emily Carpenter, Emily Townsend, George Weinstein, Gillian Morshedi, Jenny Mariaschin-Rudin, Jeri Green, Heidi Schulz, Jacob Demlow, Jaime Hensel, Jaime Semensohn, James Sie, Jasmine Warga, Jennifer Dugan, Jennifer Niven, Niki Malek, Jodi Picoult, Julian Winters, Julie Murphy, Kevin Savoie, Kimberly Ito, Lauren Starks, Lindsay Keiller, Luis Rivera, Mackenzi Lee, Manda Turetsky, Mark

O'Brien, Molly Mercer, Nic Stone, Rose Brock, Sam Rowntree, Sarah Beth Brown, Sophie Gonzales, and Tom-Erik Fure.

Mr. D would like to extend a hearty Suckle to all of you booksellers, bloggers, librarians, educators, and readers. You've earned it.

I'd like to present every member of my family with a ball of rolled-up challah, to be placed underneath twenty mattresses (and if a single one of us is kept awake, we're all royalty) (that includes all of you Goldsteins, Albertallis, Reitzeses, Thomases, Bells, and Overholtses, I don't make the rules).

In addition: to my sister, Caroline Reitzes, I present Kate's mom's old guitar, #jammin. To my brother, Sam Goldstein, I present a giant neon Bulbasaur. To my mom, Eileen Thomas, I present an early draft of this book before I had to cut the parts about Tamiment. And to my dad and stepmom, Jim and Candy Goldstein, I present you with official permission to slip out the side door after the first hour of thank-you speeches.

Anderson's Rapunzel keychain, of course, goes to Dan Fogelman.

Next, please stand and applaud as I invite my husband and kids onto the stage so I can properly embarrass them with a weepy public thank-you. You three are my stage crew and my neverending happy epilogue. It is my greatest honor to present Owen and Henry with Kate's teddy bears, Amber and Ember. As for Brian, I owe you the kind of thanks that can only be expressed with this gift of Daniel Tiger's father's nonexistent pants.

And finally, I'd like to direct your attention to the squad who taught me everything I know about finstas and f-boys. They inspire me daily with the strength and depth of their old and new friendships and, y'all, they even let me borrow their names. To Anderson Rothwell, I present this framed grainy picture of the Roswell High football field, inscribed with the caption "Whatta night #FNL." To Brandie Rendon, I present the sequel where you meet Harry Styles. To Katy-Lynn Cook, I present a limo full of hotties, chaperoned by Noah's mom. To Matthew Eppard, I present a Coke ad of your face. And, at last: to Kate Goud, I present Kate's driver's license. Your picture came out perfectly, your world is wide open, and your spotlight awaits.